Dead Letters of Laurel Cove

ELIZABETH COLLUMS

RopeSwing Press
an imprint of
Rope Swing Publishing

ISBN: 978-1-954058-26-2

Dead Letters of Laurel Cove

Cover photo: Daria Shevtsova

RopeSwing

Press

an imprint of
Rope Swing Publishing

www.ropeswingpublishing.com

If knowing answers to life's questions is absolutely necessary to you, then forget the journey. You will never make it. For this is a journey of unknowables – of unanswered questions, enigmas, incomprehensibles, and most of all, things unfair.

Madam Guyon

DEDICATED TO MY DAD

AND ALL THE OTHER MEN AND WOMEN

THAT LEFT OUR SHORES

NEVER TO RETURN THE SAME AGAIN

CHAPTER 1

LEARN NOW, USE LATER
April 1972

SHE CHANGED HER CLOTHES three times already this morning, as evidenced by the clothes strewn on the floor, while she checked herself in the mirror over and over again. And much to her dismay, each time her reflection only showed the parts she wished she could change. Gilly was thankful she had her mom's slender build, high cheek bones and full lips. But she had inherited her dad's wavy auburn hair and green eyes. What a combination. Some days she thought she was half Native American and half Irish, but then there were those days when she had no idea what tribe she fit in. Her mom had the kind of spirit she longed for, always being strong and positive, while her dad didn't really care what people thought about him. Today, if only for a couple of hours, she wanted to be more like him and not care, because every change of clothes reminded her how close to the edge they really were. And even though her mom was one of the best seamstresses in town, she knew as much as everyone else that all her clothes were no-name and tag-less. It's nothing for most people to be self-conscious about, but when you're almost seventeen and all your friends shop at Dillard's and D.H. Holmes, they know it, and you know it, when you wear homemade clothes to school every day.

"Gilly, honey, you look fine, I promise. Get going or you'll be late for the bus," Claire said.

"I know Mom, I'm just a little nervous today, that's all" Gilly answered.

Bye Joey, see you later." Gilly kissed him on the cheek as she flew out the door.

"Bye, bye Gilly," Joey said as he smeared his strawberry jelly-coated toast around in his runny, over-easy fried eggs.

Gilly hated talking in front of people, not because she was the least bit shy, but because she felt judged for things in her life that she had no control over. She slid in her desk next to the only person that hasn't judged her since she was nine years old, her best friend Kat.

"Well, I have to say that what I've heard so far

this afternoon, has been rather disappointing, to say the least. I think a full week for this assignment was more than enough time to prepare. I hope whoever comes up here next has put a little more thought into what will be a big part of your grade this semester. Okay, let's see, who's next? Gilda Stevens, come on up here and please end my day well," pleaded Mrs. Anderson.

"Oh great, now I'm responsible for ending her day well all because some of these idiots didn't put in the effort to write a decent report. Just what I needed," Gilly mumbled under her breath. She pushed away from her desk, made several steps and turned around to face her eleventh grade Social Studies class. The assignment was to write a report on how one can have a positive effect on society. Gilly's first thought on the matter was to eliminate some of the people in her class. But it would only be the mean ones who tormented and held the rest of them in this cruel daily psychological chokehold that needed to go. She just didn't understand how people like that always seemed to raise themselves to the top of the pecking order, without having one single redeeming quality. Thankfully, those were her own private thoughts and absolutely not the kind of thing she would ever share with any adult who had a good working brain. Not wanting to make any further eye contact, she took a deep breath and read her report.

LEARN NOW, USE LATER

There are no coincidences in life. The things that

come our way, whether welcomed or not, are part of a much greater plan than any human force. Why are some of us given great burdens to carry, while others seem to skip through life so easily? What we often hear is that it's because life isn't fair. Or maybe from our own individual perspectives it appears that way. But if we just take a moment to look to our right or left throughout our day, we will find ourselves much higher on the fairness scale than we would have believed. For there are always plenty of 'someones' more wanting than you, just around the corner.

Once we understand that we are free to choose which path in life to take, we must also understand there are consequences for each and every one. As we sit here today, eager to be free from the burden of rules and those in authority, there will always be accountability, if nothing more than just to be good citizens.

Even at our age, the smallest infractions can carry us far from the intended direction for success that we all should be on. We must invest ourselves in history, so that we can learn from the mistakes of those who came before us. We also must be willing to learn things that we don't think are necessary, or in our immaturity, believe we will never use. We must accept and study the courses that lie in front of us. Our work every day here is just as much about discipline, as it is acquiring new knowledge. Because, you never know what you are going to need until you need it one day.

In developing our attitudes and outlook on life,

be careful not to choose to live a sullen, unfulfilled life, with thoughts of how hard life will be one day because you have no direction. How do we do that? Come to an understanding within yourself of your passions, energy, strengths, your weaknesses and most of all, your dreams. And don't let anyone tell you that you can't. Find a dream partner. Write it down. Go back and read it, change it if you must, but make it your revision, not someone else's.

Gilly knew her face had to be beet red since her ears felt like they were on fire. She was absolutely certain, even after all her efforts that morning, that she couldn't have picked the worst thing to wear.

"Oh Gilda, that was marvelous, absolutely marvelous. I'm so impressed. Now that's what I've been waiting to hear," declared Mrs. Anderson as she stood with a heavy applause.

"Thank you, ma'am," replied Gilly.

She could feel the sting of each knife blade plunging in her back, as she walked back to her desk. Not only did some of their faces show their obvious contempt for what appeared to be a well thought out and written report, it didn't help that she got a standing ovation from Mrs. Anderson. She also had it in her head that almost everyone was mentally mocking her homemade green corduroy dress as the bell rang.

"Okay we'll finish up tomorrow. Class dismissed," announced Mrs. Anderson.

"Hey Gilly, how many wishes did you use today? Did the same leprechaun that made your hideous green dress write your report for you, too?" laughed Regina Hatcher.

"Yeah, Regina he sure did. And guess what, I got one wish left. Did you want to know what it is?" Gilly replied.

"C'mon Gilly, why do you let her get under your skin?" Kat said as she pulled Gilly out into the hall.

"I wonder what her paper is going to be about? How to move up in the world by destroying your competition?" Gilly spewed.

"Forget her Gilly, you know how she can't stand anyone to one-up her. So, about your report, that was really good. How'd you come up with all that stuff anyways?"

"Oh, that was just a collection of my mom's daily doses of advice. I really need an "A" on that paper. Too bad I don't believe any of it. I know she means well. It's just she's always trying to teach me about life, have a better attitude about things, and try to figure out what I want to be one day. And honest to God, I just really have no idea. The way things are at home right now, I just can't see my way out. Mom works so hard and sometimes we're just barely able to pay the rent or keep the lights on, you know that. I'll probably wind up being one of those little old ladies in some foundation department somewhere, selling underwear for the rest of my life, or worse yet, slinging burgers at the Double Pattie. So, I'm not sure how I can ever even think about going to college, much less what I would major in. And my grades aren't that great right now either," answered Gilly in her usual self-defeated tone.

"Well, since we are best friends, how about I'll be your dream partner. You know, like your mom said. Just think for a minute here. What kind of things do you like to do?" Kat asked.

"Are you serious?"

"You know me pretty well Gilly, but I only know some of you. You hide a lot of yourself that even you don't want to see. And you know what, it could always be worse."

"Really, how exactly?" asked Gilly, as she rolled her eyes.

"Well, to start with, we could have parents that don't care about what we want to do with our lives. I think mine actually care too much sometimes. Anyway, I think you stand just as good a chance of getting ahead as anyone else here. I mean just look around. Most of the girls here only want to talk about who they're going to marry, how many kids they want, their names, blah, blah, blah. I mean there's nothing wrong with that, I guess. And I get it that most of the nurses, teachers and secretaries are all women, and that's the direction we're all supposed to take. But this is 1972, not 1952 for crying out loud. And there are all kinds of opportunities just waiting for girls like us to grab ahold of. Don't get me wrong, I think my mom being a nurse is really cool, if that's what you want to do the rest of your life. But some of us have to be willing to think outside of the box, and that attitude of yours isn't going to get you anywhere. So, Gilly, I really do believe a lot of what your mom talks to you about. Dreams were given to us for a reason and there's no reason why any of us can't choose the one we want, or the one we think we might be good at."

"Alright then, dream partner, what's outside of your box?" asked Gilly.

"You don't seem like you even mean it, but since you asked, I want to be a fashion designer one day," answered Kat.

"You're kidding me, really! You wear the craziest clothes, Kat. Look at you with your red and white pin-striped pants and that silk yellow and pink-flowered shirt. Not exactly what everyone else is wearing, but I just thought you liked wearing weird stuff," replied Gilly. What she didn't dare tell her best friend, is that those pin-striped pants made her short legs look two sizes bigger. Gilly towered over Kat by at least five inches. She wasn't by any means a fashion designer, but Kat's petite size needed clothes to show off the athletic build she was born with. And Kat was blessed with perfectly straight black hair that Gilly would have killed for. But instead of wearing it loose, she was always coming up with some kind of weird looking updo.

"Look around, Gilly. All the girls look like they bought their clothes at the same factory. Blue jean bell bottoms, paisley print tops, mini-skirts, white boots or those ankle-breaking clog shoes. I can't help myself. I really love bright colors, patterns and materials. And what's wrong with being a little different?"

"Nothing, I suppose." Gilly hated to be preached to, even by her best friend. She would love nothing more than to have something store bought. She would die, right then and there, for a pair of those white knee-high boots.

"So, I'm waiting ..." Kat said as she stood there with her hands on her pin-striped covered hips.

"Okay, well I do like, don't you dare tell anyone, I love detective books. Like, I'm always trying to figure out who did what the whole time I'm reading them. I have a bunch of the Nancy Drew books that Aunt Maggie gave me. She sends them to me all the time. I'm seriously hooked on the Master Detective magazines. I'm always trying to talk Mom into buying me the latest one, when it comes out."

"I did not know that. You do hide things well. There you go then. You can be a detective one day."

"Those aren't real jobs," Gilly replied.

"Yes, they are. There are tons of police detectives and private detectives, and even investigative reporters. They have to do detective work to get their stories. They can't just make stuff up, just because it sounds good."

"Yeah, but not women."

"You just said you like the Nancy Drew books. Nancy sounds like a girl to me."

"Yeah but—"

"Look, didn't we take an oath to always be honest to each other? You're letting all this negative thinking inside your head revise your own dream and you haven't even written it down yet. You're already your own worst enemy. You need to try to believe some of what your mom is saying. I know our parents say stuff all the time that even they know isn't true. And they will never tell you where they messed up. Just a constant 'we don't want you to make the same mistakes we made'. But I really have to agree with her on the dream part. My parents won't even listen to the idea of me being a fashion designer. They both think it's a total waste of time. Mom wants me to be a nurse like her. She says it's about helping people and being part of the solution, and not creating more problems for women... And you know my dad is gone more than he's home. So, when he's home, he usually just sits there and agrees with Mom about almost everything. You know ever since he was made partner in his advertising company, he's gone more now than before. Sometimes I think my mom gets mad when he leaves for days at a time, and then there are times when she almost seems glad when he's gone. Go figure. That's another thing she tells me. She really wants me to have a job where I can make enough money to support myself, like her, and not worry about having to get married or stay married because I can't afford not to. Makes me a little nervous sometimes when she talks like that. Anyway, he always comes home with presents for both of us."

"How in the world would being a fashion designer

cause more problems for women?" Gilly asked with one raised eyebrow.

"Well, I think she's just way too serious all the time. You know our parents' generation just can't imagine that there could be careers out there, that someone can actually enjoy doing. She just thinks that women spend way too much time worried about how they look, rather than what they can contribute, or whatever. And if you could see my mom's face, and how tired she is when she walks in the door at the end of the day, you'd know what I'm talking about. There's just something about being around sick and dying people all day that just doesn't appeal to me."

"Well, that's easy for your mom to say considering she's drop-dead gorgeous. I mean she could literally wear a sack and look like a runway model."

"I know right, and she tells me all the time how pretty I am, but I know I'm not. I mean, I'm not ugly either, but sometimes I think that the right clothes can make a woman feel better about herself, which will give her the confidence she needs to step out in the world and fulfill her dreams. It's a win-win for everybody, don't you think? So, if I can wear my dream every day, the least you can do is write yours down and consider it."

"Yeah sure, Kat. You come up with a new outfit that will give me this confidence you're talking about so I can be a detective one day, and I'll be your first customer. But for right now, I'm getting cold standing here. I've got to hurry up and catch the bus, get home and help my mom."

"Ok, Gilly, but promise me that you'll at least think about it."

"Yeah, yeah, I'll think about it."

Once she found a seat on the bus, the first thing Gilly thought about was Regina's really cool, white knee-high boots, as she rubbed the chill bumps off her legs. She let out one long breath, longingly gazing out the window as the bus driver dropped off one classmate after another in their nice neighborhoods, with their sprawled out, ranch-style homes sitting among their perfectly manicured yards. The two-story red brick homes smattered about were still her favorites. These jerks, who thought they were better than her, had no idea just how good they had it. All she could think about was how much fun it would be to have her own space, on the second story of one those picture-perfect homes. She couldn't imagine what it would be like to have birthday, dance or pool parties in one of those nice houses. It was easy for Kat to lecture her about her bad attitude, when she had no reason to have one. Both of her parents had really good jobs, and she lived in one of those ranch-style houses two blocks from their school.

Then the inevitable came when the bus crossed the railroad tracks where her dreary little white–chipped, painted two-bedroom house sat among all the others filled with families just like hers, all of them just barely getting by. She really did believe life wasn't fair. How many more weeks did she have left to take this route, before it would soon be over, only to have to start all over again next year? And Gilly was absolutely certain, that short of some miracle, the bus would never have to stop for her on the good side of the tracks.

CHAPTER 2

THE NOT SO INCREDIBLE HULK
May 1972

FROZEN IN TIME AND space in the Sullivan's Grocery Store frozen food isle on my birthday, Saturday, May 6, 1972.

It's one of the last public humiliation snapshots I have in my mind of Joseph "Joey" Franklin Stevens.

"Gilly, get your room picked up, then we can head to the store and get a few groceries and the stuff for your cake. Do you want to ask some of your friends over this afternoon for a little birthday get together? I can make hot dogs if you want. Sylvia said that Joey can stay with them for a couple of hours so he won't be in the way" asked Claire.

"Mom, you know the only friend I have is Kat, and she said to call her when we get home. So, it's gonna be just me and her," replied Gilly.

"It's her and me. And I just don't understand why such a bright and beautiful young lady like you doesn't have more friends. Maybe you need to try a little harder."

Kat was my only friend because she seemed to understand Joey, or at the very least, she's been willing to put up with him all these years. Kat's mom, Sylvia Cooper, was also my mom's only friend as well. It wasn't at all hard for Mom and me to make friends, it was just almost impossible to keep them. So, without telling each other, I think we both just stopped trying. It seemed that for most people, no matter how old they were, being around Joey was just too much weight in the room. He would lash out at the smallest infractions on his space, and then the next minute want to hug you so tight that it would take several 'let go Joey's' to get him loose. People around us just didn't want to think that what happened to us could be their reality one day, too. Joey didn't have a disease that anyone could catch, it's just this thing that caught him. And it appeared to be comfortably taking over all of our lives. Sylvia was more than a friend, she was also a registered nurse and would sometimes drop by to check on Joey, to see how he was doing. A few times she stayed with him so that Mom could take Kat and me to Shopper's Fair, and even a movie once. It was a couple of years ago when we got to go see *Love Story* at The Paramount Theatre. I'm pretty sure Kat and I cried as much as Mom did, considering my mom still wore her black hair straight, parted down the middle and long like the star Ally McGraw, and my dad could have been Ryan O'Neal's twin. It was almost like watching our very own lives unfold before us on the big screen, but this time I was losing my mom instead of my dad. But a trip afterwards to the Double Pattie for burgers and fries seemed to bring all of us back to the real world we still had to live in, especially when Kat and I spotted some kids from school rolling their eyes at us for eating with my mom.

"Mom, really? Show me your list of friends. Tell me, when is the last time you left this house and did anything fun? I'm getting too old to play this game. It is what it is. Most of the kids in my class think that they're somehow better than me. Anyway, most of them are all fake and gossip too much. When they're not doing that, they make fun of everybody who is not just like them. You know, Mona Matthews called me one time and pretended that she didn't like Regina Hatcher. And I said yeah, she's real mean, and the whole time Regina was listening in on their other phone. Then they both started laughing at me for thinking I could be Mona's friend. I still can't believe I fell for that lame setup. Then she said all the boys called me 'Lil Orphan Annie', and Kat dresses like Bozo the

Clown. That's why Kat and I are blood sisters, and Mona and Regina are the dumb duo. Anyway, I'd rather have one honest friend with me on my birthday, than a room full of two-faced snobs."

"Okay Gilly, have it your way. But I think you're being way too judgmental. You have no idea what goes on when some of those kids get home. Maybe a lot of what you're seeing and hearing is learned behavior."

"Well, it's not my job to teach them how to be decent human beings."

"I don't know about that. Some of life's most important lessons come from the most unlikely places sometimes. Just keep that in mind, young lady."

"Okay, I'll be sure to remember that the next time I'm being publicly humilated. Can we change the subject now? Since we're already going to be out, do you think we can stop at Shopper's Fair on the way to the grocery store? I really need to get some more makeup. Aunt Maggie sent me ten dollars for my birthday, inside my new Nancy Drew book," begged Gilly.

"I'm sorry honey, but if we can manage to get in and out of Sullivan's without Joey making much of a scene, it'll be a good day. Besides, I've got to pick up some fabric from Mrs. Jennings on the way home. She's having a bridal shower for her oldest daughter in a few weeks, and she wants me to make new draperies for her living and dining rooms. It's the only work I have coming my way right now, and we need the money before the first of the month to pay the rent. With any luck, I might get a few referrals from her if I do a good enough job."

"So, what if we can't pay the rent, does that mean we're homeless again? This will be the third time we've had to move since Joey got sick. Where are we going this time, Mom? There's nothing left in town that we can afford," Gilly whined as she flailed her arms around.

"Now Gilly, we were never homeless, just a different home. You know that. And don't worry, we will never, ever be homeless. You know your Aunt Maggie will never let that happen. She said she has a place for us whenever we're ready."

"What exactly does ready mean? When we're run out of town? I don't want to move away, especially not there. I don't like it where she lives because that's a dumb, little town with nothing to do. All I have is one friend in the whole world, and you want to take that away from me too, because of Joey? Why do you let him wear those stupid outfits anyway? I'm so tired of him embarrassing us everywhere we go. I just don't understand what we did to deserve this."

"Gilda, we've been over this a thousand times. I'm sure if he could help it, he would. Now stop talking like that in front of him. You know we don't know what he understands."

"Well, obviously he understands enough to try to get his way all the time, in case you haven't noticed. Which is what we've been doing for the last, I don't know how many years now Mom, since I was nine years old?"

"Gilda, that's enough, please."

It was an old argument that she always felt guilty for afterwards. She knew she had hit a nerve when her mom called her Gilda. She only heard that name from her teachers at school, and when she crossed the line with her mom.

"I'm sorry, Mom, really. I didn't mean to make you feel bad," Gilly said as she hung her head.

"It's okay, Gilly, I'm sorry, too. We'll manage, we always do. Anyway, I've got a surprise for you for your birthday, that I think you're really going to be happy about."

Gilly just stood there, deep in her own thoughts. Her mom only had to manage in her own world, which boiled down to sitting behind her sewing machine and watching Joey all day. She had no idea how hard life was to manage on the outside for her. These people that I'm forced to deal with everyday are the kind of enemy forces she has no clue about. The teachers certainly don't help, while they stand around completely indifferent to the brutal taunting and segregation going on right under their noses, and the effects it has on the kids living on her side of the tracks. She guessed they thought it wasn't their problem. But shouldn't making people at least act like they care be someone's problem?

These outings were never anything Gilly looked forward to. They were always so exhausting. Not because she wasn't in shape physically. She just simply didn't have the capacity to keep another human being in check for their lack of social skills or self-control. There was no map or rule book that had ever been written, for what could unfold once they left the safety net of their home.

As was their usual custom, Gilly flipped the seat forward on their rusty old two-door white Falcon, while Joey crawled into his spot in the back. She settled in the passenger seat and held her breath, waiting to see if they would be going anywhere or not. They never knew if their old car would crank. It was always a hit or miss. But it was a go this time as Claire cranked the car, pushed the clutch in as they lurched backward down their driveway onto Beechwood Street, then on towards Sullivan's Grocery Store. The windows were down, and the wind was blowing Claire's beautiful long black hair, while Joey just bobbed and swayed as the radio played. 'I can see clearly now the rain is gone, I can see all obstacles in my way, gone are the dark clouds that had me blind.' Gilly sang along the whole time thinking to herself that this was a sign that today was going to be a bright sunshiny day, it just had to.

"Okay, if you can keep up with Joey, then I can run down the isles quickly and get everything I have on my list."

"Sure, Mom. I'll take him over to the magazine racks. He likes looking at the new comic books, especially The Incredible Hulk. Maybe I'll buy him a new one with some of my birthday money." Gilly always hated this duty. He was so much bigger than her and he didn't always listen.

"C'mon Joey."

"Okay, Gilly."

Gilly got Joey situated facing the comic books, while she took only a few steps to where her favorite magazine was usually kept. She flipped through Sullivan's large selection of magazines, still feeling bad for her words and tone towards her mom. She thought about the conversation she and Kat had the day Mrs. Anderson gave her that standing ovation, over her report. She knew she should be more thankful that her mom cared enough to try to make her birthday special. Her mom was running around Sullivan's, probably buying stuff that they really couldn't afford, instead of being at home, working on what would pay their rent in a few days.

Then suddenly, there it was right before her eyes. The newest Master Detective magazine, and it practically jumped off the rack right into her hands. The cover read, DOES A KILLER LIVE NEXT DOOR TO YOU? "Oh man, I've got to have this one." She flipped through the pages, reading about all the signs to look for if a potential killer lived next door, when she turned around and found to her horror, Joey was gone.

"Joey, Joey, where are you? Oh my God, Joey Joey!!!"

Gilda's face flushed in an instant and her entire breakfast of over-easy eggs and toast felt like they were well on the way up and out of her stomach.

Her heart pounded so loud it sounded like the store's loud speaker was somehow connected to her pulsating blood vessels. The thought of having a heart attack would be better than having to answer for how this might end. She just couldn't believe this nightmare was unfolding, and of all places. She never lost him before. In all these years, even her mom had never let him out of her sight, under these circumstances. She twirled around again and again, and he was still gone. She shoved the magazine back in the rack and took off past the registers, going up and down the isles jammed with grocery carts tilted in every direction. While their handlers, most in hair curlers, checked off their lists and glared at her as though she was interrupting their decision between meatloaf or trying fried Spam tonight. From the canned goods, jellies and jams, to the cereal, coffee, bread and finally, as she rounded the corner on the end of isle eight, there he was in all his unashamed glory. Joey was opening and closing the glass door that stored the frozen vegetables, shoving a Miss Debbie cupcake into his mouth. He had chocolate all over his hands and the glass doors, and the sides of his pants were smeared with the same dark brown icing and cupcake crumbs. And in his pockets, he had squished and shoved more cakes. The nearly empty box lay open on the floor, next to his old, untied black tennis shoes. Her mind, at this point, was reeling from feeling pity for him, to wanting to walk away and pretend as though she didn't know him.

She was so tired of making excuses for him, tired of cleaning up after him, and tired of babysitting him. She wanted to be someone else, anywhere else, and never lay eyes on him again. All she could think about was how unfair this was. Today was her seventeenth birthday, and now this one was ruined, too, like they have all been for years now.

"Hey kid, what's wrong with him? Are you kidding me? What kind of retard is he, young lady? And where's your mom? I'm not cleaning up this mess, and you gotta pay for that stuff now, you know!" yelled the store clerk.

Gilly got defensive, as she always did. It was one thing for her to get aggravated and talk about him to her mom, but she was still protective enough that she didn't want anyone else to, especially like that. "Don't you dare talk to him like that! You need to show some respect and stop being so mean, because he can't help that his brain is broken. And for your information, his name is Joseph Franklin Stevens and he's not a retard, he's my dad!"

Claire heard all the commotion, as she quickly rounded the corner with her buggy loaded with all the fixings for Gilly's birthday dinner. By this time, her daughter was in tears, while her husband just stood there covered in chocolate, still clutching a bag of Jolly Green Giant green beans.

She had the perfect birthday all planned out in her head, for her daughter. But now the damage was done. There was no going back. Claire was humiliated as well, but not for herself. It was never about her. She knew that her husband was innocent and never meant anyone any harm. His motives today were pure, as they've always been. That's one thing that never changed. But once again, in her heart and mind, it would only be their daughter who would suffer. Like he had done so many times before, Joey had just committed one of the most shameful of all unpardonable sins. He had just embarrassed and publicly humiliated his only child, Gilda Marie Stevens.

On the car ride home, Joey said he was sorry, like he has a million times before. He just wanted a snack, and then he saw the big, green man staring right back at him from behind the glass door. "I'm sorry, Gilly, did I get us in trouble again? I just wanted a snack like Claire promised, and then I saw The Incredible Hulk and wanted to get him for you for your birthday. You like him too, don't you?"

"Yeah, sure, just what I've always wanted, another green giant. Joey, that wasn't The Incredible Hulk, that was a pack of Jolly Green Giant green beans," Gilly answered in complete disgust. This was not the role she was supposed to play. Not at this stage in his life and certainly not at this time in her's. Of all days for Joey to pick out the clothes he had on. That stupid green sweatshirt and tan pants he had cut the bottoms off of, that made the scene today much, much worse.

We didn't have to clean the chocolate off the door or the floors. The manager just told my mom that he thought it would be best not to bring him in the store anymore. It seemed like he felt sorry for us a little bit, and didn't charge Mom for the Miss Debbie cupcakes either. And if things couldn't get any worse, the young kid that showed up to clean up Joey's mess, as we were walking away, is in my second-hour science class. The owner's son, Russell 'pimple face' Sullivan, has pestered me for the last two years to go out with him, and I always told him no. I'm sure now he was going to pay me back for turning him down, by telling everyone at school about this.

I didn't get a cake or the magazine, and Kat didn't come over. We just had toast and runny, over-easy fried eggs, the rest of the squished Miss Debbie cupcakes from Joey's pockets and watched, as always, what Joey wanted to watch, which was mainly reruns of Gilligan's Island. Mom gave me a new red, yellow and blue paisley print top and blue jean bell bottoms she had been secretly making. It wasn't the kind of clothes that made me feel confident, as Kat had talked about. Today's event only made me feel even sorrier for Mom and me. She was so upset that she didn't stop to pick up the material for the drapes. I guess we won't have the money for next month's rent now. It didn't turn out to be a sunshiny day after all. Just one more dark, cloudy day to add to my list.

I laid in bed that night, not giving in to tears as I've heard my mom do so many nights, but listening to the clattering sound of a train echoing only a few blocks away. I've imagined all the places I could go or would go, given the chance. It didn't matter if it was east or west, north or south, oceans or mountains, anywhere but here. Tonight, my destination to force into my dreams was New York City. I was sitting at my desk, dressed in a light gray vest and skirt, with a white long-sleeve blouse. I had a pencil behind my ear, and my wavy hair was suddenly long and straight, and fell forward as I reached over to answer the phone. I somehow perfected the ability to mentally set myself up where I wanted to magically be transported, and most of the time it worked. Here, I would be Nancy Drew's assistant and we had a murder to solve. Before I closed my eyes for the last time, I glanced at the bedside picture of this man that I can barely remember, pushing me in a tire swing. I can remember all the material things we once had; the two-story red brick house, my room, the yard, the garage with Dad's workshop in the rear, the tree, and even the feel of the tire under my legs. But this larger-than-life man, with the keen good looks of Ryan O'Neal at one time, that made all of it possible, wasn't even a faint shadow in my mind anymore. I've tried over and over again to go back in time and see the face of the man I used to call Dad, the man who was my dad. The times we shared together had somehow slowly been replaced with the way things were now. He just looked so handsome and happy standing over me, with his hands on the tire rope, dressed in a yellow button-up shirt and a pair of tan pants that haven't had the bottoms cut off. And me with my big, new front-teeth smile and pig tails. I should be watching my parents grow old together, rather than having to tolerate this once-great man steadily becoming an overbearing child. Mom lets him wear whatever he wants now, just to keep him calm. He could walk out of his room with shorts and a t-shirt on, in the dead of winter, or a sweatshirt on a hot mucky day, like he did today. He had on his favorite green sweatshirt, those same tan pants with his dress-blue socks and worn-out black tennis shoes. One day when we weren't looking, he took a pair of Mom's pinking shears and cut off the bottom of his pants, because he said they didn't fit over his shoes. She just said we had to do whatever we needed to do not to irritate him. So, that's why I call him Joey. I'm sure I use to call him Dad, but Mom said to just call him Joey because that's what he answers to now. She said that when people have this 'broken brain' condition, their minds have trouble with time, places and people, and it all gets lost and jumbled up in their heads. That's the craziest thing I've ever heard of, but I guess it's true. Because all he wants to talk about are people I've never met, while insisting he's been to Gilligan's Island. Then every once in a while, he announces, clear out of the blue, that he's going to take me to see the castles again one day. I just don't get it. Mom tries to stay strong and focused on what we need to do to stay together, but she doesn't know how many nights I've lain in bed, listening to her cry all the way from the living room, which had become her bedroom. She wanted me to still have my own room and space, while she stayed up most nights anyway, bent over the sewing machine.

Aunt Maggie offered for us to come live with them. She said there was a Veterans' Hospital nearby for Joey and that maybe they could help him, but I don't like it there, I never have, and I don't like Uncle Mack. There's just always been something about him that didn't sit right with me. But, tonight is the first night that I'm starting to believe we have no other choice. Mom has been carrying this burden for a long time, and I know it's not fair for her to have to deal with Joey by herself much longer. I don't want to move again. But what else can we do? I feel like my mind is starting to break, too. I want to go back to where we were, when we were a real, normal family like everyone else, before they called.

CHAPTER 3

THERE IS MORE
December 1940

JOSEPH FRANKLIN STEVENS LEARNED to accept what was given to him. Whether it was a sucker punch in the stomach, a full-handed whack on the back of his head, or an empty plate. He no longer believed he deserved better, or had the will to ask for it. Thus, he accepted that the empty desk at school would not be waiting on him either.

It hadn't always been this way. At one time, his mother, Natalie Joy Stevens, had been his favorite sweetheart. He told her so each and every Valentine's when they would exchange their cards made of white doilies and red construction paper, and on Mother's Day when she only had him to thank her. Her cards were the ones he worked on the longest. Only the best for his mom, she deserved it. He wanted a perfect cut-out heart and the most heartfelt poem that he could write, for the woman who brought him into this world. She was the sweetest girl in the whole world, according to the snippets he would write, and he promised that he would give to her, her every wish one day.

"Just you wait and see, Mom. I'm going to get you out of this place one day. I want you to have a place like Mrs. Gertie's. I've seen how you stare when we walk by, with all those pretty flowers in her yard and window boxes. You deserve it Mom, you really do. I'm going to have my own money one day, and I'll make sure you have some real roses every year for Valentine's, Mother's Day and your birthday, I promise."

Mrs. Gertie Montgomery was probably the closest that Natalie had to a friend, in the twelve tormenting years she had been married to Joseph's father. Hank Stevens was a foul-mouthed, controlling man that had no desire to please anyone but himself. And most days even that didn't seem to work, as he wallowed in his own self misery. His five-foot, ten-inch frame was as fit as it was in 1921, when he was an amateur middleweight boxer in New Orleans. The fights were never legal, as they were always held in some empty warehouse near the French Quarter. When it came to fighting, all he cared about was his nightly winnings and having his girl there cheering him on. That is, until he had the chance of a lifetime to fight Billy Murray, the official middleweight champion of 1920.

Late one night, Hank had just finished working out, getting ready for the big event where he had a chance of winning five thousand dollars. This was also the big break that he had longed for, where he could possibly make a name for himself in the legitimate boxing world. As he was heading down Canal Street in his old Monroe Coupe, a brand-new Alfa Romeo barreled right into him, hitting him broadside. The injuries both drivers sustained ended two careers that night. As fate would have it, the other broken up driver was a drunken Billy Murray. Ironically, Hank walked away with a broken jaw, cracked ribs and no way to ever earn a living, doing the only thing he loved. For when Billy Murray regained consciousness, he blamed the whole accident on Hank. With no witnesses, Hank had no other choice but to leave town.

He went on to marry his girl, Natalie Joy, because she didn't care about the money, she loved him for who he was, or sadly to say, who she thought he was. She saw Hank as her knight in shining armor, as well as her only way out of the gritty, working-class slums that she grew up in, and away from her abusive father. Unfortunately, she found herself living much the same way only sixty miles north, in the city of Baton Rouge. From the minute Hank put that ring on her finger, he controlled every minute of her life. He wanted her home, in the kitchen, or cleaning the house all the time. It didn't matter that the whole yard was an eyesore, with junk everywhere. He wanted the inside of the house spotless. Any time she was away from the house, was a waste of time to him, except for Sundays. Hank would let her take Joey to church, where Mrs. Gertie would play the organ and minister to other women. And he only did that so the church members would be sure to use him for their car repairs and gas.

Looking back, Joey also fondly remembers when he had a place at their kitchen table, with all the fried chicken and white gravy, mashed potatoes, fresh green beans and hot rolls he could eat. His mouth still watered when he thought about his favorite chocolate cake with dark chocolate icing, for report card days, birthdays and just because "you're my favorite son" (which puzzled him because he was not only her only son, but only child).

Hank Stevens thought Natalie was too soft on him. He would constantly verbally assault her, accusing her of making his son a 'sissy boy'. Hank was anything but soft on his delicate, kind and submissive wife. He was a bully and a brute, and Joey thought so many times of how much better their life would be without him. He didn't care where they lived. Anywhere but here, with a yard full of old rusted cars and tires next to his father's shop.

He remembers asking, "Mom, why doesn't Dad like us?"

Her answer was so plain and simple that even an eight-year-old could understand. “Honey, he doesn’t like himself. Sometimes I think he’s the one that believes he isn’t good enough. Like somehow, he failed us. That shop over there was never your father’s dream. He wanted to be a famous boxer and through no fault of his own, his career ended. This man pulled out in front of your dad when he wasn’t looking, and he nearly killed him. That accident ended it all. We didn’t have any money, and at that time had nowhere else to go. So, we moved in here, where his father put him to work in the shop. His father, Jack, was a heavy drinker, and still to this day I have no idea what happened to his mother. No one around here seems to know, not even your dad. Jack died right after you were born, and your dad talked often about wanting to go back to New Orleans and starting fresh. With the economy the way it is, he just feels like he has no choice but to stay right here and work. This house and that shop are where he grew up, and it became his, after his dad died. So, unfortunately, he will probably die here one day, too. He just stopped dreaming, because he thought there was nothing left.”

That’s why Joey felt like he did. He either had to roll with the punches, or get punched. Most days, as hard as he tried, he still felt like he was in that ring with his father, the middleweight boxer who lost his chance years ago.

At one time, he not only had a bed inside, but his own room. His room had sky blue walls, with a honey oak wagon wheel headboard and a yellow bedspread that had cowboys printed on it, in blue and green shirts, twirling lassos with black cowboy hats, riding their black bucking horses. Every cowboy had brown leather chaps and vests with fringe, and spurs on their boots. Rarely did he ever need the small, gold windup clock on the nightstand, because the smell of his mom's freshly baked biscuits had his feet on the floor like clockwork at six every morning. He had a matching four-drawer chest of drawers that was full of neatly pressed, folded hand-me-down pullover shirts and shorts, with a full drawer of socks and underwear, that still looked good as new. Hank hadn't given Natalie any money to buy anything new in years, so they relied solely on secondhand clothes and toys that Mrs. Gertie would bag up and give them on Sundays. She was the same size as Natalie and had a son named Buck, who was just a year older than Joey, with the same lanky build. She was good about seeing to it that the people in her church had their needs met, even if she had to dig in her own pocketbook to make it happen. Even as a child, Joey was sure that some of those toys had never been used, especially since they were still in their unopened boxes as he tore away the shiny red and green Christmas paper.

Natalie spent as much time on his hanging clothes as any presser at the dry cleaners, always making sure her son was done-up well at school or church. She didn't want any offhanded remarks about her boy being the son of a grease monkey. Although she knew that what her husband did for a living was a much-needed and well-respected occupation, she didn't want her son to have to follow in his dad's footsteps. She wanted more for him. He made excellent grades in all his courses, and she wanted him to be the first in her family to graduate and go to college. This was her way of preparing him for a different world, and hopefully a much kinder world, away from her husband, Hank.

Joseph Franklin Stevens was a genius at designing, building and taking things apart. His brown, wooden toy box at the foot of his bed was full of Tinker Toys, jigsaw puzzles and Lincoln Logs. And he was a sure shot at knocking anyone home that was at any base when he got up to bat. His wooden bat and glove were his gifts from Santa when he was just eight years old. So, she was convinced that she saw not only strength in body, but in mind, and she would make sure that those hands would be a builder of great things one day. This world that her husband had created for them, would never be her son's. She would make sure of it.

Neither Natalie nor Joey got to see the fulfillment of those promises, because when he was just eleven, Natalie tragically died of tuberculosis. The day after she died, Hank wasted no time tearing through the house and collecting all her things. All her clothes, shoes, purses, scarfs and her memory box of her son's handmade cards were thrown into a pile and set on fire in the backyard. Even the wedding picture of Hank and Natalie Stevens was taken off their bedroom wall and buried with her. The pain that her favorite and only son felt that day, could only have ended if he had been buried with her as well. She had not only been his whole world, but the foundation for all his hope and strength. It was because of her that he excelled in school. It was because of her that he could knock the ball out of the park. He did it all to make her happy. To make his mom proud. His best girl. His favorite sweetheart. He now understood the story of his father living in his own hate-filled world and he was terrified, with his mom gone, he would one day wind up right there with him.

In the days that followed, there were often times when Joey thought that perhaps his mom did raise a 'sissy boy', when he cried himself to sleep. To make things worse, his father blamed him for bringing that disease home from school and killing his wife. For years Joey believed him. He knew he would never graduate high school, much less go to college. But, somehow, like Mrs. Gertie promised on that fateful day, heaven had just inherited a new angel and she would show him a way out one day, when the time was right.

All that he had seen and heard since his mom went to heaven, only reinforced in Joey's heart and mind, that his father never wanted to remember her again. He could only guess that his father was just glad she was gone. Glad he had one less person to disappoint. But, he managed to hide and hold onto one thing. It was a Cuban Cigar box that had a dozen or so cards, that his mom had cut and pasted for her favorite son, her one and only sweetheart. The only lasting remembrance of her. It was his memory box.

Now, he was lucky if his old man brought him a cold biscuit in the morning, that he would wash down with water from the hose pipe. Occasionally for lunch, he would throw a peanut butter or bologna sandwich at him, in the same way one would throw leftovers out to a stray dog. But, when suppertime came, Hank walked next door to eat and wouldn't come back. Hank's new wife, Iris, insisted it be this way. Within days after Natalie's death, Hank brought her home one night from The Airline Bar and Grill, and she never left. This would be the beginning of the end, of the life Joey once had. His bedroom, once full of cowboys and black bucking horses, was soon emptied out to make room for a nursery for his half-brother, Tillis, who was born one year after his mother's death.

Joey, who was once the heartbeat of his mom, was no longer sleeping in his wagon wheel bed, but instead, curled up every night in an army-style cot, in the same shop where all the broken-down cars sat, on the grease and oil-stained concrete. The once freshly washed and pressed clothes had long ago been replaced with a pair of tattered and grease-stained overalls. He would not be seen as the son of a grease monkey, as his mom once feared, he would become one.

The young, beaten-down son, who was once promised the world, had for years kept his head underneath the hood of every Ford, Chevrolet, Buick and Pontiac that rolled into his father's gas station and car repair business. This had been his lot in life since he was eleven years old. There was never any room for failure, for to do so would result in one of Hank's tirades, followed by his angry, heavily greased hand.

The nights were bone-chilling cold in the winter, and the summers were worse, fighting off swarms of mosquitos, the thick air of Louisiana's sauna heat, and his recurring nightmare of his mom's final days. His only sense of belonging, in the world, came when he pulled out the Cuban Cigar box from underneath his cot. He would read his mom's notes to him, while running his young but calloused hands over the handmade construction paper cards, wondering why. Why her and not Hank?

Still, in his heart, he always tried to find something to be grateful for. That's what his mom always taught him. To be grateful. Even as she lay in that hospital bed dying, she told her son to always look up. "The world is a big and beautiful sight to see and experience. Don't forget to dream. Remember what happens when you forget to dream. I love you enough to let you go, and you must do the same thing for me. Let me go my darling Joey, you're going to be fine, I promise. Don't ever forget there's something great waiting for you out there.

Right now, you are being prepared for something so much bigger and greater than this. When the opportunity comes, you must take it." Then he would wake up and see the dusty stream of the morning daybreak, swirling like smoke through the large glass-paned window in the shop office, which had become his home.

That was where he learned to tear apart an engine and put it back together in a day's time. He was like Houdini on steroids. In other words, engine there, engine gone, engine there again.

Even though the lingering effects of the Great Depression had a profound effect on so many businesses, the one thing that kept a roof over the Stevens' house, and food on the table, was that people still needed gas and car repairs. People had little to no money, to think about anything other than keeping their old rattle traps running. Joey was brilliant at improvising for broken belts and parts that just weren't available, or that people simply still couldn't afford.

So, when a new shiny, black Chevrolet Master Sedan pulled in that cold December day, not only did Joey look up, he nearly tripped over his feet, while wiping the grease off his hands, just so he could touch it. It was such a magnificent moving treasure he knew few had seen or owned since the economy tanked over a decade ago.

The doors opened and two distinguished men in perfectly pressed tan uniforms climbed out. They both had several rows of neatly stacked ribbons and the tallest, most-decorated one did all of the talking.

"Hi, son, fill it up and clean the windows while you're at it."

"Yes sir, it'll be my pleasure. She's a real beauty. Can I look under the hood?"

"You sure can, and take all the time you want. My name is Major Thomas Mitchell. What's your name young man, and how old are you?"

The young, nervous mechanic continued to rub his hands with an oil-stained rag, "I just turned eighteen. My name is Joseph Franklin Stevens, sir, but most everybody around here just calls me Joey," he said as he reached out to shake the well-groomed man's hand. Joey looked him over, and realized quickly that he was standing in the presence of greatness. For this man had honor and integrity written all over him. Not at all like his father that demanded it 'or else'. This man in front of him commanded it, not only by how he was dressed, but in the thoughtful and kind way he spoke.

"It's really good to meet you, Joey. How long have you been working here?"

Joey was beside himself. Not one single customer had ever taken the time to really talk to him, as most people were terrified of his father. Generally, it was only a brief "fill it up" or "fix my car" that he ever got from anyone that drove up. So, he was excited to talk about himself as he answered, "Most my life, sir, since I was about eleven years old. I know engines inside and out. Can take most of them apart in my sleep... And this one here is a real beaut."

"Really, well how would you like to work on something like this every day?" asked the officer. They were on a mission today and had to sign up at least two new recruits, to meet their daily quota. And Joey was easy pickings. Young, broke and nowhere to go. "So, how much you make here at Plank Road Gas and Auto Repair?"

"Make? Awe, I don't make nothing. I work here because that's what I got to do, to have a place to live and food to eat. There's my room right over there in that corner," Joey pointed out.

Major Mitchell really felt like this was another one of their rescues. There were young men scattered all over town, with no place to call home, through no fault of their own. He just didn't understand why folks didn't have the discipline he had. If their families could've just stuck together, like his did. Times had been tough for a lot of people, but some of them just didn't understand good old fashion hope, faith and prayer.

"Well, that don't seem right, don't seem right at all. Everybody deserves to get paid for what they do. What if I tell you that not only can you make some real money doing something that you're obviously good at, but see the world at the same time, and it not cost you a dime?"

"I don't know, I'd have to ask my dad. He owns this place."

"Son, I'm telling you as an officer of the United

States Army, you don't need your daddy's permission to join the Army and serve your country. And you know what, from just looking around, I have a feeling we can work all this out. Get in and I'll take care of any permission you might need." He dared Joey's old man to give him a hard time, for saving his son from his corner cot in the shop. He had been a boxer in the Army in his early days, and didn't think he would have any problem with this guy, who obviously saw no value in his own son.

Joey thought this had to be the opportunity that his mom told him would come his way one day, and in that very moment, knew he had to take it. He ran inside, grabbed his Cuban Cigar box, and threw it in a small canvas bag. He then hurried back out, knowing he didn't have much time before his dad returned from eating lunch with Iris and Tillis. The officer already had the rear car door opened, as he crawled in and sat on the clean, pleated brown leather back seat of that shiny new Chevrolet Master sedan. All he could do was think about his mom's last words, as he made his escape from the Plank Road Gas and Auto Repair shop, and the boxing ring of Hank Stevens.

Mrs. Gertie had a puzzled look on her face, as he waved when they drove by. He would have to remember to write to her. Tell her all the things he saw and did. After all, there was nobody else. She had been the one who made sure he had an extra blanket for his cot in the winter, and sneaked him in her house, on occasion, for a nice warm bath and haircut. When she could, she would send Buck down late in the evening with a brown paper bag full of fried chicken and hot homemade bread, or a piece of his favorite chocolate cake with chocolate icing, for his birthday. She also made sure he always had one decent hand–me-down outfit from Buck, for "just in case" there was some place important that he needed to go to one day. Joey supposed that was one thing he could be grateful for, like his mom said. Just when he thought he was all alone, Buck Montgomery would show up.

The United States Army Recruitment Office was nestled in a pale-yellow concrete block building that included a laundromat, drug store and beauty shop. A slender, dark-haired woman exited the drug store with her young son in tow, just as they pulled up. Joey could still remember taking the city bus downtown with his mom, around this time of year, to see and have his one and only picture taken with Santa Claus. That was the only photograph he had in his memory box, the same year that Santa gave him his lucky bat and glove. That must have been one of the occasions when Hank would disappear for a few days. When he would take off and things felt safe, and Joey would be the man of the house. Then when he would return, it seemed like Hank hated them even more.

"C'mom son, we've got some paperwork to take care of. Need to get you downtown on the bus this afternoon."

"Bus, where?"

"Camp Beauregard. Not too far from Alexandria. You know where that is?"

"No, sir, can't say I do," Joey answered.

"Yeah, I suppose you probably haven't been around much, have you?" Major Mitchell felt strangely relieved that he had saved another one, only to go to 'God knows where' one day. However, it did his heart good knowing this young rescue would have three square meals a day and a decent place to sleep, at least for the time being.

Joey signed his name and Major Thomas Mitchell proudly announced, "Congratulations, you're in the United States Army now." That little boy that he had just seen was probably on his way to see Santa Claus, but Joseph Franklin Stevens had an even better Christmas present waiting for him. He was going to see the world, just like his mom promised.

CHAPTER 4

FROM HIGH RISE TO STICK PEOPLE
June 1972

GILLY WAS STANDING IN the kitchen that day the telephone rang. She was the one who answered it. One call she will never forget. It was Friday, June 5th 1964. She and Kat had big plans that night to go to a slumber party for Annette Bennett's 9th birthday, and it was going to be her very first sleepover with all the girls in her third-grade class. She already had her sleeping bag and pajamas by the front door, and her mom had fixed Rice Crispy treats to take along. But, this would be the last sleepover she would ever be invited to, after that life-altering telephone call.

"I'll get it Mom, it's probably Kat. Hello?"

"May I speak to your mother?"

"Yes, sir, Mom it's for you."

"Hello, this is Claire Stevens."

"Hello, Mrs. Stevens, this is Sergeant Lance Gordon with the Shreveport Police Department. I'm calling to inform you that your husband has been in an automobile accident. Well, it's really not an automobile accident like most of them are ... and he doesn't appear to be injured in any way. Matter of fact, neither he nor the other driver was injured. It's really hard to explain but, they did have to physically pick him up out of the middle of the road and put him in an ambulance. They're holding him for observation at The General Hospital. From what the doctor is saying, I don't think he'll be able to drive himself home. They think he's had some kind of mental breakdown. You're going to need to come down here and get him. I'm real sorry ma'am."

"I don't understand, if no one was hurt, then why is he still there?" asked Claire.

"I can't answer that, you just need to come down here right away. There is a witness here that may be able to answer your questions. I'm just making the call ma'am. Again, I'm sorry," replied the sergeant.

Claire just stood there for a few moments holding the telephone receiver in her hand. She felt like if she released it from her hands and hung it up, she would have to move, and in that moment, she only wanted to make time stand still. If she could just turn back the hands of time, then she wouldn't have to do as the police officer said and go collect the pieces of the broken life, that belonged to the only man she ever loved.

Gilly had stood in silence long enough "Mom, what's wrong? Has something happened to Dad?"

"I don't know but you're going to have to stay with Kat tonight, honey, I'm sorry."

The only thing Claire knew to do, as she finally hung up, was to call her friends and next-door neighbors, Sylvia and Mark Cooper. She didn't have a car and didn't know how to drive, even if she did have one. She had so many anxious days and nights, worried that this day would come. That it would maybe only take one more unexpected trauma to break him down completely. She knew her husband had some awful memories of the war that quite often caused him horrible nightmares. The blood-curdling screams and night sweats could have come from no other place or time in his life. She also knew that there was something dark harboring inside of him, that he either couldn't or just didn't want, to share with her. When they lost their infant son a few years ago, she didn't think he was going to survive that. She felt like she lost a piece of her soul the day they buried her little boy, too. However, she knew there was another piece very much alive and well that needed her, and who didn't understand why her little brother's room was now empty. She couldn't afford to lose her husband as well, so she insisted he get help, which only sent him to their neighbor and friend, Mark Cooper. In time, he finally seemed to come out of his deep depression.

Now she was faced with her husband having yet another breakdown. Hopefully, Mark would be able to once again talk her husband through whatever nightmare or flashback he was experiencing from this wreck, that according to the police officer, no one was hurt.

"Mom, what about the party?"

"Please Gilda, don't argue with me. Just grab your stuff and let's go."

Claire left their nine-year-old daughter with Sylvia and her daughter Kat, while she and Mark drove to the hospital that late, humid June night. She couldn't imagine what could have set him off, to create such a crisis. She had just talked to him before he left work that afternoon, and he sounded fine. He was headed home and they were going out to dinner, to celebrate Mark Cooper's new job. Her friend Sylvia, was excited about her husband's new career change, as the salary increase would definitely contribute well into Kat's college fund.

"Mark, I just don't understand what could've happened. You've spent a good bit of time with him. Has he ever told you anything that went on, when he was in the Army? I don't mean to sound oblivious to how traumatic being a prisoner of war must have been, but he absolutely will not tell me anything. He just tells me not to worry, he's fine.

Well, I know he's not fine and he hasn't been fine in quite a while. He's been spending way too much time alone lately, and off to himself in the garage."

"Look Claire, I know you feel like as his wife you have a right to know what's been eating at him all these years, but men don't like to share their problems, especially the emotional ones, with their wives. It's our shoulder that is supposed to be used to cry on, not the other way around. Anyway, he made me give him my word that what he talked about, I would never repeat. I'm sorry but I have to keep it. It wouldn't solve anything if I told you anyway. It would only make you feel worse and there's no way he would want that. He adores you and Gilly, and he would never want to hurt either of you. This much I can tell you, I can't believe he held up for this long," answered Mark.

For a brief few moments, Mark's last words made her thankful that she didn't know. That perhaps keeping things to himself was the most selfless act her husband could do to protect his family. Maybe it is true, as she at one time heard, that some things are best left unsaid if it changes nothing.

When they pulled into the parking lot, once again she thought that if she just stayed in the car long enough, all this would be over and he would just walk out the door. Or maybe with Mark's help again, in a few hours or days, he would come around again like he did last time.

"C'mom Claire, I promise that I won't leave your

side. If you want me to go in first I will," Mark said as he held her close.

"Thanks Mark, but I need to do this, just please don't leave me," answered Claire.

When Claire and Mark walked through the emergency entrance to the hospital, she immediately knew her husband was in serious trouble. She could already feel the sting of the gravity of the situation, all over her body. The policeman and old man standing beside him told her as much, by the look on their faces.

"Hello, I'm Claire Stevens, are you the police officer that called about my husband?"

"Yes ma'am, let's all walk over here for a minute, so we can talk in private. Like I tried to explain on the telephone, there were no injuries to either party, not even a scratch on their automobiles. So, we're not sure what has happened, but this is the fellow that was involved and witnessed the whole thing."

As the old man removed his hat and scratched his head, he said "Ma'am, I'm really sorry about all this. My old hunting dogs usually stay put when I put them in the back of my truck. I had a rope tied around the neck of this one, with the other end tied in a hook on the back of the truck bed. I know some people don't like seeing that, but he was one of my jumpers. Without me knowing, the rope somehow must have come loose from the truck. Like I said, this one was of my jumpers so he must have seen something he thought was worth going after. When he did, your husband just ran right over him. I mean it wasn't his fault. It all happened so fast, he probably didn't have time to put on his brakes, to keep from running over him. I just heard tires screeching and looked to see what all the commotion was and noticed that old Buster was gone. Anyway, when I got out of the truck and walked past his car, there he was sitting in the middle of the road, holding the dog, crying and telling him how sorry he was. I kept trying to tell him it was nothing to get all worked up about, but he just kept rocking Buster in his arms like he was somebody's child or something. It's the worst thing I think I've ever seen. Here was this grown man, all dressed up in a suit, curled up in the middle of the road, rocking a dead dog. Then it got even worse when I pulled Buster out of his arms and threw him in the back of the truck. He just kept hollering that I shouldn't be treating him that way. I hope you tell him that I got plenty of dogs where that one came from. Honest to God, I've never seen anyone act that way over a dead dog, much less someone else's. I really hope he's going to be okay."

Claire burst into tears when she was taken into the curtained-off room, where her husband had been restrained and sedated. The navy business suit that he was wearing when he left home that morning, was now draped across a chair, covered in blood, and he was lying, almost comatose, staring at the ceiling. Her mind was reeling with the events that had just unfolded, and there was just no plausible explanation for what she was standing there looking at. Whatever happened to her husband on the way home that afternoon, she knew this wasn't just about a dog. He had suffered long before their infant son died, so this couldn't have been about his death either. The dead and empty look on his face said it all. The demons, that he had fought so hard to beat down all these years, had finally won. Joseph Franklin Stevens was once again a prisoner of war. Only this time, his captors weren't the Japanese. This time it would be his broken mind.

Claire lay across his chest and cried, "Oh, Joey, what's happened to you, please tell me what to do, I don't know what to do."

Mark spoke as softly and sternly as he knew how, "Look Claire, I'm not a doctor or anything, but whatever you do, don't let them commit him. You're his wife, so you've got to do what you can to get him out of here. All they're going to do is write him up as some sort of lunatic and lock him away. The best you can hope for is that he'll snap out of it in a few weeks, like he did last time. If not, as least he won't be locked away in an insane asylum. That's what they'll do to him. I've seen it happen too many times. I promise you won't be alone. Sylvia and I will be there for you and Gilly."

Mark was spot on. Within a matter of a few minutes, Claire was surrounded by three doctors, all wanting her to sign papers to commit her husband for a thirty-day mental evaluation. They had examined him from top to bottom and inside and out, and couldn't find anything medically wrong with him, other than a possible mental breakdown.

Mark and Claire stayed with Joey until the sedation wore off the next morning. Then they rolled him out of the hospital in a wheelchair, loaded him in the backseat of Mark's car, and left the unsigned paperwork behind along with any thought of locking him up. He was her husband, and Claire was absolutely determined, that with enough love and support, she would one day be able to wake him up from this unexplained new nightmare.

From the time he returned from the war, he was always determined to put it all behind him. All he saw, all he lived through, and all he tried to not remember clinging to his mind and soul. What made things go awry that day? What invisible demon attacked his once brilliant mind? He was the best at what he did. He had, in fact, escaped from the living hell hole his dad had created for him, and the one he had been imprisoned in all those years ago. Joseph Franklin Stevens had managed, against all odds, to go beyond the dreams his mother once had for him. He had not just become a great builder of things, Joey had become a great creator of things. He had started at the bottom and worked his way up, to become the top architect at Brannon and Fields Architects. He had just finished designing the most modern and gleaming building in the south. The Mammoth Arts and Science Museum would one day sit downtown, on the banks of the Red River. The long-awaited, groundbreaking event had been scheduled to take place the week after his accident. He and his family wouldn't be there to be a part of it all. Instead, in the days, months and years that followed, he would barely be able to hold a pencil and draw stick people.

Mark Cooper didn't keep his word, to do what he could do to help. He lost sight of his commitment to his friends and neighbors, when he started travelling with his new job. But, Sylvia always kept hers. She knew what it was like to have an absent husband and father. And for years, Claire and Sylvia continued to hold one another up.

This would begin their new normal, changing the way they had to live every minute of the day, when they went to bed, when they got up. Claire had to put double locks on the doors because Joey would wander out in the middle of the night. In the beginning of his mental break down, he would get so mad if they didn't have his food ready at exactly the same time every day. It was as though he thought he would starve to death if he didn't. They learned to never, ever throw food away. No matter what their leftovers were, he ate all of it. If they left the house, it depended on how Joey was feeling every minute of the day. Gilly hated calling him Joey. If just felt and sounded weird. After a few panic attacks and temper tantrums, when he shook his fists at her, insisting he wasn't her dad, that he had no kids, it just got easier. He no longer recognized Claire as his wife, but as the keeper of whatever he needed when he needed it, and Gilly unwillingly became her assistant. They depended on him for everything, maybe too much.

It's now the end of June and, fortunately, we haven't had to move yet. Mrs. Jennings found out what happened at Sullivan's, and brought the material over for Mom to make her drapes anyway. She said she wouldn't think of having anyone else make them. I'm really starting to believe that our days here are numbered. Mom has been talking to Aunt Maggie on the telephone a lot more than usual lately. I see no other reason why she's been collecting the empty boxes, that are now sitting on our back porch.

CHAPTER 5

CAMP BEAUREGARD
December 1940

JOEY HAD NO IDEA where this place called Camp Beauregard was, only that it was where he would be trained for his new life in the military. Major Thomas Mitchell shook his hand and wished him well, when he dropped him off at the Greyhound Bus Station, where he just barely made the three o'clock bus headed for Alexandria, Louisiana. He had been assigned a seat next to a woman that immediately reminded him of Mrs. Gertie, when she reached into her oversized bag.

"You look a little hungry, son. Would you like

one of my homemade chicken salad sandwiches? I have plenty. I always try to pack for "just in case," said the stranger.

"In case what, ma'am?" Joey asked as his mouth watered.

"In case I need to share. I don't like eating in front of people that I know hadn't had a bite to eat in a while. That's just plain rude," she explained.

"Well, if you don't mind, my stomach has been growling for the last couple of hours. I sure do appreciate it," replied Joey.

She handed him two waxed paper wrapped chicken salad sandwiches and an old pickle jar full of sweet tea. Joey finished both of his off before his new friend had a chance to take the paper off of her own. It was well past his normal lunch time of the typical one sandwich thrown at him, and what this kind lady made, was just as good as anything either his mom or Mrs. Gertie had ever fixed.

"You must be heading to Camp Beauregard."

"How'd you know?" asked Joey.

"Oh, I've been going back and forth this way for a while, and I finally figured out what you young boys were doing, traveling all alone this way. You only have one bag with you, no wedding ring, and you look like you're a little lost. Why do you think I started packing more than one sandwich?"

"So, what takes you to Alexandria all the time?" asked Joey.

"My only child, Corinne, and three grandchildren live there. She comes to see me every once in a while, but it's just easier for me to make the trip. Besides, my husband passed away three years ago and it's a nice change for me to get away. That house is just too big and empty, now that I'm all by myself. I bet your parents are really proud of you."

"Well, if my mom was still alive, I know she would be. This was her dream, you know, for me to see the world. She died a long time ago, when I was eleven. And my dad, well, I didn't give him a chance to say one way or another. I just left."

"Oh, I see. I'm sorry. Well, I hope the parts of the world you get to see are kind to you, young man. I'll be praying for you, 'cause Lord knows where this world is headed right now." Then she smiled, touched his hand and closed her eyes, as the late afternoon sun quickly put her to sleep.

Joey had heard the words "just in case" before, when Mrs. Gertie made sure he had one good outfit stored away. He sat there for a few minutes, admiring his clean dark blue and green plaid button-up shirt and blue jeans, that he had changed into at the recruitment office. It was the first time in seven years that he was clean, fed, comfortable, and cared for, even if it was by a stranger he'd probably never meet again. Then he began to wonder what her last words to him meant, but couldn't keep his eyes open long enough to figure it out. Joey slept until he was awakened to get off, when the bus rolled into town. When he woke up, the kind stranger was gone. In an instant, he knew that her sitting next to him had been no coincidence, because there was really no reason why she would be eating at that time of the day. How would she know how hungry he was? He suddenly realized that she was more interested in making sure he was fed. Matter of fact, he couldn't remember her taking the first bite. Just like Mrs. Gertie said, his mom was an angel now and he had no doubt she had orchestrated the whole thing.

Just as the recruiting officers described, Joey loaded onto on old bus with the words CAMP BEAUREGARD painted on the side. Within a few minutes, about a dozen other young men quickly emptied out of three other buses and joined him. Then he, along with the other newly enlisted men, made their way out of Alexandria, driving through the back roads until they saw the posted sign that read, NO TRESPASSING MILITARY PERSONNEL ONLY.

The entire landscape of Camp Beauregard was remarkably colorless. There were no stop lights, stores or civilians, only hundreds of men dressed in their drab army gear, walking down dusty dirt roads. As far as the eye could see, there were long, gray wooden barracks that Joey would quickly learn were, unfortunately, not meant for the new recruits. These lost and wide-eyed young men would spend their first six weeks further out in the camp, in round tents that reminded him of circus tents. All of this was nestled smack in the middle of the remote woodlands in the Kisatchie National Forest.

In the first few weeks, Joey fell in quite easily

to the work outs, marching in line all over the base, as well as overall pressure to perform now as soldiers. They dug trenches and fox holes, covered them up, picked a new spot and dug some more. Living and working for Hank all those years gave him the needed conditioning over most of the new recruits. In spite of the constant berating from the drill instructors to shape up, Joey felt like he had never had it so good, except before his mom died. That was when he was 'her favorite son'. Now he was a man being treated like a man, and not his father's favorite son to use as a punching bag. His half-brother, Tillis, not only got his room and place at the table, but a remarkable amount of favor from their father, that he was never able to earn. For the first time in his life, he thought his father had taught him something that he could actually use, to be tough and not open his mouth. Although he would never thank him, he was glad that he could handle himself. He already knew how to endure all elements of the weather, and the cold, hard demands of his new disciplinarians. The best part of it all, he had three square meals a day, clean clothes, a bunk to sleep in, and he was no longer working for free.

After weeks of strength and disciplinary training, the reality of what being in the Army was all about, finally hit home. That was the day they had to pack their gear and head out for their first official Louisiana Maneuvers. In this part of Louisiana, the terrain was about as close as they would come to a ground war in the jungle. The air was hot and humid and the landscape was swampy and dense, with thick underbrush and trees. This is where he would meet the only friends he ever had beside Buck. This is where Joey, Oscar and Marty also learned that they would soon be part of the United States Army Forces in the Far East.

Joey had yet been able to repair the first automobile, much less look under one single hood. There were very few on their base, and the only mode of transportation that he spotted their entire five-mile hike, had been about a dozen horses that were saddled by a handful of the officers. The sight of these beautiful animals suddenly released all the resentment he had silently held, about not putting his hands to use under the hood of a car. This was the promise that was made to him weeks ago, and was the only thing that he thought he could ever be good at.

He had never seen a horse in person, much less been this close to one. The only horses that Joey ever had contact with were in the dreams he had, sleeping underneath his printed cowboy riding, bucking horse bedspread when he was just a child. If he could just touch one, if he could just sit on one, he would be happy to be a part of caring for one of those amazing creatures instead of working on cars. The flood of memories of his wagon wheel bed and his mom's oven door creaking open in the morning, made the weight of his backpack and mud-laden boots suddenly disappear, as he drifted off down memory lane.

"Joey, man where's your head, we're dividing up. Me, you and Marty need to go this way. We're getting ready to do some ground training. Get with it!" yelled Oscar.

"What do you mean dividing up?" asked Joey.

Marty rolled out his sarcasm, "Well, if you'd been paying attention, you would have heard that we're now part of the Blue Diamonds American Army, and the other side are the Red Devils, which is going to be our enemy out here. So, get your head out of the clouds. I don't want to get pretend killed. Not yet, anyway."

Over the next two weeks, the Blue Diamonds and Red Devils fired blank rounds at one another, while recorded battle sounds echoed through the Kisatchie National Forest. When they weren't in a make-believe gun battle, they rode on used tractors for pretend-like tanks. The whole thing appeared to be nothing more than fun and games to most of the new soldiers, as an appointed referee of sorts called out who the winners and losers were, until one day, a real-life event occurred. As they were crossing the Cane River, one of their guys disappeared under water. Apparently, as he was crossing, he was pulled in by an undercurrent and his body was found floating about a mile down the river. Not one of the officers, much less the new recruits, thought they would be returning with any serious injuries, much less a fatality. The entire training exercise came to an abrupt end, and there would be no winners called for that day's exercise.

On their hike back to the camp that evening, Joey's heart was heavy as he remarked, "Man, I can't believe that guy died over a stupid game."

"Joey, this ain't no game. Look, I don't know what they told you when you signed up, or how much you've been listening, but there's no doubt that we're heading into a war and we need to get ready for it. I mean no one has said it out loud yet, but the Germans are invading Europe and the Japanese are trying to take over the Pacific," Marty said.

"How you know all this stuff?" asked Joey.

"Because he's one of those know-it-all New York Yankees that think they know everything. Somehow, he thinks they get the news first up there, before we do down here. But don't listen to him. There's no way Roosevelt is going to get us involved," answered Oscar.

"Don't bet on it," Marty answered.

Joey wondered if this was all of the world he was ever going to see. He knew he was more than physically fit to go wherever the Army needed to send him. He just didn't know, from what Marty said, if there was going to be a world left for him to see.

In the weeks that rolled on, they would continue to rotate groups of men in and out of the thick forest, trying to plot and plan different strategies for different attacks. When it wasn't their turn to do their Louisiana Maneuvers, Joey, Marty and Oscar would either hitchhike into Alexandria to see a movie, or play cards in their barracks. They had now become inseparable. After their first hike into the woods, the new recruits had finally been moved into the regular army barracks. Joey wasn't quite close enough to let his friends see the one thing that he still needed from time-to-time. When they were gone, or he knew they were not looking, he would reach into his metal foot locker, pull out his Cuban Cigar box, and try to remember the good part of where he came from. He promised himself he would write Mrs. Gertie, but had no idea how, until the day Lt. Col. Murray Hayden walked in their barrack.

"I'm looking for Private Joseph Stevens," the officer said as he stuck his head in.

Joey stood quickly with a salute. "Sir, yes sir. Private Joseph Stevens here."

"At ease private. Look, I hear you're pretty good at fixing engines. Need you to take a look at my car. It's been around the block a few times, but she's still my best girl, if you know what I mean," Lt. Col. Murray Hayden said with a wink and a grin.

"Yes, sir, it will be an honor," answered Joey. He couldn't believe it. He was finally getting a chance to do what he did best. He really hoped that whatever repair work he did for the colonel, would be good enough to leave a good impression. That's all he wanted and that's all he ever really needed from his father. Joey had waited for years for just one single pat on the back.

They walked past the old wooden barracks until they reached the officer's quarters. The officer's 'best girl' was a 1932 two-door black Chevy sedan. This was not the tear apart and put back together engine work he had hoped for, because it only took Joey five minutes to find and reconnect one loose wire. However, the officer was thrilled to have his 'best girl' up and running. "Great job son, anything around here you want to learn that we haven't shown you yet?"

Joey had received more than a simple pat on the back, he had a reward waiting for him and quickly took advantage of it. "Well, sir, I'd really like to be spending more time working on cars, like they promised me... or tending to the horses. But, other than that, I heard that there are some reading classes around here. I'd like to work a little more on my reading and writing, sir. I had to drop out of school in the sixth grade, and I really think I have some catching up to do," Joey answered.

"I'm sorry son, but right now we don't have much to work on. The military doesn't have much of an inventory of anything right now. We're working on it. Trying to get some more funds headed our way from Washington. They need to seriously work on increasing our defense budget. That's why ya'll are out there in the woods, using tractors for tanks. As you can see, we only got a handful of Jeeps here and there. Those things hardly ever break down, but when one does, I'll make sure to send for you. As for the horses, I can't really help you there either. Every officer tends to his own. For the other, consider it done. See that building over there? Believe it or not, that's our library. Not a whole lot to pick from. We rely mainly on donations from civilians back in Alexandria, but you make sure to show up next Monday and the fellow at the desk will help you with your reading and writing. I'll line up everything," assured the colonel.

"Oh yes sir, thank you sir."

A lot of what Joey thought he forgot, came back quickly. With the encouragement and teaching of the young librarian soldier, Joey was eventually able to read and write with the confidence of any high school graduate. He had been in the Army for six months, when he was finally able to write Mrs. Gertie his first letter home. While all the other guys were writing to their wives, girlfriends and the ones they wanted to be their girlfriends, Joey only had Mrs. Gertie to exchange letters with. He was made fun of, his 'Gertie girl,' until the packages of homemade chocolate chip, oatmeal raisin and butter cookies started coming in. Then she became the mom they all wished they had, just like he did all those nights on that army cot inside the Plank Road Gas & Auto Repair Shop.

CHAPTER 6

THIRD TIME'S A CHARM, MAYBE?
July 1972

GILLY PULLED OUT THE diary that was given to her a few weeks after her dad completely fell apart. Kat's mom meant well when she arranged for a social worker to visit her neighbor and friend, after her husband had his accident. She knew all too well, from her work at the hospital, that sometimes the patient isn't the only one that needs help. Depending on whatever kind of illness or injury the patient was being treated for, there were many instances where the whole family could be deeply affected. She was already seeing signs that Claire and Gilly were having difficulties 'coming to grips' with what could possibly be their new permanent reality. Her own husband had already left for his first week-long convention with his new job, so she already knew he would be of little help in the near future, to any of them. However, the only thing that Mrs. Weaver's visit did for Gilly, was make her even angrier.

She sat Gilly down on their sofa as though she was going to somehow be their savior, and she began her empty words, "Gilly, I understand that you and your mom are having some difficulties coping with your new situation. Maybe it will help if you just keep a diary and write down your feelings every day. That way you won't keep things all bottled up inside. You know, even at your age you could be dealing with ulcers, stress headaches, or any number of medical issues if you don't find a way to manage your thoughts and feelings. Here, I brought a brand new one for you. It even has a key so you can lock it if you want. Oh, and here are some really good reading materials that might help also."

"Are you serious? That's your advice for me? So, you're saying if I write my feelings down, then all the bad ones will just magically disappear? Gosh, if my dad had only just kept a diary. I wonder why he didn't want to write all his feelings down about his mom dying, his dad being a jerk, being a prisoner of war, and oh yeah, let's not forget the day my little brother died! If only he had done that one simple thing, he probably wouldn't have cracked and lost his mind." Gilly sneered.

"Gilda, Mrs. Weaver is just here to try to help us. You need to apologize to her right now!"

Gilly just sat there with her arms crossed in total defiance.

"It's okay, Mrs. Stevens, this isn't the first time someone has taken their anger out on me, and I'm sure it won't be the last. She sure does talk like someone much older than nine. I'll just see my way out."

"I read a lot. It helps me with my feelings," remarked Gilly.

"I'm really sorry. It's just been really rough around here these last few weeks for all of us, my apologies. Thank you so much for coming by. Gilda, you can at least tell Mrs. Weaver thank you for that beautiful diary she just gave you."

"Thanks for the diary."

Every page in the diary was as blank as the day Mrs. Weaver left it, over eight years ago. She refused to write one word in it, and still didn't understand why she hung on to it after all this time. Why would she want to record the events of her life? Wasn't it enough that she lived it day in and out? Besides, some of the feelings that Gilly found herself struggling with over the years she would never, ever want her mom to see. She didn't care if there was a way to lock it up or not. The last thing she wanted to ever do was hurt her mom. Gilly had long ago pitched the pamphlets in the garbage where she thought they belonged. The one entitled "Losing Someone You Love" incensed her so much that she wanted to wad it up and throw it right back in Mrs. Weaver's face as soon as she saw it. She had, in fact, not lost her dad. He had just lost them.

She knew, all too well, the sad reality and consequences of war. In school, they had studied all about the very war her dad had served in. She could barely bring herself to look at the black and white photographs taken from one of the concentration camps in Poland. She knew that her dad had been captured, and was held a prisoner, along with thousands of other men in the Philippines for over three years, but was eventually rescued in 1945. The thought that he had been held in something even remotely like that was something she just couldn't think about. Like her mom said, when he finally got home, he just wanted to put it all behind him and he was just so happy and thankful that she waited for him.

They got married right after he finished college and he got a really good job. Then they bought the two-story red brick house on Michigan Street, next to Mark and Sylvia Cooper's, with pink lace curtains in Gilly's upstairs bedroom. And within no time the two young couples became best friends doing almost everything together including welcoming home their daughters the same year in 1955. But the one thing they didn't do together was lose a child.

Suddenly Gilly threw the diary across the room

as she broke down. Why have so many bad things happened to us, I just don't understand? Even though I was only five, I can still remember holding sweet little Joey in my arms. He was the cutest little thing I ever saw. As soon as he was born, Dad went right out the next day and bought him a little bat and glove, Tinker Toys and Lincoln Logs. Then one afternoon, Dad went in to check on him and found him in his crib, completely still and not breathing. He was only six months old. Mom said Dad kind of had a nervous breakdown when Joey, Jr. died, but in time, he seemed to be able to pull himself together. Mom told me about his mom dying when he was young, and him not being close to his father. All that stuff that happened to him in the war was such a long time ago. I just don't understand how he could go through so much, accomplish so much, and then lose it all in a split second.

Claire knocked softly on Gilly's door, "Gilly, honey, are you okay?"

"Yeah, Mom, I'm fine." Gilly answered.

I'm perfectly fine now that one of the worst birthdays I've ever had is finally behind me, at least for now, since school is out. I know without a doubt that no one has ever been as embarrassed and humiliated as I was that day, when mom and I were thrown out of a grocery store, after someone called my dad a "retard."

All the things that they probably were thankful for, had come and gone. Life didn't seem fair at all and I'm not sure I want to be a mom one day. Now that I'm thinking about it, I'm not sure I want to be a wife one day. Mom has given up everything to do as she promised in her vows. For better or worse. To me it just seems like all she has to look forward to now is the 'worse', for as long as they live. Yet she still has it in her to tell me every chance she gets, "Just look around Gilly, there's always someone who is more wanting than us, just around the corner." I just can't imagine. I don't know what fix there is for this. It just seems like he can't be the only one, out of all the hundreds of thousands of men and women that have served during the war, that's come back like this. That is, unless they've all tried to hide it, too.

Now with this horrible scene at the grocery store, I really think mom is at her breaking point. After Dad lost his job years ago, it didn't take long for us to run through all their savings. Mom made some money off the sale of the house, which put us in a smaller home. Because she made this commitment to take care of him, finding work that she could do at home and afford that house, just became too much. This place we live in now has been the second house on the wrong side of the tracks. Aunt Maggie has offered, and all but insisted, that we move to the coast and stay with them. That way, Joey can be taken in as a patient at the VA Hospital, just a few miles away.

Aunt Maggie and Uncle Mack have a small apartment on the beach that we can live in for free. The other burden of paying rent would be off Mom, and she and I would be able to settle into some kind of normalcy. However, Mom has fought every move to let go of Joey. She somehow believes that she can 'will him' to one day come back from this other side that we have no sight of. Even I know that will probably never happen. Yet she insists that, 'Love suffers long and is kind, love does not envy....', Yeah sure, tell that to all of our so-called charitable sisters and brothers who have mocked, ridiculed and banned us from the drug store, library, bank and now the grocery store. Why do people have to be so cruel? Why would a grown man have to lose everything about him, just to survive in such a childish way? Can't they see how much this affects us? I get mad at Joey, too. They don't have to live with him day in and out. They're just an audience for a brief, few moments to our 24/7 nightmare.

Even after Mom worked on Mrs. Jennings' drapes several nights in a row, she didn't get the referrals she was hoping for. We got a slight reprieve when Aunt Maggie sent us enough money to get us through July. I think she must have done that, to give Mom a little bit more time to figure things out, knowing how hard it had been each time we had to uproot Joey. Good old Aunt Maggie, she has always come through for Mom and me. Sadly, now it's the middle of July and it appears that there's no hope left.

I was just told, not asked, that my senior year will not materialize here. If we move now, we'll have time to get settled in before school starts in that miserable place called Laurel Cove, for the fall. I think, like most difficult decisions Mom has had to make over the last several years, once she makes her mind up, that's it. She was like that when it came to our survival. I didn't want to move all the other times either, but it was her stern voice of conviction that let me know quickly, that it was a done deal. This will be our third move, and at this point, the only remaining hope for all of us is to start over somewhere else. Mom said she should be able to get a regular, good-paying job over there, and with that, a possibility of me going to college. Maybe one day, with the right kind of help, Joey would know what was going on again and be happy that I followed in his footsteps to be an architect like him. One of the few memories I do have of him is sitting side-by-side at the dining room table, drawing pictures of my family standing in front of our two-story red brick house, while he worked on some of his architectural masterpieces at home. It wasn't a clear vision of our two faces, it was more like a dark silhouette of a father and daughter sitting alone together, before the cruel circumstances in our world began to tear us completely apart.

Kat's mom dropped us off at the Double Pattie, for our last meal together, the night before we left. Thankfully, it was family night and we weren't tormented by the likes of Regina, Mona or any of the other jerks from school on our last night together.

"Here's the address for the apartment that we're going to be living in, or should I say, the place where

I'm going to die. I'm going to miss you, Kat. You're the only 'blood sister' I've ever had or ever will have, you know that, right?"

"Sure, I know. You're always going to be my one and only blood sister, too. I don't know what I'm going to do without you. You've been my rock. No one else gets me like you do. I asked Mom if I could just quit school now. I don't need a diploma for what I want to do. I thought the top of her head was going to blow off right then and there. I'm pretty sure she's got her mind made up that I'm going to be a nurse one day, whether I want to or not. I'll run away first. I swear I will. She promised me that I could make new friends if I just tried to fit in a little more. Like I told her, if fitting in means that I have to be like the dumb duo, I'm not interested. Not now, not ever."

"Look, Kat, I think you're gonna be a really awesome fashion designer one day. I really mean that, too. I probably should have told you that the same day you were encouraging me about my detective stuff."

"Thanks, Gilly. That means a lot. I promise I won't change if you won't. We've got to stick to our plans no matter how many miles apart we are."

"Deal," answered Gilly.

The blood sisters sat there quietly for the rest of the evening, eating their burgers and fries, while watching all the other customers enjoying themselves as they ate, talked and probably made plans for things Gilly could only dream about now.

Kat promised she would write and so did I. I told her that her letters to me would for sure be considered special delivery, since Aunt Maggie was the Postmaster of Laurel Cove and would make sure I got each and every one.

With all this upheaval, and now yet another move, I didn't have the heart to tell Mom that I didn't want to follow her dream for me either. Being an architect was actually the last thing that I wanted to do. After all, it was her idea. "Write your dream down, Gilly. Don't let anyone revise it." I had finally put the words down in writing. The one and only thing I decided deserved to be written in my diary, and I purposely didn't lock it. I wanted to become a detective one day and maybe solve the mystery of what happened to the once-great mind of Joseph Franklin Stevens, the man I used to call Dad.

CHAPTER 7

IT'S ALL GRAVY FOR NOW
October 1941

HIS UNIT GOT THEIR orders. The men moving out would consist of nearly every soldier and officer from their Blue Diamonds/Red Devils Louisiana Maneuvers. The recruitment numbers had really picked up in the months since Joey enlisted; and much like Marty said, there were now consistent rumors of an impending war. He watched as entire busloads of young men arrived every week, and was stunned to see just how thin and bony most of them looked. Many of them had probably been scooped up from their dead-end lives, much like he had been all those months ago. This place was certainly not someone's home away from home, if they had a real one. But, it had definitely filled Joey's plate in more ways than one. He was sure he would miss Camp Beauregard. It was a place where he was not only clothed, fed and strengthened, but where he finally experienced decency, honor and respect for and from the men that helped him become one.

The old yellow Camp Beauregard buses made several trips back into Alexandria, where they all boarded Greyhound buses that took them to New Orleans. When their bus rolled into New Orleans Union Station, the only thing that Joey could think of was Hank's boxing career that ended abruptly. He always hated this city for being the source of the very thing that caused him and his mom to be terrorized all those years. With Hank out of the picture now, the beauty of the city seemed to bloom right before his eyes, and his dad's boxing days would no longer define it. It appeared to be a charming and fascinating city with elegant stately homes, moss-draped trees, red and green street cars rolling down Canal Street, and large crowds of well-dressed people carrying shopping bags. The sweet aroma that wafted through the air, as they were unloading, wasn't anything he had ever smelled before. It was a mixture of hot cocoa, caramel and vanilla. Jazz music seemed to be filtering through the station as though it were being piped through the ceiling.

"Hey guys, what is that smell? Is it coffee or candy?" Joey asked.

"Both, probably. We just rolled into one of the best places on earth when it comes to food, coffee and candy, especially pecan pralines. We got a couple of hours to kill, let me introduce you to a good old fashioned New Orleans Po'boy. Then if we have time, you've got to try you some café au lait and beignets." Oscar said.

"Some what?" Joey asked.

"Just trust me. This is one part of the world you don't want to miss out on."

"How you know this place so well?" Marty asked.

"Had the distinct pleasure of living here for a couple years during my foster care days. Worked in one of the bars down on Royal Street, sweeping floors and stuff like that. If old man Pardue hadn't got himself shot and killed, I'd probably been raised here. It wasn't a bad place. He gave me three squares a day and a cot in the back storage room. Best life I ever had, 'cause at least I had a solid roof over my head, and didn't have to work out in the fields all day. And I had more than one woman looking after me, too."

"What do you mean more than one woman?" asked Joey.

"Well, that's why Mr. Pardue got shot. He was married, but he had a bunch of girlfriends. They all thought I needed looking after."

"Awe man, you're crazy," Marty said as he slapped Oscar on the back.

The trio hustled their way down Canal Street into the French Market, where Joey and Marty experienced their first real taste of the south. Joey had a loaded, hot roast beef and gravy po'boy and onion rings, while Marty and Oscar ordered the famous shrimp and crawfish po'boys from Germaine's Po'Boy Restaurant.

"Well, what do ya'll think, some good stuff, huh?" Oscar asked.

"It's okay, I guess, but nothing beats good ol' pastrami on rye from Fat Louie's place back home," Marty answered. But, he had to admit that the po'boy bread was about the best he had ever had.

"That was delicious. How long do we get to stay here?" Joey asked. He wanted more. He loved food more than anything else in the world now. Before, his world consisted of what his dad threw at him, but now it seemed like it was his for the taking.

"Just long enough to grab a cup of café au lait and beignets."

Oscar weaved his way through the long line in Café Du Monde, "Please, we got to catch a train, we're getting shipped out, can I get through?" In a matter of minutes, he had three cups of coffee and a bag of white powdered sugar beignets, all paid for by one of the generous customers.

They walked, drank, laughed and ate. By the time they arrived back at the New Orleans Union train station, all three were covered in the white powdery sugar. Anyone not knowing, would have thought a bag of flour had blown up on their clothes.

"I don't think I've ever had that much fun eating, since my mom used to let me lick the spoon when she made my favorite chocolate cake," Joey laughed. This was the life that Joey had long been aching for. Gone were the days of abuse at the hands of his father. Although he continued to miss him, he did not miss the nights he prayed to hear Buck tapping on the shop window. If this was what seeing the world looked like, he could hardly wait for the next stop. Before they loaded onto the train, Joey asked a stranger to take their picture. This was one memory he never wanted to forget.

They boarded a shiny Silver Steam locomotive, along with hundreds of other young soldiers, waving goodbye to the city that care forgot. If only for a couple hours Joey, Marty and Oscar left behind their troubled pasts without any thoughts of their fragile futures.

During their train ride, they made stops in Houston, San Antonio, El Paso, Tucson, Phoenix and Los Angeles, then finally San Francisco. Each and every one was a new experience for the young man who spent most of his life with his head underneath the hood of an automobile. He saw black-tail prairie dogs, mule deer, coyotes and grey foxes scurrying throughout the deserts in Texas and Arizona. There were prickly pear cactuses with bright yellow flowers, desert Christmas cactuses and huge barrel cactuses scattered here and there, jutting out of rocks and sand, flittering outside his window like one silver screen movie after another.

The sky was so clear at night; he swore he saw a shooting star somewhere in the deserts of Arizona.

They slept, ate, played cards and watched darkness come and go for three days, until they finally arrived in San Francisco. To think just a few months ago, he was going to sleep at night, mostly with an empty belly, on a cot with grease under his fingernails. Now he had on a clean, pressed uniform every day, a fresh haircut, a full belly, could read and write like all his buddies, and he had even saved enough money to buy a new Canon 35-millimeter camera from Brumfield's Drug Store in Alexandria, the day before they left. He now not only had something else to store in his memory, but the ability to share these new memories with someone else, as he continued to take one perfect shot after another, starting the moment he walked out of the drug store. Mrs. Gertie was his lifeline now. She was the only one from his escaped, tormented life that had a soul and knew the life he once had, and for that he was grateful. Not only that, in one of her last letters, she was excited to write that Buck had also enlisted in hopes of being a Navy fighter pilot. She wrote of how proud she was of her boys. He had not had anyone call him 'her boy' since his mom died, and was more determined than ever to keep in touch. Joey didn't care if he ever laid eyes on the Plank Road Gas & Auto Repair Shop again. He had already mentally buried that place, along with Hank, Iris and Tillis, just like his father did with his mom's wedding picture the day she died. If he ever returned, it would be to make sure his old man was six feet under, for all the abuse he and his mom suffered.

Once their train arrived in San Francisco, they were informed that they had exactly three hours to get to the docks "or else."

"Okay guys, there's one place we gotta see before we leave this place," Oscar announced.

"I don't know, Oscar. I don't want to be late. I sure don't want to find out what the 'or else' means. I think I'd rather head over with the other guys," answered Joey.

"C'mom, you said you wanted to see the world, didn't you? Well, this is part of it. It won't take long," insisted Oscar.

"I'm in," Marty said.

Within a few minutes, they were standing right in the middle of Chinatown. Joey thought he had somehow been magically transported to another country. Not only did he not understand the sounds coming out of everyone's mouths, he couldn't read any of the signs hanging in the dozens of storefronts. They were all dressed in clothing he had never seen before, and he didn't quite know what to make of the smells all around him.

"What's that weird smell?" Joey asked.

"Oh, that's probably incense. I've smelled that a few times myself. We have a Chinatown too, down around the lower east side" Marty said.

"Here, you gotta try this," as Oscar threw seventy-five cents at a Chinese street vendor. He handed them each a bowl of noodles and some chopsticks.

"What the heck am I supposed to do with these?" asked Joey.

"You do this," as Oscar held the chopsticks between his fingers, while picking up the noodles effortlessly.

Marty snickered, as he easily followed suite, while Joey finally just gave up and used his hands.

Joey continued to take pictures until they reached Geary Street, where he saw dozens of beautiful, overflowing flower stands everywhere. It suddenly occurred to Joey that Oscar's quick little excursion was probably the best idea he had so far. Within the next block was a drug store, much like the one he purchased his camera from, back in Alexandria. He not only had a finished roll of pictures to send Mrs. Gertie, but he also paid the store clerk in advance for developing, as well as his time and expense to send them to her. He quickly purchased a money order made out to her and dropped it in the mail, as well. Joey wanted to be sure to follow through on his words to his mom long ago. Even though she was no longer here, Joey would send Mrs. Gertie enough money to keep flowers on his mom's grave for at least a year. That was one promise he could now afford to keep, to make sure she had a vase full of real roses every year for Valentines, Mother's Day and her birthday. He had no idea how long they would be in Manila, but according to Staff Sergeant Murphy, no more than a year or two.

As they sailed away, Joey had already loaded a new roll of film. The first on this roll, and the last sight of the country they loved, would be The Golden Gate Bridge, one of the greatest engineering marvels in the world. Joey smiled, knowing that one day when he returned, he would without a doubt be a great builder of things.

Standing on the deck with their hands on the railings of the USAT Washington, these young men were beginning one of the most courageous journeys that had ever gone before them. Joey and his new brothers would spend several weeks on this great ship. After all the loss and hurt he had suffered, he just couldn't believe what a lucky man he was.

However, their destination would the Philippine Islands, a place where few lived to tell the tales, and those that did live, never wanted to speak about it again.

CHAPTER 8

LAURAL COVE
August 1972

IT WAS A LONG, hard, almost self-defeated ride for the only two people in the car that had any idea what was going on. Claire felt like a failure for her inability to help her husband overcome his trauma. And Gilly already knew that at the end of this trip, the only thing waiting for her would be this horrible little split in the road called Laurel Cove. She had no idea why anyone under the age of twenty would intentionally want to live there. From what she remembered, all it had was a post office, a diner, a hardware store, grocery store and after that no more than just the basics. No Double Pattie to hang out at, if for some miracle she made any friends. They certainly didn't have a movie theater, which she could one day go on her first date to. Her regret now was that she probably should have at least given Russell Sullivan a chance, even though he was a pimple-faced pest. At least she could have mentally recorded her first date of seeing some Academy Award-winning movie like Love Story, instead of ordering a plate of tuna salad in the town's diner. Russell swore to her that he didn't tell anyone about her dad's incident in the grocery store. She's pretty certain he didn't, because she almost had him in tears when she confronted him about it. It didn't matter now because no one would ever meet Joey, since he wouldn't be living with them anymore.

As the miles before them began to dwindle, Gilly began to have an unexpected sense of heartache that Joey would no longer be a daily part of their lives. He could be funny at times. The way he got so excited every time Claire let him eat in front of the television on his TV tray. When he would act like he was busting out of his clothes like The Incredible Hulk. The way he could flip his green peas from his spoon, across the kitchen. She could still see him blowing bubbles through a straw in his chocolate milk, as though it was his very own special invention. Also, he absolutely, without a doubt believed in Santa Claus. Besides his birthday, that was his favorite time of the year. It didn't matter what Claire gave him. She could wrap a box of Corn

Flakes cereal, and as long as the tag on the present said FROM SANTA, he was as happy as any young boy would be seeing his first new bike. He knew every episode and all the characters on Gilligan's Island. That was one thing that Gilly just couldn't understand. How he could remember all the names of all those people, but not remember her and her mom and what happened years ago. It's almost as though his brain took a break, one big, long, dark break somewhere during early childhood, and didn't sign back in until after the accident, only to still be six years old again. Not one single event or person in between was stored in his head anymore; at least none that she knew of. When he was in a good mood, he loved to cuddle with Gilly like she was his favorite stuffed animal. When he was having a bad day, he was almost impossible to bear. How would the people at the Veteran's Hospital know that he liked his eggs over easy, with strawberry jelly on his toast? Or that the only way he would drink milk, was with two big heaping tablespoons of Nestle's Chocolate in it? Who would tease him about being Mary Ann's boyfriend when he watched Gilligan's Island?

"I'm hungry, Claire. When are going to eat?" asked Joey.

"In just a few minutes, I promise. There should be a Stuckey's Restaurant in about five more miles."

There was absolutely no chance they would eat inside with the rest of the customers. So, Gilly and Joey stayed in the car while Claire went inside, ordered their hamburgers, fries and milkshakes to go, and then parked their Falcon under a tree while they ate in the car. Gilly choked on her food, as she thought there was a chance that this could probably be the last time the three of them would eat together as a family.

"Mom, I know you said that Joey probably understands more than we think. I wonder if he has any idea where he's going. How are they going to know all the things he likes and what he doesn't like? What are we going to say when we leave?" asked Gilly.

"I don't know how he's going to handle things, but don't worry about all his favorite foods and things like that. I've already made a list. The social worker insisted on it. She promised me that the head nurse on his floor was as good as they come. She said her name was Lydia Bennett, and she assured me that they would do whatever they needed to do to help him settle in. He will have plenty of company with men just like him, unfortunately. She said they have all kinds of group games, and they even have a big TV room. Who knows, maybe he'll wind up making a few friends." Claire answered.

"Yeah, he'll have friends now and I won't," muttered Gilly.

They finished their last meal together and Gilly teared up as she wiped the ketchup off of Joey's chin. She just wished she knew what he was thinking, like she had so many times before. It seemed so cruel that he had no idea where he was going, and that his whole world was going to be different. Maybe that wasn't such a bad thing, to not know. She didn't want to think that he was as terrified as she was.

As they turned off Beach Boulevard onto the driveway of what was supposed to be some broken down old building in her mind, Gilly was surprised to see just how peaceful the hospital looked. Nothing at all as she expected it to be. It almost looked like an oversized mansion that sat among all the large, oversized oaks and blooming hot pink azalea bushes.

Gilly sat alone outside the front office, while Claire completed all the final paperwork. The large foyer inside had a massive chandelier hanging from at least thirty feet above her head. Right in the center of the foyer, was an oversized staircase with wrought iron railings that she could only guess led up to the patients' rooms. This was so much grander than she had ever imagined. All this time, she thought Joey was going to be locked away in some deep, dark dungeon. Now she could at least be settled that his new home was a hundred times nicer than the run-down, two-bedroom house they just left.

Without any resistance from Joey, Claire and Gilly walked out of the hospital without him. It was almost as if he reconciled himself to this, long before the idea that such a thing existed. His room was laid out much like the one he had at home, with just the basics, a bed, nightstand, small lamp and chest of drawers. But he had one thing that seemed to grab his attention right away. He had a perfect view of the Gulf of Mexico and the beaches that held it back.

As we backed out of the parking lot, I just wasn't sure which part of her life Mom was hurting for. The one she had, or the one she should have had. All I know is, this isn't the answer I had hoped and prayed for. I would give anything to have our old life back on Michigan Street, with the pink lace curtains in my bedroom, the tire swing, the big garage in the back, and my dad cooking on the barbeque pit in the backyard. Kat was my next-door neighbor and best friend. It's where we pricked our fingers and became blood sisters one Friday night during a sleepover. It was where my little brother was born and died. Even though I remember it being a sad time, it was the last place that I could still call out to my dad and he would answer. Today, as we were leaving him in his green sweatshirt and cut-off tan pants, sitting in his new room, all I thought I was going to say to him just seemed empty. The only thing I could pull myself together to say and do, was to lean in and kiss him on the cheek, just like I did every morning before I left for school, "See you later, Joey." The only thing he had to say to me was, "I think the castles are getting closer, Gilly."

Mom told him that Nurse Lydia was going to be his new friend, just like Nurse Sylvia had been. Then she said, "You be good for her just like you were for Sylvia, and Gilly and I will bring you a special treat." She then kissed him on his forehead and we walked out the door. It was too soon for me to size up Joey's new caretaker, although the kindness on her face pretty much aligned with the patience and tenderness in her voice, as she welcomed Joey to his new home.

Mom held herself together and so did I, but I'm certain that we'll probably pick up where we left off in that run–down, two-bedroom house. She won't be able to hold it in forever. Her crying will once again filter down the hall when she thinks I'm asleep. We may be in a different place, but I have no doubt it will be for the same reason.

As we headed towards the last place I ever wanted to live, I finally had the nerve to ask what I had been thinking for days. "Mom what can they do for him there that you and I couldn't do? We have given him everything he wanted, everything he needed. Even Ms. Sylvia said she thought there was little anyone could do for him at this point."

"I'm not sure, Gilly. It's a Veterans' Hospital. It's a fascinating time we're living in right now. New drugs are being developed and discovered. New treatments are coming out all the time. Maybe they'll have some kind of therapy that we just don't know anything about. I never told you because you were just too young, but Mark Cooper told me the night of the accident, that he was surprised your dad held out for as long as he did. And the reason why he didn't want to get help was his fear of coming across as weak or being called a sissy."

"Why would he be afraid to get help? Wasn't he worth it? Weren't we worth it? I would never, ever call him a sissy. Where'd he come up with something like that, anyway?"

"I think what he had inside was probably an overwhelming collection of pain and suffering that started when he was really young, and the rest of it, only God knows about. I just believe that he thought if he dwelled on the past too much, it might bring out a lot of things he just didn't want to remember. Anytime I tried to get him to talk about his nightmares, he would just say, 'It's all in the past Claire, let it go Claire, I'm okay Claire.' Something about the accident that night, when he hit and killed that dog, just destroyed him."

"Yeah, go figure. After all he went through, why would accidentally running over someone's dog push him over the edge?"

"I don't know. I'll visit him during the week, and we can come together on the weekends. You can go visit him anytime during the week after school, if you want to. There's a bus stop from Laurel Cove that stops right across the street. We're not that far away. Let's just try to think about getting home now and get ourselves unpacked and settled in. Okay?"

It was nestled off the main road that anyone could miss it if they didn't know there was a town hidden behind the overgrown entrance of trees and bushes. Off to the right side of the narrow road, was a weathered sign that read LAUREL COVE, POP. 849. Aunt Maggie had given me a history lesson of the town years ago. It had been established in the early 1800's by Raymond Bolton's family, whose one and only remaining descendent was Walter Bolton. He runs the hardware store where most of the town's inhabitants hang out, when they're not catching up on the local gossip in the post office or Mimi's Diner. One remaining descendent was enough for me to know that everyone else either died or moved elsewhere. Case closed.

Our apartment was clustered in with three others. Aunt Maggie owned two, and the other two were owned by Mr. Bolton. Fortunately, ours was on one end and Aunt Maggie's was on the other. I was always thrilled to see her, but only when she was without him, that is, Uncle Mack. The thought of having to see him every day was almost more than I could bear. I would definitely have to figure out his schedule, if he had one, so I could avoid him for the next year, until I'm old enough to get out of this place. Maybe Kat and I can get our own place one day. A place away from the likes of people like Regina, Mona, Uncle Mack and places like Laurel Cove. I'm sure there are some apartments further away from the beach, but yet close enough to still visit and see Mom and Joey. Kat has already said she was ready to run away. So, like she once said, it would be a win-win for everyone.

It was the same small, two-bedroom furnished apartment that we would stay in when we would visit, before Joey got sick. When I could call him Dad. We made several trips to this little town to visit Aunt Maggie before there was an Uncle Mack to deal with. The beach was the same and so was this misfit little town. I was always glad to see it in the rearview as we pulled away, back to where I at least had some marginal feeling of belonging in a real city with grass in our backyards, ranch-styled and two-story, red brick houses, movie theaters and places to eat like the Double Pattie. I did have Kat to go back to, a neighborhood with sidewalks and bikes, and kids playing in the street. Long after we stopped coming, when we lived on the wrong side of the tracks, I could at least cross over from time to time. Here, there was only one side of the track with nothing to do, no friends, and tons of sand, unnerving, unsettling, never staying put, blowing, irritating sand.

When we walked in our new home, it was obvious even to my eye, that Aunt Maggie worked really hard to make it warm and welcoming. She had hung new blue draperies in the living room and pink ones in mine. I didn't have the heart to tell her I had outgrown pink years ago. She had replaced the dull, worn-out bedroom furniture in what would be my room, with a white lace and pink bedspread covering, over a white iron twin bed, along with a chest of drawers and a matching white desk and chair, with a small silver office desk lamp. There were seashell decorations scattered on top of my chest of drawers, bathroom cabinet and living room coffee tables, which was fitting for life in a beachside community. Unlike most people, I had never been drawn to the beach. I never liked to sun bathe, and even though the feel of the sand between my toes felt curious and comforting at times, it annoyed the tar out of me when it got trapped in my bathing suit. Those tiny grains of sand would inevitably find a way into every crevice in my body, which to me was at times more irritating than it was worth. Sleeping in an apartment on the beach for the unforeseeable future, would definitely take some getting used to. The slapping sounds of the Gulf of Mexico were a little too close for comfort. What little memory I have of this place are the nightmares and uneasiness that the water would reach in and swallow us up, in the middle of the night. That somehow the gravitational pull, that worked the tide back and forth, would forget to pull the tide back and we would be washed out into the Gulf of Mexico.

Mom promised me that we wouldn't be strangers here for long, as Aunt Maggie and Uncle Mack were quite well known. Aunt Maggie was the Postmaster for the Town of Laurel Cove, and Uncle Mack was supposedly a bit of a celebrity for being the one and only local artist. However, I really never saw anything he made that looked as though he could get five cents for. It all looked like junk to me. He would bring his handmade gifts every time they would visit. Mom said it was considered modern art and not to be so snotty and ungrateful. Maybe that's what Uncle Mack is, a modern weirdo. I was never comfortable around him, nor could I sense that he was comfortable around us, especially Joey. I'm not sure what Mom thought about him, but I think she was just glad that Aunt Maggie had finally settled down, gotten married, and seemed happy. It wasn't until after Dad got sick that we finally got to meet this "love of her life." He just showed up in Laurel Cove one day, looking for a room for a few days. Aunt Maggie rented the apartment to him, and if there's a rest of the story, at least I don't know it. She just called one day and said they got married. Don't know where he came from and what he does to contribute, other than collecting trash off the beach and making souvenirs to sell to the tourists. So, they were, in fact, well known and for the most part, well respected.

Mom packed her sewing machine, but it was put away in her bedroom closet. I was happy for her about that. I hope she can get a job she likes and meet new people, and not have to make draperies anymore. It just seemed like, when she wasn't tending to Joey, her back was bent over the sewing machine. I don't know if she knew what day of the week it was, unless I told her. The rest of the things that we didn't sell or throw away, like Joey's toolbox, his briefcase, boxes marked "important papers," Joey Jr's toys, and some of my old dolls, were put either under our beds or on the top shelves of our bedroom closets. The feel of the handles on his toolbox and briefcase, while moving them in, gave me a sense of what a strong and talented man he had been at one time. Now, I'm almost certain he couldn't tell you what a hammer or a pair of pliers was, much less what to do with them.

Aunt Maggie's friend of a friend managed to get Mom a job as a teller, at the First National Bank of Gulfport, and I reluctantly enrolled in Laurel Cove Academy. We were free and unencumbered for the first time in years. No Joey to watch, guard or pacify. We didn't have to double bolt our doors at night. We didn't have a schedule to go by for when we had our meals, and we could watch what we wanted to on the television at night. Yet, somehow, we both felt empty and lost. This would be the beginning of the unbending and remolding of our day-to-day lives, as we began to learn to live without Joey. The very thing we endured, wanting and wishing would somehow change, was gone. I should be happy or relieved, but I'm not.

At the end of the first week, I had already fired off my first letter of misery and discontent to Kat, complaining about the people, this lifeless little town, and how much I missed her, now having nowhere to go and no one to talk to who really understood me. There was only sand and water in the back of our apartment, and more nothingness out our front door.

The second week quickly came, and so would be my first week at Laurel Cove Academy. Surprisingly, it was not as bad as I thought it would be. I didn't realize how much the dumb duo had an effect on me, until I walked into my new school and they weren't there. I would never have to see their faces again. All their hateful comments about what I was wearing or where I lived, would have to be directed to another victim, or either they would double down on Kat. Poor Kat. She probably won't last long at all. I really feel guilty for leaving her.

There were only twenty-two students in my entire senior class, and most of them seemed curious and excited just to see a new face. It seems that for the most part, families moved away and rarely did anyone new move in. Again, that was no surprise to me, considering there was really nothing here to move to.

The academy required that we wear uniforms of white button-up shirts and tan skirts or pants, so there was definitely not going to be any worry with dressing in the latest styles. Mom said that sometimes you have to figure out a way to celebrate the little victories in life, and I guess this would be one of them. However, this would not have set well with Kat. She spent hours picking out her outfit for each day, and I don't think I ever saw her wear anything twice. This new victory didn't last long, when I realized these new uniforms would have to be bought with money. Money that we didn't have yet. We used what little money we had for the pull behind U-Haul, and lunch at Stuckey's. Mom hasn't worked long enough to get her first paycheck.

However, Aunt Maggie came to the rescue once again. A few days after school started, without me asking, she left her only employee, Gabriel, in charge of the post office and we drove into Gulfport to a uniform shop and then stopped at The Gulf Shore Grill for dinner.

"So, how were your first few days, Gilly? Did you make any friends yet?" asked Aunt Maggie.

"It was okay, I guess. How'd you know I needed uniforms?" Gilly asked.

"I just knew. I know all this is overwhelming right now. Just try to give it some time. I know life has been pretty rough for you and your mom, for a long time now. I also know this is nothing like where you came from, but there's a lot of good here, Gilly. You just have to look for it. It's peaceful, quiet, no crime, there's a lot of sunshine, and the beach is here anytime you want to enjoy it. The people, well, I know they're a bit different, but there are really some here that are nice and quite interesting, if you'd just be willing to give them a chance. I don't think I would want to live anywhere else."

"How did you end up here, Aunt Maggie? I mean it just seems really strange you would pick this of all places?" said Gilly as she worked her french fries around in the ketchup.

"Actually, it was the post office that brought me here."

"How?"

"I started out working at one in Shreveport, where you just moved from. It's where your mom and I grew up, too. Well, I wanted to run my own post office one day. When this one came open, I applied and got it. It's been the best thing that ever happened to me. I'm the boss and I can run it like

I want. In these small towns, the post office always seems to be the heart and soul for everyone. It's what keeps them connected to the rest of the world. It didn't take me long to get to know everybody and everything about everybody," winked Aunt Maggie.

"What do you mean? Do they tell you?"

"Pretty much. Sometimes too much. Then what they don't tell you, whether you want to know or not, you see when their mail comes in, where it came from, late notices, magazines and all that kind of stuff. I probably know more about some of them than they know themselves. But, that's our little secret, okay?"

"That's where you met Uncle Mack?"

"Yes, it sure is."

This would be my chance. Learn to start asking questions. C'mon Gilly, get it out. Start digging for the truth. This seemed like a really good first assignment. Even though I didn't like him, for whatever reason that I still couldn't put my finger on, there must have been something that attracted Aunt Maggie to him. I felt like, not only did I need to know these things, I really thought I needed to know how these things worked. I've never had a boyfriend because I was always too embarrassed to have anyone over. Now with it just being Mom and me, what would I do if someone asked me out? Mom just said she knew from the minute she saw my dad, that he was the one for her. But how? Uncle Mack always seemed so dull, so quiet, and in my opinion, lazy. Aunt Maggie worked six days a week, while he, for the most part, walked up and down the beach picking up shells and pieces of wood that washed up, turning the finds into stupid, useless souvenirs.

"So, you didn't answer my question, did you make any friends, yet?" Aunt Maggie asked again.

"Not yet. This one girl named Hope wanted to know where I moved from and already invited me to her house. I'm not ready for a new best friend yet."

"Well, that's a start. Give yourself some time, not only will your telephone be ringing off the hook, but you're probably going to find yourself fitting right in before you know it. I promise."

Here's my foot in the door. "Aunt Maggie, speaking of meeting new people, you said you met Uncle Mack when he moved to Laurel Cove, but where did you meet him? Where did he move from and why did he want to move here? How'd you know you wanted to marry him?" Gilly thought to herself how that didn't go well at all. She just sounded like she was interrogating someone who had just been arrested for murder. She would have to definitely work on her investigative skills. And she needed to find something else to do with her hands when she got nervous, other than chewing on her fingernails.

"That's an awful lot of 'where and how' questions all at once."

"I'm sorry, but since we're going to be living here now, I just wanted to get to know him more, that's all. He never really has had much to say."

"Well, that's kind of the way artists are. They're

usually quiet and rather introverted. So, don't take it personally. Let's see, he used to live in Florida, wanted a change, stopped here for a visit and decided he wanted to stay awhile. Then, one day he walked into the post office and swept me off my feet. Does that answer all your 'who, what, when and where' questions?"

"Kind of but... I think I'd like some place a little more romantic to be swept off my feet one day."

"Don't get smart. You sound like your mom."

Well, that didn't get her anywhere except she now knew the weirdo was from Florida and wanted a change. A change from what, though?

CHAPTER 9

MANILA BAY
November 1941

ON THANKSGIVING DAY, NOVEMBER 27, 1941 their time at sea ended. How fitting, to soon be stepping foot on such a tropical paradise as this. Joey felt like he was a pilgrim landing in this new part of the world he had only seen on a map. He knew that Mrs. Gertie had probably spent hours preparing turkey and all the fixings, for a special sit down for her and her husband, since Buck was out there somewhere too. Although their Thanksgiving meals weren't big and fancy, his mom always made it a point to say the blessing before Hank walked in and growled at such utter nonsense. Joey understood when his mom said that Hank didn't like himself. Who would like such an angry, bitter man who had no one to blame but himself for such a negative and fiendish outlook on life?

Joey didn't want to ever live that kind of life again, and as he stood there staring at this lush and tropical landscape, all he saw was a little piece of heaven that was going to finally be part of this new memory he wanted to desperately build on. The closer they got to shore, the more elbowing that went on between Oscar, Marty and Joey as though they were major league baseball players and had just won the World Series. Much like Joey, they had also left behind lives of human servitude and hopelessness. They had not only shared the small, cramped quarters over the last several weeks, but nearly every meal along with almost every back story. There was something about their time, all these weeks on board that caused all three to let their guard down. Where they came from and all they had left behind. Maybe it was the bond of brotherhood that had started to form during their first days being on the Blue Diamonds team on their first Louisiana Maneuvers, or perhaps it was the uncertainty of what lay ahead of them. Either way, their quiet exchanges of each other's family tree's rotten fruit seemed to forge them together even more. Oscar Wilson had absolutely no memory of either parent, and had gone through a series of neglectful and abusive foster families, with the last one being a sugarcane farmer's field hand in Louisiana. Marty O'Reilly had left behind the filthy, tenement apartment and crime-ridden streets of New York City, where you were either in a gang or a victim of one, as his father had been. His mom, Eleanor, insisted he join the Army as his only way out of what she thought was a hopeless situation. She had great plans for her son, much like Natalie had, at one time, for Joey. These three living, breathing testimonies to where they came from and why they were there at that moment, were among hundreds of stories onboard that held onto their hope for a different future, as the USAT Washington slowly drifted into Manila Bay.

The sky was the same brilliant blue that Natalie Stevens had painted his bedroom, from his days of tinker toys, cowboys and freshly baked biscuits in the morning. It had been a long time since he had given God credit for anything, but he could just see both Him and his mom brushing the sky ahead of this grand, ceremonial entrance.

As the officers and enlisted men disembarked, the celebration continued all around them with cheers from the crowds of the Filipino men, women and children. Were he and the rest of the men somehow seen as some sort of celebrities? The natives of this island truly loved the Americans, as they had continued to bring liberty and prosperity for over forty years as a friendly, occupying force. Were these uniformed men going to once again be their salvation amid the growing upheaval and unrest in the world? Joey knew they were here to protect and serve, not only the country they left behind, but this small island country, and others alike, from all the dictators and madmen who wanted to rule and consume every inch of the world. He thought about what Marty had said that day, when they were getting ready to do their first make-believe battle training. The Germans were invading Europe and the Japanese wanted to claim every inch of land in the Pacific. They weren't in some place that they could just leave if they wanted. The Philippine Islands were surrounded by the Pacific Ocean, and there was no going back anytime soon.

They only had a couple of hours before they had to report to the American base of Fort McKinley, which was located on the outskirts of Manila. Much like their brief visit to New Orleans and San Francisco, Joey was once again enraptured by just how enchanting the island of Luzon was. All this time, Joey thought that the Philippines was one island, but had been enlightened during their trip, that this island country actually consisted of more than seven thousand, six hundred individual islands. How long would that take to see every one of them? "One at a time Joey, one at a time," he thought quietly to himself.

The views were once again picture perfect. Every shot he took with his camera was an ongoing photo book collection, to be sent to Mrs. Gertie. After all, what good is it to see the world if you have no one to share it with? The low, large stone walls that seemed to border every street were covered in red, violet and yellow flowers, much like those Joey remembered sprouting from the yard and hanging from the window boxes of his old friend. He recognized the roadside roses and violet rhododendrons as his mom had taught him, but the rest were simply bursts of colors for which he had no name. Right in the center of it all was a beautiful fountain, blowing water straight up before it cascaded down in a giant pool surrounding it. There were spotted ponies with small, grass woven hats on top of their heads, pulling along their island drivers with their loads of fresh fruits and vegetables in the rear. The roads, albeit narrow, were covered in bricks and stones which echoed the footsteps of both humans and animals. It was almost like a carnival scene that didn't at all fit, with the reason why they were there.

They were approached right away by an older Filipino man in one of those carts full of pineapples. It was like a magic trick before their eyes, as he made one quick whack, removing the top before he began pulling off the small individual chunks. With the juice from a chunk of pineapple running down his chin, Oscar announced, "You know, General Douglas McArthur is here somewhere. I overheard Colonel Warren talking about him. We might get to meet him."

Marty raised his eyebrows and said, "What do you mean might? I'm sure it was his order that brought us all over here in the first place. The least he can do is make an appearance for the rest of us peons."

Looking over in the distance, Joey spotted a white and gold encrusted church steeple rising into the blue skyline, and for a few seconds, all the excitement and exhilaration that had been pulsating through his body emptied out, and was replaced with an instant conviction that this was somehow the calm before the storm. His interest was more in meeting one of the army chaplains that had travelled with them aboard ship, than a five-star general or continuing the street party. That would have to wait, as their celebration was abruptly called to an end.

"Load up, get your butts in gear. This ain't no street party!" yelled Lt. Col. Gerald Pitkins.

There was only a small collection of barracks at Fort McKinley, built much like those they lived in back at Camp Beauregard. However, here they would be segregated again, but in a much different way. The officers were given the luxury of the barracks to live in, while the soldiers were ordered to set up tents on the fort's drill field, located directly in front of the barracks. Here they would have to cook and eat around a fire, and spend their nights sleeping in the tents on cots. Joey was again relegated to sleeping on another army cot, as those memories still continued to haunt him. At least there would still be plenty of food. One thing for sure, he hadn't missed a meal in a long time.

It was a cold, November afternoon when their

train left Louisiana. The San Francisco Bay was cool and windy when the USAT Washington pulled out. Now sweat was pouring down the faces of the men in this suddenly hot, humid midday sun. "Get good and used to it, soldiers. I know for some of you it was cold when you left the states. You can pretty much forget that. This is your reality now. I know it feels hot as hell, but you're on the other side of the world now!" Lt. Col. Gerald Pitkins roared with his belly laugh.

They set up their tents with two to each one, and for the first time in months, the three amigos were separated. Oscar and Marty bunked in one tent, while Joey was assigned a bunkmate that only his angel in heaven could once again have arranged.

"Sorry you stuck with me, son. I don't snore, but I've been told that I do pray a lot in my sleep. Nice to make your acquaintance. I'm one of the assigned chaplains for this battalion. They wanted me to stay over there in the barracks with all the other officers, but I thought it would be easier this way, to get to know you guys. Can't really do much preaching over there, if you know what I mean. You can call me Chaplain, Chaplain Shimley, or just Shimley. My first name is Albert, but I prefer my last name. It has a nice ring to it, don't you think? Anyway, I answer to just about anything. But you might want to keep it proper in front of the officers," said Chaplain Shimley as he reached out and shook Joey's hand.

"Nice to meet you, Chaplain Shimley. Sir, are

you an officer?" asked Joey as he searched for the right words. He had some memory of going to church with his mom. But for the most part, he only remembered his mom's excitement as each Sunday got closer. Natalie looked forward to it every week when they could get dressed up, leave their home-bound prison, walk freely down the street, and see her friend, Mrs. Gertie. One of the few things he remembered about being in church were a few soft pokes from his mom, while trying to stay awake, handing the collection plate over to the next person and the bags of clothes and toys that Mrs. Gertie would occasionally pass off to them. He had never been in the full and complete presence of a man of God, at least not this close. Now one was going to be his tentmate. He knew about being reverent in front of a man of the cloth, but this would be a double honor.

"I'm a commissioned officer. I'm here for counsel, prayer, last rites and things like that. Not allowed to fight in combat, but I'm going to be here to do all the spiritual fighting you guys need."

"Oh yes sir, we're probably gonna be needin' a whole lot of that one day."

For the next several mornings, they worked with the Filipino Army Scouts, training them as they had been trained at Camp Beauregard. From five to eleven every morning, they trained in hand-to-hand combat with fake weapons again, instructing them on how to dig trenches and foxholes, while the

Filipino's drew maps to get the new island occupiers acquainted with the terrain and surrounding areas.

If they didn't have any kind of work on the field or the docks unloading supplies, Oscar and Marty headed to the bars for drinking and dancing with the women, or gambling with the men. They were his brothers, but this would be one of the things that he didn't want to be included on. The memory of Hank bringing his stepmother home from that bar that night had never left him, and that's the last place he ever wanted to meet a woman. So, Joey took instead to rambling up and down the streets, trying to get a feel for the city and the people that he would be sharing it with for some time.

On one of his first early afternoons in town, Joey purchased a small bag of souvenirs of handmade jewelry, that he planned to mail back to Mrs. Gertie, along with the pictures from his last roll of film. If he could no longer be a good son to his mom, he could at least try to continue to be one to Mrs. Gertie. Just as he was leaving the small souvenir shop, a young Filipino boy approached him.

"Can I show you the city, sir?"

"What's your name, son?" asked Joey.

"Eddie, sir. Everyone around here just calls me Eddie," answered the small, frail boy.

"Why aren't you in school? You're a little young to be trying to make a living already," Joey remarked.

Joey already knew the answer. He had lived it. You're never too young to be thrown away. To become a servant to the dark hearts of men. He had, at least for a short time, someone to instill hope for a better life. This young boy appeared to have never known that. He wasn't wearing oversized, grease-stained overalls, but that would have been better than the clothes he had on, that appeared he had outgrown years ago. His eyes were dark and sunken into his light brown face. One of his ears appeared as though it had stopped growing when he was an infant. And his top lip was disfigured in the most remarkable way unlike anything Joey had ever seen before.

"I'm eleven, soon be twelve, I think. Not real sure when my birthday is. So, Father Ray just said to celebrate it on Christmas Day, the same day they found me in a basket by their front doors. Don't know what my last name is. The church has been my home for as long as I can remember. Father Ray and the rest of the priests have been my family," answered Eddie.

Joey couldn't believe it. This poor kid was probably dumped there the day he was born. He had heard stories of children living in orphan homes in America, because they were born with physical defects or because their mother couldn't take care of them. If the church was his home, why was he working the streets and not in school? Why did he appear as though he hadn't had a 'just in case' change of clothes in years?

He could still remember, as they passed the donation plate on Sundays, the preacher would pull on everyone's heart strings, as he did for each and every cause. “Reaching into your hearts is easy. Today, I need you to reach into your pocketbooks. The Baptist Children’s Home needs our help. It’s up to us to help these poor, forgotten children.”

Natalie Stevens always had a secret hiding place in her purse, where she would dig into and drop a handful of change, while telling her son, “Joey, remember to pray for these little souls. They have no one if we don’t help.”

Joey thought he had left all that behind him. He thought it was only in America that children were discarded, where one was made to work for a cot in the corner and a sandwich thrown at them for lunch.

He wanted to get to know the people of this island, but of all people to stumble upon. He didn’t travel halfway around the world to get involved with someone who obviously needed so much, but there was nothing he could do to stop the words from coming out of his mouth or his hands, as he dug in his pockets.

“Well, today sounds like a perfect day to celebrate your birthday, son. And what’s a last name anyway? I can’t say that I’m proud of mine or where it came from. I tell you what, I’ll pay you double whatever your rate is to show me around, how about that?” Joey replied.

“Oh, yes sir, get in, I’ve got some places to show you nobody knows about,” Eddie answered with excitement.

Joey reluctantly left Eddie right in front of the

same souvenir shop every night, wishing there was more he could do for him. He talked about him to Chaplain Shimley every evening, questioning God's hand in such cruel circumstances. Not wanting to waste the opportunity given to him, he had confided to his new preacher friend about his home life and his father's treatment of him. This wasn't the same telling of his story, as it was with Marty and Oscar. With them, he kept a tough and unbroken exterior, but with Chaplain Shimley it was more about allowing his hurt to come to the surface.

"I just don't understand how God works. Why would he take my mom, being the wonderful and kind person she was, and leave me with my dad? If God really does know all things, then he knew ahead of time that my old man would beat me, and yet he took my mom from me anyway? Why would he have left Eddie on his own? That kid has no family. He had to be taken in by some priests for crying out loud, and it doesn't look like they've done much for him either. We were both kids. Just young, defenseless kids," Joey all but cried out loud.

"Joey, there's just some things I don't have any answer for, but sometimes rather than looking at why things were the way they were, maybe we just need to try to look at how much different we would be if they weren't. I mean, the minute you met this young fellow, you felt his pain. If you hadn't gone down that road yourself, you probably wouldn't give him the time of day. You see, Joey, you have what a lot of people don't have. That's knowing someone else's pain and suffering firsthand. In other words, you have the great virtue of empathy. That's a really special gift. Some gifts are wrapped up in really ugly paper, but once they're unwrapped, it becomes this beautiful gift that few have the ability to understand."

"I guess I never looked at it like that before. So, what you're saying is that God allowed me to suffer, so that I would know how to help someone else just like me, one day?"

"In a way, yes. You can make a mark in this world, but a much different one than your father did. It's your choice. Look son, we're over here in the middle of a war. It may not seem like it now, but it's closing in. I just want you to have peace with not only where you are now, but where you've been. You're going to have to find a way to forgive your father one day, not for his sake but your own. You know everyone is fighting a battle you know nothing about. I just don't want you to live with his demons, too. Maybe he was afraid your mom was being too soft on you and he just got lost in his grief when she died. That happens more times than I can count. Every father wants a son who is tough and can hold their own. Who knows, maybe that's how his father raised him. There are a lot of generational curses out there, that just need someone with the wherewithal to put an end to it. I'm not saying you'd ever hit your son, but unforgiveness can break you, too."

"Yes sir, I guess you should know. I never really

studied the Bible like you and my mom. She talked a lot like you, so I guess that's where she got it from. Never could really read that good until a few months ago. So, I promise to work on it, if you think that's best."

Chaplain Shimley reached into his metal footlocker and pulled out a black, pocket-sized New Testament and said, "Let me help you with that, I've got one right here and it's got your name on it."

Joey knew Chaplain Shimley felt like his anger was keeping him from moving forward with a clean and pure heart. But, right now, he somehow needed that fire in his belly to go forward. One that he never knew he had, one that he never willingly worked on until he left that day. Maybe that was part of his unwrapping, too. All those years of torment, deprivation and abuse had gradually filled every fiber of his body. Perhaps, when he was working at the shop there was somehow still the presence of his mom that made him want to be the best at what he did. He still wanted his mom to be proud of him. Whatever it was that kept his anger tapped down, was gone now. He hated Hank to the very core of his being, and hoped he would reap what he sowed one day. He would never be that kind of a father, and he would certainly never be that kind of a husband. He felt like this fury inside him would keep him alive through whatever circumstances life threw his way. But, maybe Chaplain Shimley was right about one thing. All those horrible memories helped him to see what he needed to see in Eddie's eyes. He had no idea it would one day have a name but this thing called empathy would be the glue that would bind these two for decades to come. One thing he was sure of, he would never be beaten down like that again. He took the gift from his friend, put it inside his Cuban Cigar box, and would pull it out to read every night until he couldn't reach for it again.

Eddie was always waiting in front of the same shop, proud and ready to show Joey different parts of the city. For the first time in a long time, Joey felt like he had someone who needed him, someone to look after, a little brother. Not like Tillis, who seemed to revel in his position, in what used to be his home and his room. The day before Joey drove off in the back of that Chevrolet, he had to polish Tillis' shoes, while he watched. Tillis taunted him the whole time. He didn't think it was possible, but Eddie had it far worse than he ever had. He really didn't blame Tillis, for his dad had taught him well how to be a selfish tyrant and bully. Maybe what he saw in Tillis, was that very generational curse that Chaplain Shimley talked about. That would have to be between his half-brother and God, to make or break. All he knew was that for the rest of his time on this island, whether months or years, he would make sure his new, little adopted brother had everything he needed and more.

CHAPTER 10

THERE IS A LOT OF GOOD HERE
December 1972

THANKSGIVING WAS A DISASTER. Joey had one of his temper tantrums that neither Mom nor I have seen in a long time. He said they put way too much gravy on his mashed potatoes, and he didn't like the way that Mr. Bentley was staring at his food. He was absolutely convinced that Mr. Bentley was going to take his plate away, before he was finished eating. It didn't matter that Mr. Bentley was there only to pick up after everyone was finished, just like he had always done, but once the paranoia set in, there was no going back. So, we finally had to take him and his plate back to his room. Nurse Lydia told us not to worry, she would make sure to let Joey fix his own plate for their next big gathering at Christmas.

It had always been unnerving to see him get this upset, as it seemed to set the tone in the house for the rest of the day. Even though we've been living separate and apart for all these many months, we're still working on relaxing our previously set meal times, while Mom is still adapting to her new routine of taking her time when we go somewhere. Whether she tried or not, it didn't take long at Harvey's Market—which could've filled one corner of the big Sullivan's Grocery back home. The people working there seemed to be a lot friendlier than we were used to. Or maybe it was because we didn't have The Incredible Hulk with us now, causing a scene and making everyone uncomfortable. Either way, we never stayed long. For me, because even though they had a small selection of women, teen stars, and gossip magazines, there were no detective ones for me to look through. They didn't even have The Incredible Hulk comic books for me to buy Joey anymore.

We visited him every weekend, but each visit left Mom and me both sad, and at the same time relieved. It didn't matter what day of the week or what time of the day we went, it seemed like Nurse Lydia was always there. She wasn't just a nurse that took care of her patient's physical needs. It was as if she thought their emotional needs were just as important. Sometimes we would walk in to see her seated at the tables, helping one of them with a jigsaw puzzle or digging in the Crayola box for just the perfect color.

"Look at how good you are at staying in the lines Joey, my goodness that deserves an extra cookie!"

"Yeah, extra cookie," as Joey clapped and giggled the same way he would when Mom would let him eat on the TV tray. It was as though the lines on the paper were completely invisible to him, just as they had been for years. Here, the mere notion that he could still hold a crayon and scratch it across the paper was enough to celebrate. Gilly could only assume that some personal interaction was better than none at all. And much to her dismay, Joey seemed to really like spending time with his new friend, Nurse Lydia.

I guess I found myself getting a little jealous, that not only did he not seem to miss us, but he was actually having fun at this place. Here I was thinking about how hard it was going to be on him, and it appears the only ones having a hard time were Mom and me. Nurse Lydia was a lot more patient with him than I think I ever was. Then again, I was just a kid when this nightmare started, and had no idea how to deal with it all. And Mom was just trying to figure out how to keep a roof over our heads. This amazing woman, Nurse Lydia, chose to go to school to be a nurse, and learn how to help people like Joey. I'm going to have to tell Kat about this. Maybe her mom was right about this kind of stuff. Now that I'm thinking about it, it would be really cool if Kat became a nurse one day, and took over for Nurse Lydia. She could be right here, not only being my blood sister again, but Joey's nurse.

The down side of all this was, he hadn't had much to say to either one of us lately when we visited, and would rarely look at us either. We didn't know if he was mad at us for leaving him, or maybe he thought we were mad at him for another one of his disastrous events. Maybe Mom was right after all. Maybe he still knew us and how we still belonged together, and felt we had abandoned him.

As we were leaving one Saturday afternoon, feeling like this was all we had to look forward to, Nurse Lydia stopped us in the hall. "I can tell by the look on your faces that you're disappointed with his lack of any real improvement. It's just going to take some time for all his doctors to agree on his treatment. Things don't move very fast around here. There's just too much bureaucracy. Hopefully, in the next few weeks you'll start to see some improvement. In the meantime, don't put your lives on hold. Both of you doing that won't fix what's going on in his head. I do know that he really looks forward to seeing the two of you, so don't think he doesn't miss you. Here, when you get time, just take a look at this." She handed us a booklet entitled "Adjusting to Life After. How to Pick Up the Pieces."

I've never been one to be into any kind of self-help books, as most of the information always seemed useless and superficial to me. Once again, I was ready to toss this one, just like the ones that Mrs. Weaver tried to give me, right when all this started. Life after what? After you've abandoned your dad because his brain broke into a million pieces after he ran over a dog? Where's there a chapter on that? How does a family, or what's left of one, meld back together when someone is missing? Why did this happen to him, to us, in the first place? Wasn't it enough that he served in the Army, and then held as a prisoner for years? Nobody has wanted to get into the details with me about what happened over there. I'm sure Mom knows more than she's letting on. If he had no problems talking to Kat's dad about it, why on earth wouldn't he tell Mom as well? Maybe I'm just not as grown up as Mom thinks. If he can still walk, talk, blink, see, hear and eat, why can't he understand where he is and who we are? If he sees The Incredible Hulk as his hero, then why doesn't he see me as his daughter, or Mom as his wife?

I had, however, grown to trust and admire Nurse Lydia, so on the way home I reluctantly flipped through the pages and read through the chapter "Don't Forget Your Dreams." This was one takeaway that made some meaningful sense. The idea was to try to follow up on one's dreams, that had been put on hold, because that would be what your loved one would want you to do. I wonder what Joey would think about my dream. Would he think that it's ridiculous? Would he be hurt that I didn't follow his interests? We never talked about it. We just didn't have enough time to.

Out of boredom, every day after school I started stopping by the post office just to hang out with Aunt Maggie. Maybe it could be here that I could figure things out. It was too quiet at home, with Mom at work all day, and I just wasn't ready to bare my soul to Hope. She was much too agreeable and never held her own opinion about anything.

Just as you entered the town, the post office was located on one end of a whitewashed, weather-beaten, lap board siding building that had Bolton's Hardware store in the middle, and Mimi's Diner on the far end corner. There was a huge glass picture window that had the words stenciled in big, bold black letters, LAUREL COVE POST OFFICE, ESTABLISHED, MARCH 1915. The door had a glass insert on the top half, that had the words 'WELCOME' printed in the center, with an 'OPEN' sign hanging from the inside. There was also a small bell attached to the door, that jingled all day long as people came and went. To the left, in a small alcove, there was a collection of sequential numbered, gold-plated post office boxes, and on the right of the door, in the corner, stood a hand carved, six-foot wooden statue of a Native American. His left hand held a long, carved-out spear, while his right hand was held up with the palm facing outward. His head was weighed down in an enormous headdress, filled with multi-colored feathers, and the bottom of his torso was wrapped in a carved out brown leather skirt.

Aunt Maggie said it was a replica of Chief Tonaka, from the Biloxi tribe. Apparently, the very land we're standing on was once a Native campground. She said there was an old tale, that if you honored him with a salute, your wish would be granted. So, needless to say, I saluted the big guy every chance I got. Once everyone made their customary salute, customers were able to check out the bulletin board on the right wall, that served the town with weekly announcements. Since the local newspaper had shut its doors years ago, everyone who was anyone posted news on everything from school and church activities, weddings, baby announcements, items for sale, as well as a list of the post office official posting of the 'FBI's Ten Most Wanted.' These were ten of the most dangerous criminals in the country, with their photographs and list of the crimes they had committed. Not the sort of sleuthing I'm ready for yet, because these guys looked like they'd kill you just for looking wrong-sided. I think I'm just going to concentrate on finding out who's who around here for now.

Much to my surprise, there was a lot of activity in the lobby of this small post office. For such a little town, I found myself somewhat curious and a little entertained at all the comings and goings of the customers that came in every day.

There was Oliver, a big black Labrador, who had wandered in and made himself at home about eight years ago. He was the post office's friendly guard dog and town mascot, who loved everyone. From day one, Oliver became my new confidant. He was just as good a listener as Kat, and didn't smother me to death like Hope. He had his designated spot behind the counter and I had mine. Depending on the level of chattering that went on, he would rarely pick his head up unless someone had a treat for him. Aunt Maggie has let me sit behind the counter for weeks, just so I could get acquainted with most of the regulars, as she put it, but I didn't see anything regular about most of the people that came in. However, a few of them slowly began showing me small doses of what gratitude meant, the very thing that my mom had tried to drill in me for years. If we would just only look to our right or left throughout the day, we would find ourselves much higher on the fairness scale than we have ourselves to believe.

Gabriel Simpson, or "Gabe" as everyone called him, was the one and only mail carrier. He was a lonely widower that had to be in his seventies, and had been a fixture at the post office for as long as anyone could remember. Aunt Maggie said he didn't see that well, and she constantly got complaints about him misdelivering mail, but she just didn't have the heart to let him go. This was the only thing he had left in his life, since his wife died years ago. She said it was just easier for her to slip out of the office and go fix those mishaps herself. It took him most of the day just to deliver mail to around three hundred or so homes. She said he probably spent most of his time visiting and no doubt having lunch at someone's house each day along the way. So, he was usually leaving for the day when I walked in. He reminded me a lot of old Mr. Palmer, who owned the Double Pattie. You didn't want to order any burgers if you saw him working in the kitchen. He was old too and burned everything he cooked. His wife didn't have the heart to make him quit either. She would just make you a new burger, when he wasn't looking, and give you extra fries for the wait.

One of my favorites so far has been Mrs. Hattie, who told everybody that Jesus loved them, she loved them, and "isn't this such a beautiful day," even on days when it was gloomy and overcast. Oliver always raised his head when he heard her voice. She was one of his favorites too, for always bringing him a special treat. Her weather-beaten, ebony face was a roadmap of decades of hard work and strife. Yet, somehow her voice only echoed unabashed thankfulness and hope. How was her mind still intact, and her soul full of so much grace, when Joey's fell apart? Life surely hasn't been easy for her either, which made me ashamed for my own ongoing self-pity.

I found it unusual that so many older folks lived here. Apparently, at one time this had started out as a small vacation resort, but throughout the years, morphed into full-time living by northerners yearning for a slower pace of living and year-round sunshine. It appeared that many of them had gradually been burdened with raising their grandchildren, or simply taken in their own adult children, who couldn't make it elsewhere. I hoped, as Aunt Maggie filled me in on their back stories, that she didn't feel burdened with my mom and me. Like somehow, we couldn't make it on our own either.

For hours throughout the afternoon, I would just stand in awe, while some of the older customers, with their hands so bent, twisted and buckled from arthritis, could barely work their wallets and change purses. Others, with their backs so crooked, it hurt just to watch them shuffle in and out. Once again, these seemed to be the happiest people I've ever met. They were always glad to 'wake up this morning', and the men would let me know 'as long as my wife tells me I'm happy, then I'm guessing I'm still happy.' Then there were a few that, in my opinion, should have had a room down the hall from Joey, in the hospital ward of broken minds.

Anastasia seemed to live in her own cloudy, delusional and disenchanted world. She was in the post office daily, but made only one weekly transaction when she would mail letters to anyone that had a title which included the Governor, Queen of England, President Nixon, the Russian Embassy, and even a couple of the astronauts. It was as though she was there, but not on the same planet. I never knew if she was talking to me or to her imaginary friend, Arthur. Yet every time she walked in, I got homesick. Much like Kat, she put on a display every day of clothes that didn't match, didn't fit, or should have been thrown out decades ago. God, I miss Kat. I still haven't heard from her.

Then there was Leon Miller, who Aunt Maggie called Leon the Detective, because he wrote down in a little pocket notepad all the names of the FBI's ten most wanted every month, after it was posted on the bulletin board. Of all that went on in the Laurel Cove Post Office, it was this man that Aunt Maggie found the most amusing. Of course, I did not. She said he was some sort of amateur detective. It was this revelation when I suddenly felt there was a reason why we were here. All my misgivings about Laurel Cove Academy, sleeping in an apartment on the beach, this stupid little empty town, Uncle Mack, and no Kat to talk to, suddenly vanished. I didn't care if he was a real detective or not. Just the fact that he had it in him to want to catch the bad guys and solve crimes was enough for me, and getting to know Leon Miller could just be the catalyst I needed to seriously believe the words that I had written down just a few shorts months ago.

"Oh, Gilly, I have a letter here for you from your friend Kat," Aunt Maggie announced as she was leaving for the day.

Gilly was beside herself. She couldn't imagine what had taken Kat so long to write her back. She had already mailed her six letters and made three telephone calls, and so far hadn't gotten a reply or answer from either. Her separation from Kat was now well into its fourth month. She was beginning to think her one and only friend had forgotten all about her. She shoved the letter into her booksack and couldn't wait to get home. Finally, some news from home. She had so much more to tell her one and only friend and blood sister. Gilly just hoped she's was doing okay. She hoped that Regina and Mona hadn't tormented her too much. Hopefully, she's still on track for her dream, because Gilly was absolutely positive of her's now.

Dear Gilly,

Sorry, I haven't written sooner. I've been really busy. Mom and Dad are getting a divorce. Seems he's been busy with more than his job while he's been away. Mom said she wasn't surprised and was just glad she made enough money to support us. Dad will be paying child support, but not the kind of money we were used to. Guess we'll soon be moving one day, too.

So, to help Mom out, I got a job working part time at the Double Pattie after school. I have to wear this ridiculous-looking uniform there every day. But other than that, it's been more fun than I ever could imagined, so I really don't mind.

There's a really cute boy that works there. His name is Martin. He's not at all like the stupid boys at school. He's already in college. I can't wait for you to meet him. He said he's only going to college because that's what his parents want. But, get this Gilly, he plays in a band. Can you believe it? I really think he likes me because he invited me to go listen to them practice at his house tomorrow night!

Hope you can come visit real soon.

Love, Kat

Kat didn't ask one time how Gilly was doing. After all, it had been her world that had been totally turned upside down when they had to move away. It didn't matter that they would have to move soon, too, because she knew they would never wind up living in a run-down house, on the wrong side of the tracks. It was obvious to her that Kat didn't miss her at all. She had been replaced. Gilly suddenly had a small window into her mom's world. She now knew what it felt like to not only lose someone you loved and cared about, but she had also just lost her best friend. Just like she heard her mom do so many times before, Gilly cried herself to sleep that night.

The next morning, while she was waiting for her Pop Tart to pop up, Gilly had another 'gut punch.' Her head and heart were colliding. Why did Kat seem happier than she had ever been, even though her parents were getting a divorce? Did the dumb duo suddenly decide to make nice after she moved away? Kat made absolutely no mention of either of their sworn enemies and what they had been up to.

Claire broke her downward spiral when she announced, "Gilly, I know we've both been busy, but in case you haven't noticed, Christmas will be here before you know it. We need to get a tree up and I need to get busy with my shopping."

"Yeah, I know."

"Is something wrong?"

"Mom, have you talked to Kat's mom lately?"

"Oh, I'm sorry Gilly. I haven't had a chance to tell you. Sylvia and Mark are getting a divorce. I have to say that I really wasn't surprised. I think Mark's traveling so much finally took a toll on their marriage. From everything Sylvia said, they would make it, but poor Kat, she's had to get a job after school to help out."

"Yeah, poor Kat. I think she's already moved on. She'll be fine, Mom. It's just going to be really weird without Joey here this year. He just made it so much fun."

"What? She's moved where?"

"Nothing. Why are we decorating this place? Joey won't be here."

"Well, we can spend the day with him there. It will almost be the same. Plus, there's no reason why you and I can't celebrate it here, too."

"Yeah, I guess."

Gilly decided to skip the post office that afternoon. Instead, she went home and pulled their Christmas decorations out, and spread what they had throughout the apartment. She felt like she needed to do something to get her mind off Kat and Joey. How is it that they both seemed to be so much happier without her? Had she been the one holding them back all those years? She had never been insecure about what few relationships she once had. Now she felt like she needed to write a letter to someone who had clout, like Anastasia did every week. She needed someone that had some authority, who could maybe cue her in on what was going on. When she was done with the decorations, she made a salad, fried pork chops, homemade mashed potatoes, and popped a frozen apple pie in the oven. The last thing she wanted, was to think her mom could be happier without her one day, too.

Claire was delighted with the change she saw in her daughter, that happened almost overnight. Gilly had endured more than most her age, and maybe this move had been the best thing for all of them after all. She had a good, regular-paying job now, and she would make sure that this Christmas would be one of their best.

As they rode to the hospital on Christmas morning, Gilly no longer felt or looked like she lived on the wrong side of the tracks. She didn't know if it was the letter from Kat, Joey's disposition, or her time standing behind the counter at the post office that opened her eyes. Something had really started to help change her mindset. And today, it really helped her overall outlook, as she ran her hands over her new pearl necklace that draped over the neckline of her beautiful store-bought, red velvet Christmas dress. As she crossed her legs, she couldn't help but admire her mom's other generous gift. She finally had a pair of those long admired white, knee-high boots.

As Joey carefully unwrapped his present FROM SANTA, both Claire and Gilly, if only for a few moments, thought they were all at home together again when he smiled and propped his elbows on his new 'The Incredible Hulk' TV tray.

CHAPTER 11

THE SECOND RAID
December 1941

ON DECEMBER 7, 1941, Joey crawled into his army cot with the most foreboding feeling he had ever had. Something didn't feel right. He could smell it in the air. Almost like he could smell Hank several yards away, before he walked through the door at the repair shop. There was some kind of evil encroaching on this island paradise. It bothered him so much that he even shared this mortal terror with Chaplain Shimley.

"Sir, what if I told you that I'm afraid? Would you think that I'm a coward or a sissy?" asked Joey.

"Son, fear is a good thing, especially in these times. If you weren't afraid, I'd think you a fool. You've got to hand it over to God. I have to remind myself of that all the time. Talk to Him, tell Him what's on your mind, what's in your heart. If nothing else, fear God, respect his omnipotence. No one knows what tomorrow will bring. It doesn't matter where you live or who you are. Life is fragile. Always has been and always will be."

"Yes, sir, I lived it. My Mom was lying in that hospital bed one day and the next day she was gone. I believe she's up in heaven right now. Guess God didn't have any use for my old man. Good night, Sir."

"Good night, Private Stevens."

Joey had nightmares all night. First, of his mom lying in her casket with his dog tags clinched in her hands. Then he saw this huge bonfire behind the repair shop, where all of their clothes, Tinker Toys, Lincoln Logs, and his Cuban Cigar box were being thrown in and burned, while a man poked the fire and howled like a wild animal with wicked laughter. When this man turned around, it was his father, with a big evil grin. And then suddenly, there were bright lights and yelling, "Joey, man, get up, Pearl Harbor was attacked by the Japanese! We just got word. It's started. We're at war," hollered Chaplain Shimley. This was no longer his nightmare this would be the entire world's.

With the deafening sounds of the air raid sirens, hundreds of tents emptied out, some of them collapsing with their inhabitants still inside. They had all trained for months, both stateside and in their current surroundings, yet there was nothing that could have prepared them for this. As pandemonium spread all throughout the encampment, Lt. Col. Gerald Pitkins ordered everyone out of the open area, back into the thick brush and woods behind the officers' barracks. In spite of the fear Joey had the night before, his thoughts weren't on his safety. He was suddenly consumed with the whereabouts of Eddie. He was sure his newly-adopted little street urchin was probably already out and about, trying to make a few dollars this morning. He now needed him somewhere safe. If he had to personally escort him back to the church, then he supposed that would be what a responsible big brother should do. No matter how many times he tried before, Eddie always put up a fuss about not wanting to go back yet. Joey was beginning to have his suspicions on just how much Father Ray was involved in Eddie's life. This was not a comfortable feeling at all, and he was surprised at how this orphan, who he had only met a few days ago, had already made his way so deeply into his heart. Much like he felt when his father would mistreat his mom, he had already gotten protective of Eddie.

By midmorning, word came that they could return to their camp. Joey didn't know why he had the premonition the night before, but was now sure this was the beginning of something much more sinister than his dream. Chaplain Shimley didn't have to ask twice, if Joey wanted a ride into town.

Details of the attack on Pearl Harbor were slowly coming in, over the radios blaring, in every shop in town. The attack commenced at 8:00 a.m. Hawaiian Time, when the base was attacked by 353 Imperial Japanese aircraft that came in two different waves. All eight Navy battleships were damaged, with four of them sunk and 188 U.S. aircraft completely destroyed. The death count right now is still coming in, but is expected to be over 2,000, and the wounded at least 1,000. Men, women and children were gathered around the opened doors of cafes, listening to the news, wondering if they would be spared, while others milled about in their normal routines. Joey and Chaplain Shimley could not believe what they just heard.

"Sir, I don't understand, why?"

"Power, son. Power."

It had been only a few short weeks since his ship, the USAT Washington, had sailed through those same waters. Joey wondered if that was where Buck was. Mrs. Gertie never said. He knew he needed to pray, but he would need Chaplain Shimley's help because he just didn't know where or how to begin.

Joey finally spotted his little friend waving at him like it was just another day. "Eddie, I've been looking all over the place for you. I need you to go back to the church and stay there. We could be under attack here any minute. Don't you dare come out for any reason, and you need to mind

Father Ray. You go where he tells you to, do you understand me?"

"But I don't want to stay there. I want to go with you. They're just a bunch of old men that only know how to hide. I want to fight with you, Joey! You promised you'd show me how to be a soldier one day. Now's just as good a time as any, don't you think?"

"Look son, don't get smart. This isn't a game. If and when those planes start heading this way, no gun, even if you know how to shoot one, is going to save you. You just need to get yourself in a safe spot. I'm hoping they won't fire down on the church. That's probably the safest place in town right now."

The San Agustin Church was empty, and after Joey hollered for a few minutes, Father Ray finally appeared. He appeared to be much the same size as his father, but did not have one single whiff of intimidation about him. His voice was kind and soft.

"Can I help you?"

"Yes, Father, I just wanted to make sure Eddie stayed put here. Not really safe out there right now."

"Of course, but I can't lock him up. He's never been one that's minded much. Have you Eddie?"

"No, Father."

"He's always been a bit of a free spirit. We finally made a deal that he could leave in the morning, but he had to be back by dark. He works you know. Somehow, he thinks he needs to pull his weight around here. We definitely need the money, no doubt. Have to rely on donations to take care of the little ones we take in. We have over sixty now. We've taken in three newborns, in just the last year."

Joey was so taken back. He thought of all the times that his mom pulled her coin purse out, and now he knew why. They had so little and still she gave. He could have easily wound up in a place much like this, had he not had a corner cot in the shop to sleep on. All those years he thought he had it so bad; at least he had Buck and Mrs. Gertie.

"Where will you stay if the Japanese start bombing here?"

"We've got a basement. That's where we've been all morning."

"Okay look, this is all the money I have on me. Take it. Use it for the kids. But can you please do me a favor and make sure Eddie doesn't leave?"

"All I can do is try."

"Joey, what if I don't see you again?" Eddie's voice pleaded.

"You will, I promise."

Chaplain Shimley swung around the corner, and hollered at Joey to get in as they hurried back to camp, "You got the boy squared away?"

"Yeah, I hope so. He wanted to come with me, but I told him that wasn't happening. Chaplain, are you going to lead a prayer meeting when we get back?"

"First thing."

Chaplain Shimley's plan was to gather the men together and have a short service, with the hopes of instilling some calm in the increasing panic-stricken looks he was seeing on the soldiers' faces. But, before he could put things together, Lt. Col. Gerald Pitkins ordered them to break camp, collect their belongings, and evacuate Fort McKinley. The only thing the chaplain could do at this point was silently pray that God would cover them.

As Joey and Chaplain Shimley had just finished packing up their tent, the air raid sirens went off again, followed by sounds of low-flying planes overhead. Before they could move, it seemed as though the big moving, painted red suns were spitting fire on them. It was six Japanese bombers and this was the real thing, now they were being attacked. Hundreds of holes were being punched in the ground, the tents and the soldiers. Men were jumping into the newly dug trenches and fox holes, while others were running for cover into and underneath the officers' barracks. The attack only lasted ten to fifteen minutes, but it unfortunately took the lives of twenty men. Like Marty said that day during their first Louisiana Maneuvers, this wasn't a game and these men weren't pretend killed.

Joey never knew most of the men that were killed, as he had been spending all of his free time with Eddie. He had never been so happy in his life when he finally laid eyes on Oscar and Marty after the attack, and relief washed over him, knowing they were safe. He had been so preoccupied with Chaplain Shimley trying to save his soul, and getting Eddie in a safe place, he almost forgot why he was really there. Joey now realized there was nothing he wouldn't do to save those two. Even if it meant a beating, he swore would never happen again. This was different. This time wouldn't be a humiliating beatdown by a bully with a heavy hand. It would be for the courage and commitment that had grown in him over the last few months as a soldier. He suddenly, finally felt strong and defiant. This was now about good against evil. For the first time since his mom died, he knew this was what it was supposed to feel like when you had good people in your corner. He may have no longer been in that boxing ring with Hank, but this was a new fight, and one he just knew they had to win.

The rest of the day was spent transporting the dead and wounded out of Fort McKinley, and finally arming everyone with real weapons and ammunition, while they wrapped their heads around what had just happened, and what tomorrow might bring.

CHAPTER 12

MEMORIES AREN'T THE ONLY THINGS THAT DIE
January 1973

"MOM, I KNOW IT'S a little early to bring this up, but how do you feel about Valentine's Day? I mean it just seems to be a day that half the world loves, while the other half dreads it. Did you and Dad ever do anything special?"

"Oh Gilly, I think it was probably one of his favorite days of the year. He always brought home a dozen red roses and took me out to eat at one of the finest restaurants in town. He was such an incredible romantic. He always brought you home a big, red, heart-shaped box of candy. You would sit at the table and make your little cutout heart cards for us. It was such a sweet time for us. I wish you could remember those days. And I hope you're never part of that half of the world that doesn't look forward to it one day."

"Me too, Mom."

"Why do you ask? By the way, I know all about the Valentine's Banquet at school. It's one of the biggest events in town. Everyone's already talking about it. Has someone asked you already?"

"God, no, Mom. How does news spread around here so fast?" Gilly laughed.

"Have you already forgotten who my sister is? Your Aunt Maggie knows what's going on around here, before most of Laurel Cove gets out of bed in the morning," Claire replied.

"That's a little scary."

"So why aren't you going? This would be a really good chance to mingle. I'm sure you don't have to have a date to go."

"I think I'd rather stick a fork in my eyeballs first. I mingle enough there, as it is. Don't get me wrong, it's nowhere near as bad as back home, but there are only nine boys in my grade, and most of them are absolute losers. I'm sure they have no plans to make anything of themselves. When they're not trying to make those grotesque noises with their armpits, they're trying to figure out how to sneak a smoke in at lunch period. You know, I have the highest grades in the whole class. Can you believe it? Me, Gilly Marie Stevens, at the top of her class!"

"Honey, that's amazing!"

"Thanks Mom, but like I was saying, none of them care to try at school, and the girls just rotate from week to week who they like and want to marry. Maybe they can all get a job helping Uncle Mack to collect junk off the beach one day."

"Gilda Stevens, what a horrible thing to say!"

"Mom, you know it's true. I asked Aunt Maggie about him, where he came from and what made him so special, and she didn't have a good answer. Not for me anyway, and I didn't mean to disappoint you so quickly. It just seemed like she was avoiding the whole conversation. We met, we fell in love, and we got married. What really attracts men and women to each other in that forever way? I mean, I get the whole thing about feelings, looks and personality, but how do you know that person you're sitting next to or going to the movies with, is who you want to spend the rest of your life with? It's got to be more complicated than I met, fell in love and got married."

"No, you just think it's complicated. It's just a matter of personal taste. Just like the kind you have right now about the boys in your school. But, don't be so judgmental. It takes a while for some people to grow up, especially boys. You're just a little ahead of most of your classmates because you've had to grow up faster. You've had a lot of responsibilities most don't ever have, and I have to say, I'm really proud of you for how you've handled it all and how you've settled in here. I don't think you've complained one single time for weeks now. So, I'm just going to pretend I didn't hear that. Just, please don't judge your Aunt Maggie. Not only does she have this big, selfless heart, she's a much more well-thought-out person than you give her credit for. Besides, if it weren't for her, we probably would be homeless right now. By the way, one day when you're ready to open your heart, you'll know forever love when it comes your way, I promise."

It was nice for Gilly to hear her mom talk about a happy memory of how her dad loved her mom that much, to want to make Valentine's a special day. Since there weren't enough boys to take all the girls, some of them wouldn't have a special day, so a lot of them were already pouting about it. Gilly didn't dare tell her mom that Rory Turner already asked her to the Valentine's Banquet, and she had absolutely no problem telling him no. He had stalked her pretty much from day one, and she just thought the whole Valentine's thing was stupid anyway. She didn't care that his dad owned Harvey's Market, and that Rory was going to run it one day. It was really weird to her, that another boy whose dad owned a grocery store, wanted to go out with her. Maybe she just spent way too much time in the grocery stores or something. She had given her Aunt Maggie a pass when she laughed about Leon the Detective, but if Rory had only ordered The Master Detective magazine when she asked him to, instead of making fun of her, he might have had a date to one of the biggest events in town.

She was actually glad now to be in Laurel Cove for Valentine's Day. She didn't think she could stomach seeing Kat all dressed up in normal clothes, going to their banquet with Martin. For someone who didn't want to conform and try to fit in before, it had to be this forever love thing for Kat to change so quickly.

Gilly walked in, saluted Chief Tonica, and looked over the bulletin board. Same old stuff, no break-ins, no murders and she could have cared less about who's getting married or having a baby. She wished there was an actual newspaper in town. That's where she would prefer to spend her free time, doing some real investigative reporting. Like, who knocked down Mrs. Audrey Lambert's mailbox at the end of Dry Dock Lane? Mrs. Lambert swears it was Gabe's mail truck, but he said she probably did it herself backing out of her own driveway. Nobody knows exactly how old she is but she's blind as a bat. She doesn't have a real, valid driver's license anymore and couldn't get one again if she tried. She always confuses Gilly for Aunt Maggie every time she visits the post office, even though they don't look anything alike. Aunt Maggie looks just like an older version of Claire, never mind that she's at least thirty years older than Gilly.

"Good afternoon, Gilly, how was your day?" asked Aunt Maggie.

"Oh, the same. Only four more months and I graduate. I'm kind of getting excited about that."

"Still no plans yet?"

"Not yet. Mom said after everything we've had

to deal with, she wasn't going to give me a hard time about college... YET. She does really want me to go, though. She said she nearly has enough money saved up for my first year at the University of Southern Mississippi. I just don't know what they would have to offer me if I went. I don't want to waste Mom's hard-earned money if I'm not sure."

"Well, I understand and you won't get any pressure from me. It wasn't my thing either."

Gilly was so relieved to hear that, "Really, it wasn't, what about Mom?"

"She wasn't interested either. She always said that all she wanted to do was be a wife and mother one day. I have to say, I was a little jealous when it happened for her and not me."

"So why didn't you have kids. I mean, you and Uncle Mack didn't want any?"

"Well, yes and no. It was always finding the right guy first, that just never seemed to work out for me, like it did for your mom. By the time I married your Uncle Mack, having kids wasn't this thing that I felt like I needed to do anymore. Don't get me wrong, I love kids. You have always been my best girl. I don't know, after I started working here, the people of Laurel Cove really became my extended family, and my life is very full. So enough of that. Since you don't appear to be going anywhere else anytime soon, how about you come on back here and let me show you a few things. You've handled yourself really well up here at the counter, and I appreciate you coming by and helping me out up front. What if I start paying you for a little more responsibility around here?"

"Really, can you just do that?"

Aunt Maggie lifted her voice, with one hand on her hip while the other moved about showing the contents of the back office, "Of course, I can. I'm the Master and this is my domain!"

Gilly gazed at the backside of the post office boxes where all sixty-eight labelled and numbered small, open tunnels would get their mail every day, "Sounds good to me, where do I start?"

"Right here," Maggie handed her a handful of mail, ready to be delivered into those small open tunnels.

The inner workings of the post office had been off limits to Gilly, for the most part. She had seen the bags of mail, packages, equipment, shelves and her Aunt Maggie's cluttered desk, but really never left the counter after she threw her booksack underneath it after school. Other than sticking her head in from time to time, she had never officially been invited all the way in, and didn't want to wear out her welcome. Going there every day after school had been her salvation, since it appeared Kat had dumped her for Martin. Even after Gilly attempted a couple more phone calls, Kat was getting more and more distant, to the point where Gilly thought there was really no point of calling her again. So much for the finger-sticking blood sister oath they took. She had always thought they would be friends forever. She thought Kat was different. She just thought she was much deeper than that. All it took for Kat to move on, was for her to move away. Maybe her mom was right. She had to grow up faster than everyone else, and obviously took her commitments more seriously. As far as she was concerned, Kat was officially now part of the dumb duo. Only now, she would refer to them as the dumb trio. So, she and Oliver spent nearly every afternoon together, waiting on the handful of customers that came in. Now she was going to be involved in the business of getting to know everyone else's business, in the town of Laurel Cove. This was going to be better than any detective magazine.

Maggie was just as patient in training her new employee, as she had been an aunt to her very best girl. It didn't take long for her to memorize each and every name, who they owed money to, where their relatives lived, and where their friends and family went on the vacations, that they wished they were on. Reading the back of every postcard did seem wrong at first, until she saw Aunt Maggie shaking her head and doing the same thing. Then one day, she had a letter addressed to Earl Herring, Box 22, Laurel Cove, Mississippi. Oddly, the name on the box was for a Barbara Winters.

"Aunt Maggie, what do I do with this letter? It's not the same name as on the box."

"Okay, let me look at it. There's not a return address to send it back either. That's too bad. This upsets me when it happens. Unfortunately, we'll have to add it to the other dead letters. I always feel so bad when that happens."

"So, you bury it somewhere?"

"Heavens no, we have to keep it right over here in this box, that I keep on the shelf, right behind my desk."

It appeared to Gilly that Aunt Maggie's desk looked like she had business that hadn't been taken care of in years. The four-foot-long shelves behind her desk were riddled with countless notebooks, wire trays full of papers, and books. Among all the clutter, Gilly finally spotted a dusty, old, white shoebox with the words 'DEAD LETTER BOX' written in black.

"Huh, I thought only people died. I've never heard of letters dying, too."

"Well, we can't deliver it and we can't return it, so it just kind of sits there, dead. Nowhere to go."

"So, you do kind of bury them, but it's in a shoe box?"

"I suppose you can say that. It's not like I forget about them. I know most of them by heart. I rifle through them occasionally and try to find some connection in town, but for the most part, they do just sit there. Some of them have been in there for years, some for decades. It's sad really."

"That doesn't make any sense. Why can't we open them? Maybe find some more information about the person who wrote it so we can return it or something."

"Because that's against the law. It's illegal to open any first class mail, for any reason."

"Well, that's a stupid law. What if there's some really good news, or bad news, or even a big check or something like that inside?"

"Then the news will never be told and the check will never be cashed. I know it doesn't sound right or fair, but that's just the way things work around here."

Gilly's mind was already swinging into overdrive. No letter should ever be left undelivered, unreturned or unanswered, much less sit in an old, dusty shoebox forever. Someone had taken the time to write their thoughts, feelings, confessions or maybe even their last wishes. She knew that this couldn't be a real law. She couldn't imagine going to jail just because she opened someone's letter. It wasn't really breaking and entering into anything like a house or a car. Besides, she knew that if Gabe thought blind, old Mrs. Audrey had fallen and hurt herself in her house and needed help, he wouldn't hesitate to break in and help her. Aunt Maggie had told her that it was her post office and she could run it like she wanted. This was probably her way of protecting her adopted Laurel Cove family of secrets, just like she had with her Uncle Mack. Aunt Maggie had deemed herself the protector of the secrets of Laurel Cove, but Gilly had come to despise secrets. Secrets were the very thing that had her dad sitting in that Veterans' Home. All his secrets had been tucked away, and now he was entombed, much like these letters, waiting to be opened and freed. If she couldn't help her dad come back to life, then at least she could help finish the journey for one of these personal, handwritten souls. She already knew who could help her. It would be none other than Leon, Leon the Detective.

CHAPTER 13

THE BATTLE AT BATAAN
March 1942

ON THE DAY OF the attack on their campground, they quickly moved from Fort McKinley into Manila. The city had been attacked the same day, but the damage had been minimal and there was no loss of life. Along with the men in the Philippine Army, American soldiers helped in clearing out the shattered remains of a half dozen homes and businesses. The souvenir shop, where Joey had bought the bag of hand-made jewelry for Mrs. Gertie, happened to be one of them. The grief and shock that he saw, as he looked into the swollen eyes of the elderly shopkeepers, nearly broke his heart. The brutality and destruction of war was already beginning to take a toll on him, and this was only day one. It just didn't seem fair. Half of the young men killed, would get a decent burial with their friends and families here on the island, while the other half would only get a letter of sincere regret and deepest sympathies. This would be one of the many heart-breaking duties that the chaplains working here would have to do. They may never be called to do combat, but fighting evil on a different front was just as important.

No one knew when or where the Japanese would return, but there was no doubt they would. So, the American soldiers were buried in a cemetery in town, next to San Agustin Catholic Church, that was also Eddie's home. Joey checked in one last time to make sure he was staying put, and Father Ray promised he would do everything he could to keep him secured in the church and safe.

"He's been quite a handful, but that's just who he is. Poor fellow, until you showed up, he never had anyone give him a second look. Most of the time people just wanted to look the other way. It was just too uncomfortable for them to look right into the face of someone that love forgot about. We've taken in hundreds of orphans over the years, but he's been here the longest. We don't have many resources around here to care for someone his age either. He should be out playing, but he insists on working in the city every day. I think it's always been his hope that he would meet someone like you one day, that wouldn't take too long a look at his physical deformities, but rather, his heart. It's been hard trying to convince him that he was made in God's image, but now he's absolutely convinced that somehow you were sent to save him. He really thinks of you as his big brother. I do hope you can come back one day and spend more time with him," said Father Ray.

"Just tell him, well... just tell him for me that I love him, and I promise to do whatever I can to come back for him." Joey could not believe he had said those words out loud. The last and only person he had ever said such a thing to was his mom, and he was sure as ever, that in that moment she was standing right beside him.

On the morning of the third day, they got their orders to load and head towards the Bataan Peninsula. There had been so much confusion, with orders flying from the mouths of every officer, that had more than one bar on his uniform. It was then that Joey realized there was a chance that many of them might not ever return.

There was something about the dream he was having, when all hell broke loose, that kept haunting him. He had managed to hold onto it all these years. It was the last remnants of his cherished time with his mom. He knew that most people would think it was childish, but he didn't want to ever lose his memory box.

"Guys, I have some stuff I don't want to take a chance on losing out there," Joey said.

"What are you talking about, your head?" snickered Marty.

"No man, just some things that I brought over here. My camera and things like that. Help me think quick, where can I hide something so I can come back for it later?"

"You know, I've got some stuff too," Oscar announced.

Marty looked around and spotted the truck with their belongings loaded in the back. "C'mon, let's grab our stuff off that truck before it takes off."

Joey, Marty and Oscar dumped out the contents of Joey's metal footlocker, and quickly turned it into their time capsule, hoping that one day, one of them could come back and retrieve it. In went the two hundred pesos and a Bulova watch that Oscar had won in a poker game. Marty had been stowing away bottles of whiskey and cigars the last a few weeks from a local vendor, and then Joey stuffed in his Cuban Cigar box, Bible, Mrs. Gertie's souvenirs and camera, surrounded by a couple of thick army blankets. They then hauled it over to the same church, where they had just laid to rest some of their brothers, and buried it next to a landmark they hoped would always be there, a statue of Mary. Then all three jumped into the back of one of the last remaining trucks, as they made their way out of Manila, headed for the Bataan Peninsula.

By the middle of the day, they had orders to stop

and try to worm their way into the jungle. Now Joey understood why they had trained as they had, all those months in the deep, thick forest of Kasatchie National Park. There weren't any banana trees in Louisiana, but the terrain was almost identical, as was the same sauna-like heat. He had studied the maps drawn by the Filipino Scouts, but he could have just as soon been standing on the moon. Nothing looked familiar. Thankfully, the island soldiers had, for the most part, travelled with them. He also realized that the fight they might soon be involved in, would not be from the air, but here, face to face. Joey had never met anyone from Japan, much less had the thought to kill one of them. Yet, it was these same strangers that tried to kill all of them from miles in the sky.

Lt. Col. Gerald Pitkins hollered out, "Okay, men, grab a shovel and get busy. We're going to hunker down here for a while. It's just a wait and see right now."

Joey picked up a shovel for the first time since they left Camp Beauregard. In the short time they had been here, they had only watched as the Filipino Scouts dug out and constructed dozens of trenches and foxholes. These would be much wider and deeper this time; this was serious and not for practice. It was here where Chaplain Shimley received his most captivated audience. He would move about, from one fox hole to another, praying with all the temporary inhabitants as they now burrowed themselves in their earthen bunkers.

For the first few hours, Joey held tightly onto his semi-automatic rifle. One he had never fired before. The only time he put his weapon down was to eat. That was the one thing that still brought him comfort, food. Then the hours turned into days, to the point of the men being comfortable enough to crawl in and out without fear. Then, without any warning, during the early morning of December 15th, gunfire erupted on the Bataan Peninsula. Several feet away, Joey could hear one of the machine guns rattling off, into an area not more than one hundred yards away. Sweat was pouring down Joey's face, as he faced this unknown enemy. All he knew was that any movement south of their camp would need to be stopped. This was no longer a pretend practice, like the Louisiana Maneuvers had been. He was afraid, but Chaplain Shimley had assured him that was okay. He saw movement ahead, and then he met the eyes of his enemy and fired. All he could hear were the sounds of gunfire and the squawking sounds of wild chickens flying through the woods. Did he just kill a human or an animal? At one point, his pants were so drenched in sweat, he wasn't sure if he hadn't peed on himself. He was a sissy boy, just like his father said. Then a body fell in with him.

"Hey man, are you okay?" Marty asked.

"Sure, not sure what or who I'm shooting at, but I'm still here," Joey answered, relieved for a moment that his friend was next to him. Out of all three, he knew Marty had the strongest mind for this kind of battle. He told them story after story, of the times that he weaved in and out of the dark alleys in New York City, doing everything he could to avoid gunfire in the ongoing turf wars.

"Good, look, just got word that we've pushed back pretty good. We're gonna head south a bit. You're going to join us?"

"Do I have a choice?" asked Joey.

"Only if you want to have dinner tonight in Mariveles. That's where we're headed next. Listen, you need to take it easy on your food. Need to make it last. We might be in this awhile. I know how you don't want to miss a meal."

"Hey Marty, did we lose anybody?" Joey asked.

"Are you kidding? We're all just a few days older, that's all," Marty laughed.

They pulled into the city of Marivales on Christmas Eve. The only thing that Joey could think about was that his orphan friend was going to spend another birthday without a real family. If he ever got out of this place alive, he would make sure it would be his last one alone. He had already made up his mind. He didn't know how he would work out the details, but somehow, someway he was going to do the right thing, just like his mom said in church, when they would pass the collection plate for those poor orphans who had no one else. It would be up to him to help this little boy. He was going to become his legal guardian and take him in one day, as his little brother.

When they thought they had Marivales fortified,

death began to fall all around them. The Japanese ground troops had them outmanned and outgunned. The battle continued on, getting worse every day. For Joey, the only thing that mattered out in these woods, at the end of each day, was finding out that Oscar, Marty and Chaplain Shimley were still alive. They represented his hope, strength and faith.

Chaplain Shimley did his duty to pray for the dead, each time one of their own was buried in place. Sometimes, they could do nothing more than remove the poor soul's name tags and continue on.

Joey tried to close his eyes at night and collect in his mind, a place far away, where he could build a life for himself and Eddie. He knew for sure he would never return to the place where he was born. Maybe it would be somewhere further north. As good as he was at working on cars, that was not what his mom wanted him to do. Joey would find his dream job out there one day and be a great builder of things. He wouldn't be the only one trying to mentally remove himself from his foxhole.

"Hey Marty, do you know what day is it?" Oscar asked.

"No man, all I know is I was just sitting in this cozy little restaurant with this really hot blonde, with my plans for the night all laid out, and you just ruined it," Marty growled.

"When day breaks, we're going to have a prayer breakfast," Chaplain Shimley announced.

"Oh, yes sir, Chaplain, I wasn't trying to be...

count me in," Marty replied having no idea he had an audience.

"It's okay, no harm done. I just want to keep everyone's spirits up. That's what I'm here for. So, no need to mince words around me. It's not like I haven't heard it all before. Besides, dreams are not a bad thing. It's sometimes the very thing that keeps us going. There's not a fellow here right now that isn't dreaming of the day we can all go back home. So, go on and try to get you a few more winks while you can," answered Chaplain Shimley.

It was becoming apparent in all the confusion, when they hurried out of Manila, that they didn't pack nearly enough food, medical supplies or ammunition for this ground movement. They had no idea when they left, that their time away from the city would take them into March of the following year. With each day, there were more casualties and less food and supplies, to treat the sick and injured. When a retreat was ordered, it was too late. There weren't enough healthy, able-bodied men to transport all the wounded, and over two-thirds of their ground transportation had been destroyed. Chaplain Shimley had steadfastly remained in their ranks, praying over the sick, injured and dying.

Joey, Marty and Oscar thought they still had a chance to fight their way through. The three amigos had joined the Army because they refused to surrender to the brutal lives they had all escaped from. However, on the early morning of March

29th, without knowing the reason why, plans were already in the making to raise the white flag.

CHAPTER 14

RISEN FROM THE DEAD
February 1973

BACK HOME, SHORTLY AFTER the disastrous Sullivan's Grocery Store event, Gilly found herself chewing her fingernails. She had never had any nervous habits before, but this somehow rocked her world like none other before. Maybe it was because Gilly knew in her heart that this was the last straw, or it could have been the relentless taunting she was getting more of at school. Apparently, when word got out what Joey did at the store, the dumb duo asked her one day in the cafeteria if she had any Miss Debbie cupcakes on her. From then on, she thought if she didn't put her fingers in her mouth, Regina and Mona would probably wind up with a fist in their faces.

Here, Gilly's life had finally calmed down, enough that she had given that bad habit up but without realizing it, had created a new one of cracking her knuckles. Although the life she left behind had been one of chaos and uncertainty, at times, she at least had some familiar base left. Here, however, everything was still new, different and unstable for a seventeen-year-old girl, who had to leave behind her last bit of belonging. Her friend Kat, to whom she was able to freely expose all her innermost thoughts, without any reservation of being mocked or ridiculed, was now hundreds of miles away. They made a pact to that. A finger pricking, rubbing the blood together, pact to always keep their secrets safe. Her 'want to be fashion designer one day friend' was the one that insisted she pursue her dream, only to fall head over hills in love with some guy in a garage band. She knew she needed to let Kat go, but she was tired of letting people go. Her mom had already praised her for not complaining, so she didn't want to talk to her about how she felt Kat had abandoned her. The only person at Laurel Cove Academy, besides Rory Turner, that her given her the time of day was Hope Dugas, and she somewhat reminded Gilly of Kat in some ways. She tried to act like she didn't care what other people thought, but you could always see it in her face. Gilly was beginning to think that's what Kat did. She wore those crazy-looking clothes to keep people from looking at her sad, rejected face. Unlike Kat, Hope didn't mind showing just how much she wanted to fit in. She was the type of person that would rather give than get. They couldn't display their outwardly styles here, but they all seem to still make it up once again in their small segregated groupings. Like choosing from a group for teams, there's always the one that is chosen last. And it appeared everyone's last choice was always Hope. She clung to Gilly from day one, like she was her last hope. It wasn't long before she found her way to their apartment, as well as the post office, on a regular basis. It's as if that was yet another one of her battles to try to win, before surrendering to the constant rejection of the world all around her.

Although Gilly knew that she would never do that finger pricking, blood sisters vow thing again, it was comforting to at least have someone her age to spend time with. Hope shared her dream of wanting to be a social worker, which was no surprise. She not only had a big, generous heart like Aunt Maggie, she also had a forgiving soul, much like Mrs. Hattie. Nothing anyone did or said to her seemed to create or stir any kind of hate, bitterness or resentment. She just kept putting one foot in front of the other, believing that something better would be waiting for her just around the corner. She would just liken their meanness to her, as nothing more than immaturity and a lack of wisdom, as to what was important in life. As time went on, Gilly found herself inspired by Hope's thought process, as she eliminated all the possible reasons why their classmates were the way they were. Then, one day, as easily as one disrobes for bathing, Gilly found herself pouring her guts out about her desire to be a detective some day. It was Hope's jaw-dropping response that gave Gilly the courage to do what she knew she needed to do.

"You know Gilly, I think people that do detective work are really brave. It's kind of like walking into a dark room, that you've never been in before, and nobody knows where the light switch is. Well, someone has to be willing to feel around to find the switch, and not be afraid of what they're going to find when the lights come on."

"Man, I would never have thought about it that way. I just always thought that I liked solving mysteries, but I guess you do have to be prepared for the unknown."

"Exactly! You never know what you're going to uncover."

"Thanks, Hope. You have an interesting way of looking at things some times. You know what, I think you're going to make a really good social worker one day, too. Why don't you come over Saturday night for dinner, and we can find something to watch on TV or maybe play cards."

"Really, Gilly?"

"Sure. Look, we'll talk later, but right now, I need to go help Aunt Maggie. She's paying me now, so I can't be late."

"Okay, I can't wait."

Just as Gilly walked through the door, Aunt Maggie said, "Oh good, you're here. I need to go fix a mishap that Gabe made this morning. I'll only be gone a few minutes. You think you can hold the fort down for me?"

"Sure, Aunt Maggie, no problem," answered Gilly.

As soon as the bell on the door stopped ringing, Gilly was more than ready to hold down the fort. If she didn't make her move now, she thought she probably never would have this brief moment of courage, that Hope had just instilled in her. She walked straight into the office, picked up the Dead Letter Box off the cluttered shelf, took the dusty lid off, and started flipping through years of sealed and undelivered letters until she spotted the very one. She knew the author needed her help, as she shoved the mystery letter into her booksack. It was addressed to MR. SAMUEL WATERSON, EDITOR, PERSONAL AND CONFIDENTIAL, LAUREL COVE NEWSPAPER, LAUREL COVE, MISSISSIPPI.

For the rest of the afternoon, while working at the post office and later at home, all Gilly could think about was that letter. Why would someone send a letter marked 'personal and confidential' to a newspaper editor, and not put a return address on it? It had to be something written by someone who wanted to remain anonymous. Maybe this person was Mr. Samuel Waterson's source for some big story he was working on. Gilly knew she had to be prepared for whomever this letter was about. She had found herself quite fond of most of the customers now, and hoped that it wasn't about any of them. The town newspaper closed its doors six years ago, when the editor and only remaining employee died, and this letter with the postmark of May 3rd, 1967 had just barely missed its appointed delivery.

"Mom, thanks for supper tonight. I promise to have something hot and ready for you tomorrow night. I like it that we're taking turns. I'm really tired, and I think I'm going to go ahead and go to bed"

"Okay, honey, I hope you're not overloading yourself, by trying to work and go to school. You know we're okay now. You don't have to work to help make ends meet."

"Yeah, I know, but I really like what I'm doing at the post office. It makes me feel like I belong around here. I'm learning a lot."

"Well, don't learn too much or get too comfortable. I don't want you to forget about college."

"Sure, Mom."

Gilly went to her room, closed her door, changed into her pajamas, crawled into her bed, and turned off her bedside lamp. The room was dark, but underneath the covers with her, she had her dad's old flashlight and a butter knife from the kitchen. With one long breath, she turned it on and slowly slid the knife underneath the sealed flap, that had been holding it in place by years of dried glue. It was just a simple, typed one-page letter as the eyes of this new, young detective began reading about her very first case.

Dear Mr. Waterson,

Just visited your town as a tourist this weekend. It's a lovely town, but you have one problem. Mack, the artist, isn't who he seems to be.

He's a traitor and not to be trusted. So, you need to watch your back.

Sincerely, Anonymous

The only time Gilly had heard the word traitor used, was when Joey was still her dad. She saw his army uniform still in the closet and asked why he kept it.

"So, I can always remember the brave men that served with me, and never forget the traitors that were amongst us."

"What's a traitor?"

"The best way I can explain it to you is, someone who betrays you, but in this case, it was in the worst kind of way."

Gilly already knew there were plenty of people just like that out there. They'd sell their souls and everyone else's to save their own hide. "So, there were traitors in the Army with you, when you were in the war?"

"One for sure, that I know of. But, where we

were, one was one too many. Now, I've already said too much. Don't worry, you're too young to fret about such things."

"No Dad, we got those at school. Only we call them two-faced. They'll pretend to be your friend, only to get help with their homework and stuff, and the next minute they're pretending they don't know you. So, I guess some people might just be born that way."

So here in their midst was a real, bonafide traitor. Surprise, surprise. And it was none other than her Uncle Mack. Her gut feeling had been right all along. She had to turn off the flashlight and regroup her thoughts. She was shaking all over worse than any public speaking that she had ever done. Just like Hope had said, you never know what you're going to undercover, and this was the kind of hurt that would be absolutely unforgivable. Gilly adored her Aunt Maggie, and the very thought that she had been deceived by this wretched man made her blood boil. Who else could it be? There was no other 'Mack' who was an artist in Laurel Cove. The letter was typed, so she couldn't tell if it was written by a man or woman. Aunt Maggie said he just showed up here one day, needed a change of scenery and a fresh start, but a start over from what? She couldn't wait for the night to be over, school to be over the next day, and for Leon Miller to walk in the post office.

Gilly felt really bad that she had to shake off Hope again, with the excuse she had way too much work to do after school. She would have to make up for it Saturday night, and be much more attentive. However, she didn't know how she would ever be able to tell her not to be so needy all the time. Her new friend seemed to be starved to death for the least bit of attention. Maybe it was much like her mom told her one time, maybe this was Hope's learned behavior. Maybe she didn't have a mom like she did, one that cared. Right now, she had to get there to make Leon's usual timeline for checking his post office box, which was every afternoon around three.

"Good afternoon, Mr. Leon. Can I talk to you for a minute?"

He was startled that anyone would want to talk to him. He had always been in the habit of checking the bulletin board first, then checking his mail without much interaction from anyone. He knew most people thought he was a bit eccentric, but keeping a low profile in this little town was what he had done for years. No one knew much about him and he wanted to keep it that way. It's the way he had pretty much lived his entire adult life, until he met his young, new protégé.

"Of course," answered Leon.

"Have you ever found anyone on the FBI's ten most wanted list?"

"I've come close a few times."

"Really, are you serious? Just how close?" Gilly kept her hands in her pockets, not wanting to expose just how nervous she was, about this whole undercover operation that she had brewing in her mind.

By this time, Leon's pride was beginning to take over, that someone was actually taking him seriously. "Well, there was this fellow by the name of Garland Frank that was wanted for armed robbery over in Georgia, and my guys and I had tracked him into Tennessee, but lost him somewhere close to Knoxville. The Tennessee Bureau did finally catch him up in the mountains, but I'm sure it was with our help."

This was more than Gilly could process. Leon was actually part of some sort of manhunt team. And all of this was going on right under her nose in Laurel Cove.

"What do you mean 'your guys'?"

He didn't know how or why, but Gilly had touched something in him that, in that moment, he couldn't control. He had lived in Laurel Cove for the last ten years without one single person ever showing an interest in who he was. This young, fresh face with a thrill in her voice overshadowed any attempt not to share his resumé. "Oh, I belong to a private detective club. We're just a bunch of amateur sleuths that meet about once a month over in Atlanta. Nobody takes us seriously, but we've busted a few criminal organizations."

"I can't believe this! The Master Detective magazine has always been my favorite. I had every issue until I moved here. Is there any way that I can join? I'll do whatever. I can answer the telephone, write letters, whatever you need."

"Oh, I don't think so. Like I said, people don't take us very seriously, but it's a serious undertaking for us. You have to be very careful when you start digging around in other people's business."

"Well, what if I told you that I know for sure there's a case that needs to be investigated, right here in Laurel Cove. I have it in black and white."

Leon was hesitant. Nothing had happened in Laurel Cove since he moved there, other than a few mischievous pranks by the hands of some of the young boys. Even that didn't take but a few hours to figure out who the culprits were.

"What kind of case, exactly?"

"I'll tell you, only if you let me help. Please..."

"Okay, I'm not going to make any promises, but let me hear what you got and then maybe I can make you my unofficial apprentice."

"We close at 4:30. I'll meet you at Mimi's Diner at 4:35!" squealed Gilly.

Gilly pulled out the letter and began nervously cracking every single knuckle on both of her hands, while she watched Leon, as he read over it. He then looked up, nodded his head, and swore her in right there on the spot. She had finally arrived in the place she had longed to be, and this was way better than any finger pricking blood sister thing could ever be.

CHAPTER 15

THE DEATH MARCH
April 1942

MANY OF THE MEN that hadn't died in combat, over the last four months, were gradually succumbing to malaria, malnutrition and dysentery. Other than Oscar taking a hit in his left shoulder, the three that came together were remarkably still in one piece, as was Chaplain Shimley. The only thing they had to look forward to now, was their official surrender somewhere, on the same path they travelled in on. Once that occurred, they would be held as prisoners until the war was over, and then go home. It didn't sound quite so bad to most of them, after it was all explained a few days ago. After all, General McArthur had just been evacuated off the island. He was their commander in chief, and they had no doubt there was a plan underway for a surge and rescue, unlike the Japanese forces had ever seen before. How could they possibly be any worse off than they were right now?

That wasn't the case for Joey. When it was decided that their days were numbered as free men, they were ordered to destroy all remaining weapons, so as not to fall in the hands of their enemies. Once again, Joey heard the word 'sissy' playing over and over in his head. He had never been so scared before in his life. He didn't want to die. The picturesque scans of the days before they left the states flashed in his head. From the smells, as the Greyhound bus drove into New Orleans, his first po'boy, the train ride to San Francisco, and the last picture he took of the Golden Gate Bridge, as their ship sailed away. Would he ever experience such a carefree life again?

Blankets were attached to tree limbs, to form small hammocks, to carry the men who could no longer walk. The ones that still could walk, had little to carry their own dead weight, as the rest of the able-bodied men formed in something less than formal marching formation.

"Oscar, Marty, we have to stay together. Remember, all for one and one for all. We came to this place together and we're going to leave together.

Are we still all in?" Joey said, as he was trying so hard to keep a courageous front.

"Not like we have much choice now, is it?" answered Marty.

As they headed east out of Marivales, on the main highway, within a few minutes Joey and the rest of the soldiers, both American and Philippine, were met by a full Japanese battalion. Little did they know, this would only be the beginning of the life-long nightmares that so many would keep tucked away in their hearts and minds for decades to come.

Their Japanese captors took great delight in stripping them of any and all personal belongings. Dog tags were ripped from their necks, and their watches were stacked upwards on their tormentors' skinny arms, from wrist to elbow. The American prisoners had their helmets knocked off their heads, and used as collection plates for the rest of the plunder of rings, wallets and any other valuables. It was then that Joey was thankful he had the forethought to leave behind his most precious valuables. That was one thing he would have killed for, his Cuban Cigar box, full of the only tangible remnants of his life, when he was loved. After they were robbed of all personal belongings, they began what would become known as The Bataan Death March, surrounded by hundreds of armed thugs and brutal pied pipers.

Those unfortunate ones who had their helmets stolen, seemed to fair the worst in the hundred-plus-degree blazing heat, so the men would take turns throughout the day with those who had no head covering. They refused to allow the prisoners to have any food or water on the first day, taking great victory at such an easy defeat. As they walked, the Japanese soldiers would beat and execute those that were too weak to continue. Joey was more worried about how he would react, if he became the target of their cruel vengeance. He didn't want to be the cause for his fellow prisoners to suffer any additional torment, because of any flashbacks he might experience from the days of his father's angry hands. When darkness finally arrived, their weary and broken bodies were allowed to collapse on the side of the road.

"Man, I don't know about this. This is not how it's supposed to end for me," Marty said.

"You? I'm so hungry right now I think my insides are eating themselves. If this is what it's like to starve to death, they can just shoot me right now," Joey murmured.

"Take it easy, there's something out there called the Geneva Convention that all these countries signed and agreed on, how prisoners of war should be treated. They have to eventually give us food and water," stated Oscar.

"The Geneva what?" asked Joey.

"Just take my word for it. It's a humanitarian agreement, made a long time ago, that is supposed to protect us if we're taken prisoner. Just like you Marty, I know a few things about war," Oscar continued.

"Well, I don't know where you've been today, but there's been nothing humanitarian about some of our guys getting shot today just because they couldn't take another step," Marty said. Just as soon as the last word came out of his mouth, he felt a sharp blow to the back of his head.

"Urusai!" yelled the guard.

Joey moved in quickly. His empty stomach suddenly filled with rage, he stood in between the two men, without any thought of his own personal safety. Within seconds he received the same sharp blow, but this time it was to his empty gut. He doubled over and fell to the ground, knowing full well more blows were sure to come. As he rolled over, the Japanese soldier that struck him, kicked him in the ribs, then spit on him.

"Joey, don't be stupid. I'll be okay. We don't need any more dead heroes right now. Besides, I've been hit harder than that back home in my old neighborhood." Joey laid there groaning. Oscar pulled him up and got him to his feet. Marty continued on with his own personal survival story, as Joey grimaced in pain. "There was this gang that sent muscle out every single day, trying to recruit new members. If you didn't join, then they would beat the tar out of you. That guy is nothing more than a little coward with a big stick. I'm not joining his club either. Don't put yourself in the way for me next time, buddy. I can handle it. That little punk can kiss my...."

"Okay guys, don't give the devil any more wiggle room here," Chaplain Shimley interjected.

"Yes sir," Marty replied as he continued to rub the back of his head.

This was not at all what Joey had signed up for. His mind had changed, as he was now feeling the bitterness and resentment toward whoever's idea it was for them to surrender. They could have won if they had just hung in there a few more days. Now, not only did they have to try to survive hunger, heat and sheer exhaustion, their captors wanted to torment them in the worse kind of way. He had survived this attack because that guy was a runt. Either the guard didn't kick him hard enough, or he was a little punk just like Marty said. Although his side was sore and bruised, he was sure that the kick he got didn't break any ribs.

The sun rose and set for three days on this long treacherous walk, and then just as Hank had done so many times, one of the Japanese soldiers began throwing food from the back of a seized American Jeep, that he had probably taken apart and repaired himself. The irony of it all was too great to bear. It wasn't a bologna sandwich, but a small handful of rice wrapped up in a piece of a banana leaf. The fortunate ones, that were able to make their catches of food, shared with their brothers without any hesitation.

As they entered their fourth day, Joey's mind

took him back to the day those two well-dressed men pulled into his father's station, and the promises they made. See the world; make some real money doing the thing that he was good at. As the sun beat down and Joey's throat filled with dust, he became more and more angry that General McArthur had let this happen. Within a matter of hours, dozens more of his fellow soldiers began to wither and fall. One after another, the Japanese shot them as though they had nothing else to do.

"Look guys, we got to keep our heads. We can't give up. When you feel like you can't take another step, get in the middle and we'll lock arms to hold one another up, okay?" Joey said. He had finally toughened himself up again. Like in the beginning of his terror-filled days with Hank. His mom had always been the buffer between them. She had been his protector from his dad's brutality. Now the urge had surged inside of him to protect his friends. All that he had endured, was the training he needed, not only to keep himself alive, but to keep the ones he had come to love and care about in his fold.

"God, I can't believe this is happening. We can't go on like this," Oscar said.

"Yes, you can, Oscar. Don't you dare give up. It's going to be dark soon. We'll have to stop then. Just make yourself dream of where you want to be right now, or better yet, where you see yourself one day when this is all over. I've done it hundreds of times already. Surround yourself with that. Take yourself away Oscar, you can do it. We got you man. We got you," Joey pleaded.

Oscar mentally left the march and drifted off, while Marty and Joey held him up on both sides. They couldn't lose him to the litter of dead men that were now lining both sides of what felt like their dirt road to hell.

Finally, as night fell upon them, they were allowed to stop. Those that could, passed out right away, while others just passed away, because they had simply given up.

"Have you guys seen Shimley? I lost sight of him sometime in the middle of the day," asked Joey.

"Well, he's either probably trying to bring up the rear, or trying to save the souls of these sons of devils that captured us. Considering they probably ain't got one to save, I'm sure he's holding some kind of prayer vigil somewhere," answered Marty with a smirk.

"Don't knock it man. I'd rather believe in God and be wrong, than take a chance that he's right about everything," Oscar chimed in.

"When did you convert?" asked Marty.

"Yesterday," answered Oscar.

"What part of the day did you see the light?" asked Joey.

"When we were the only ones that got food. I don't know how ya'll didn't notice it, but it's like he singled us out. Why?" answered Oscar.

For what it was worth, Lt. Col. Gerald Pitkins was still somewhat in charge. He, at least, had the painstaking responsibility of trying to keep up with who all had died that day, so that at some point he and Shimley could notify their families. Those that fell along the way weren't even given a proper burial, but were left for their corpses to rot in the sun or be picked apart by the vultures. As the days went on, taking a head count for those remaining became even more difficult and disheartening. Within five days, over six hundred men had disappeared from their first day's march.

In the days that followed, they had been reduced to collecting water from caribou mudholes, that were steadily infecting the men with more cases of water-born bacterial diseases. When the Japanese weren't shooting the men that fell in exhaustion, they were continuing their beatdown on what was left of any human dignity.

"You, you there, come. You want water?" asked the Japanese soldier.

"Yes, yes sir, for me and my friends, please," answered one of the prisoners.

"Okay, here you drink." He pushed the butt of his rifle into the ground and made a small hole in the dirt, then poured some water into his manmade dog bowl, while laughing hysterically.

At this point, they didn't care. Water was water. The other Japanese soldiers also found it amusing, as they continued to make dozens of water-filled dog bowls, while their captured prisoners kneeled all around the holes, lapping up the water. Joey and his friends refused to participate in such cruel and subhuman treatment. They would rather die of thirst first. When Joey thought they couldn't be reduced to less than human any further, they were ordered to bark. The memory of that would be one of among many that would haunt him for the rest of his life. The memory of that would be the very thing that would never allow him to ever want to own a dog.

This inhumane and humiliating death march continued until they reached the town of San Fernando. There, they were finally given rest, a handful of rice, and one cup of water. Joey couldn't understand why after seven days of complete and total brutality, they were finally being shown some glimpse of humanity. However, they would all later learn that this was just a running game of the control they relished in, just barely keeping them alive.

Joey was a measly one hundred and thirty pounds on a five-foot-eight-inch frame, when he rode away in the back of that shiny new Chevrolet last December morning. After a growth spurt, and months of hearty eating and workouts at Camp Beauregard, he shot up two inches and gained forty-five pounds. All of that was gone. Gone in less than four months. He had run out of holes to adjust his belt, and had taken to tying it in knots just to hold his pants up. He still felt he was one of the lucky ones. Many of the men had defecated so many times on themselves, either from their sick, watery bowels or simply fear, and they no longer had pants to hold up. These men had been subjected to walking for miles in their stained underwear. Luckily, Joey had bought new shoes the same day as he bought Eddie's, so his were still intact while others were completely worn out. Every night, when his mind could erase, for a few brief moments, the hatred he had for his captors, Joey prayed for their continued survival and for Eddie's obedience to his last wishes. The deaths of the men have been bad enough, but the bodies of the civilian men, women and children left in small villages along the way were making Joey doubt God even existed anymore. Innocent Filipino people, murdered for just wanting to hand them food and water. None of them trained for this. None of them were prepared for this. Who could be? What did any of them do to deserve this unending murderous hell? Where was Chaplain Shimley?

Then they were again ordered to fall into place on the last leg of their death march. The ones that survived, the ones that fought to keep their sanity, wouldn't be walking this time. Over three hundred suffocated to death on their nightmarish train ride, stuffed like sardines in over 120 degree heat, left for hours with the doors closed.

Those that lived tumbled out into the fresh air, while the dead were again left to rot. The very thing that Joey fought so hard to do, had finally taken over. His mind had become numb. Numb to the death that had now become ordinary. Numb to the brutality that they had come to accept, just like he had to do when he worked at the Plank Road Gas and Auto Repair Shop. At least for now, the death march was over. What they didn't know, what they didn't understand, was how fortunate those who died before them really were, as they entered through the gates of their new hell on earth.

CHAPTER 16

TRAITORS AND THIEVES
March 1973

IT HAD BEEN WEEKS since Gilly had been sworn in as a real detective's assistant, and she still had no word or even a second glance from Leon, when he came in the post office. She didn't know if he was ignoring her or maybe she had somehow been tricked. Just because he said he was a detective didn't necessarily make him one. What if he had told her Uncle Mack what she was up to, or worse, what if he had ratted her out to her Aunt Maggie? Neither one of them had been treating her any differently. Maybe she was just being paranoid. Not a good sign if she wanted to do this kind of work. Paranoia and delusion always seemed to have a way to rear its ugly head when it goes unchecked. Gilly had first-hand experience of exactly what that looked like.

Today, what delusion looked like was a bright red, sleeveless dress that had a huge matching red bow on the right side. It was slit up the other side to her knees, with white fishnet stockings and black ankle rain boots. Covering her arms was some sort of green crocheted shawl, and to wrap it all up, was a red baseball cap covering her long, gray matted hair. No one, absolutely no one, ever gave Ms. Anastasia a second look. It was as if she was part of the landscape, that everyone around here had come to fear and accept. The men just nodded their heads with a respectful, "Good day, Miss Anna," and the women all smiled as though she had the power to make or break what little social status that existed around here. There was no way to accurately tell just how old she was, but you could tell this was her way of escaping the real world. One that had broken her down a long time ago, and just like Joey, she had never recovered.

"Good morning, Miss Anastasia."

"Where is it?"

"Just a minute, it's in the back, as always." Aunt Maggie, being the generous soul she was, had always seen to it that Anastasia has had at least two good meals a day, since she took over as Postmaster about fifteen years ago. It was a package deal when she was sworn in. She always packed her two sausage biscuits every morning, along with whatever she could put together for lunch, in a paper bag. I only get this important paper bag duty on Saturdays and when school is out, since these are the only mornings I work. She always reminds me in her typical fashion. Just like most people around here, I try to avoid any confrontation with her. Sometimes Aunt Maggie just sends her whatever leftovers she and Uncle Mack had from the night before, and other times she makes whatever Anastasia tells her to. She always has it prepared and sitting in the same corner spot on her cluttered desk. In order to protect what little dignity this poor old woman has left, one of us always tries to deliver it when no one else is looking, but everyone knows. Mr. Walter Bolton, who is probably one of the kindest men I've ever met, built her a little, two-room apartment behind his hardware store. He didn't put in a kitchen because he was worried, in her state of mind, that she might accidentally burn the place down. So, Aunt Maggie just picked up the duties of feeding her from the previous Postmaster, and Mr. Bolton makes sure she has some kind of dinner every night and three meals on Sundays.

"Here you go, ma'am, anything else?"

"You know what else."

"Yes, ma'am, of course."

At least once a week, without fail, she would pull one letter that she had carefully addressed to whatever dignitary she thought would hear her plea, and then slap a nickel down to mail it. Then, like always, Aunt Maggie would take money out of her pocket to make up the difference, as was another one of her duties to continue this mad woman's ritual.

"I'll take care of it, have a good day!"

"What's good about it? Until I have my boy back, there'll never be another good day. It's like they cut my heart out that day they kidnapped him. I can still see my beautiful baby boy staring at me with those beautiful, dark brown eyes. He had a head full of dark brown, curly hair with perfect fingers and toes. God gave him a big, special kiss on his right wrist with a birthmark in the shape of a perfect strawberry. I can still see his face smiling up at me. To this day, I'd know him if I saw him. I blessed him with the name of Rudy right then and there, after my favorite movie star, Rudolph Valentino."

I heard the same story dozens of times by now, and could easily mouth the words in rhythm every time. Aunt Maggie made me promise to be kind to her and never, ever roll my eyes. She said that from everything she heard, she really did have a baby boy. He wasn't kidnapped, but taken away by social services because she couldn't take care of him; she had no family and no one knew who the father was.

"Yes ma'am, I know, I'm terribly sorry. I'm sure one of your letters is going to land in the right hands one day."

Knowing good and well they were probably tossed as soon as they arrived, that is if they arrived, we always mailed them. We had to. Aunt Maggie said it wasn't up to us to judge whether or not what was in her head was real. It was our job to make the customers happy. In my opinion, she had lost sight of any happiness a long time ago. I made a mental note, every time she came in, that she had the face of someone I never wanted to be. Just like Kat had said that day, another poor soul that fell into that black hole, of being her own worst enemy.

The post office was empty of its master of the domain again this morning, and Gilly fought hard not to search through the dead letter box again. Aunt Maggie's words kept ringing in her ears about all the rules and regulations of the post office. She was starting to feel guilty for betraying those rules. Yet, she wondered, how did feeding Anastasia every day and covering the difference on her postage, fit in the post office rules and regulations? Help was help in her mind. Just like her Aunt Maggie went over and beyond the call of duty, that's exactly what she felt she was doing. Even though it had been explained to her that opening any first-class mail was strictly prohibited, as well as against the law, she understood that rule was for 'if the mail was actually deliverable.' To just box away letters for years as dead letters didn't seem right or fair to anyone. She had plenty of good reasons why she did it, and putting her hands on that particular letter had to be the kind of fate that she had only dreamed about. This was her chosen path now, and getting to the truth was the only thing that mattered, as well as finding out that her Uncle Mack was a potential traitor made her somehow rationalize breaking this rule. After all, shouldn't her Aunt Maggie know who her husband really is? What if he was some sort of spy, or maybe some kind of double agent? Maybe that's why he spent so much time walking up and down the beach. Was he sending signals out into the Gulf of Mexico, to agents of another country that wanted to attack them again, like they did Pearl Harbor? Her family had been torn apart because her dad fought to save his country, and whatever the consequences, this was one thing she would gladly follow in his footsteps for. Gilly didn't have any idea what her dad had been through during the war, but this was one traitor that wasn't going to slip through the cracks. Like her dad said before, "One traitor is one too many." Suddenly she felt more alive and driven than she had ever been in her entire life, because 'Leon the Detective' had just walked in and was heading her way.

"Good afternoon, Gilly."

"Good afternoon, Mr. Leon. How are you today?"

"I'm fine, can you take care of this for me?" he said as he slipped her a note that read,

I've got some information. Meet me today at the same place, same time.

She didn't have to wait for him this time, as he had already ordered her coke and his coffee when she walked in. This had been a long wait, too long. The brisk walk to Mimi's Diner brought up the same old feelings, from the day she stood in front of her class reading her report, in that green corduroy jumper. This was important to her. She needed to know if her Uncle Mack was a traitor, just as much as she needed an A on that paper. Although, if Leon was going to make fun of her long-held suspicions about Uncle Mack, she would just have to strike out on her own and figure this mystery out herself. When she sat down, Leon took one sip of coffee, grinned and nodded like he had once before.

"Okay, first things first. I've found out some stuff that I'm sure you're not going to like. Now having said that, I'm not sure there's anything that can, or even needs, to be done over something like this. We're talking about something that happened a long time ago, so you just need to be prepared to let it go. Is that clear?"

Gilly just sat there for a minute. This was her case and her uncle. She had found, or stolen, the letter, whichever way someone wanted to look at it. She was the one who had the courage to open it and turn the light on it. "I guess, but why can't I decide if I want to let it go?" Gilly asked.

"Because I really think this is one can of worms that probably needs to stay right where you found it. However, I have to admit that it was definitely an eye opening and interesting set of facts. So, are you going to listen to what I've found out so far, or do you want to argue about who's going to do what here?"

Gilly slumped back in her chair and said, "I'm listening."

"Ok good. First of all, I know people around here

think I'm some kind of nut, and I kind of didn't tell you everything about myself either. I still have a lot of contacts all over the country. I'm retired military myself; spent twenty years in the Army, and about ten of those in the War Department Military Intelligence."

"Are you serious?" Gilly sat back upright and her eyes grew wider as the suspense grew.

"Why do you think I make it a point to check out the FBI's Ten Most Wanted List regularly? I can't help myself. It's in my blood. I know where to go and who to go to. So, the postmark of Pensacola, Florida and the word 'traitor' wasn't a big stretch. I just put two and two together, and made a phone call to an old buddy of mine in Fort Lauderdale. There were several military bases in Pensacola, and during World War II, ground and aviation training was huge in that area. Anyway, he made a few calls and it seems that Mack was more of a thief than an actual traitor. When you're in the military, anything you do that doesn't live up to your code of honor, is considered a stab in the back to those guys all around you. I mean, if they can't trust you, then you're done."

"What kind of stuff did he steal? Did he ever get caught? Do you think they're still looking for him?" Gilly spilled out breathlessly.

"Will you be quiet and listen for a minute? So, the information I got is that Mack spent ten years in prison for theft of military property, while he was training to be a fighter pilot. He was dishonorably discharged back in 1953. How or why in the world he would end up here, when he did, is anybody's guess."

"So, let me get this straight. Aunt Maggie is married to an ex-con?"

"It appears so. Look, I admit this case, as you call it, has been one of the most interesting things that have happened since I moved here, but there's little for either of us to do about it now. You can't just go off on some tangent and confront him about it now."

"Why not?"

"First of all, how would you explain yourself? Also, how would you explain how you found out? If this gets out it could turn this whole town upside down, never mind what it would do to Maggie. She's a good woman, and I don't want her to get hurt because you went snooping somewhere that you weren't supposed to."

"But, don't you think she has the right to know?"

"Maybe she already does know and doesn't care. He paid his debt to society. We all have our past, Gilly, and not all of it is good."

"Yeah, but this is different."

"How so?"

"If you knew where Mom and I came from and why we moved here, you would understand."

Leon just sat there drinking his coffee, not wanting to share anymore. He had already exposed too much of his hand, with his new little protégé, and didn't know how he would ever be able to put this genie back in her bottle. He just rubbed his hands together, took one last sip of coffee and said, "Okay, tread carefully. Whatever you do, you can't get me involved. I'd just as soon have everyone continue to think that I'm just a harmless wannabe amateur detective."

Knowing deep down he didn't want to be left out on another chance like this, Leon finished their meeting, "But, if you decide to open another dead letter and need my help, you know how to find me."

"I will. I think I'm going to go see Joey and talk to him about it."

"Just be careful, Gilly. You could get us both in real trouble."

"Oh, don't worry, Joey won't tell a soul. I can swear my life on it."

Gilly didn't want to get into the details of why they had moved here and who Joey was. But, she didn't need to, because Leon already knew. Like he just told her, he still had contacts everywhere.

Claire had told her over and over again that Joey probably knew more of what was going on around him, than anyone realized. And it always made her heart hurt more, if she believed anything less.

This was something that just couldn't wait. It was too late in the day and she needed to go back and help Aunt Maggie. She would just have to go see Joey the next morning, after she knew her mom had already left for work. Gilly had never skipped school a day in her life, but she knew that the mornings were always their best time of day. That was one of their routines, when they had breakfast every morning. Claire would have already left the kitchen to start her day behind the sewing machine, and it would be just her and Joey before she left for school. That's when she would share all the things that went on in her life, most of which were the problems she was having managing her world on the other side of the tracks.

Just as she was signing her name in at the front desk, she noticed Uncle Mack walking out. She was sure he didn't see her. If she had seen him before reading that letter, she would have probably not thought much about it. Now knowing that he was a 'traitor thief' walking about on the sacred ground of the VA Hospital, the only thing she wanted to do was report him to the first 'white coat' she saw. What was he doing here anyway? The only place he belonged was at his stupid souvenir stand on the beach. He had no business being here. Her dad was here because of the war. The place was full of men and women all broken up because they had done the right thing and served this country with honor. Right now, they were in the middle of a war in Vietnam. Many of them would probably spend their final days broken up and beyond repair here, instead of being at home with their families. This guy had no business breathing the same air as some of these heroes. Her anger was burning, and she didn't care what the consequences were. She would leave Leon out of it, but she was going to tell her Uncle Mack exactly how she felt. First, she had to clear it with Joey.

As she walked into the room, her opening line was still the same "Hey Joey, how are you doing today?"

"I'm okay, Gilly."

She sat on the windowsill while he stared out across the Gulf of Mexico. Nurse Lydia told her and her mom a few months ago, that the doctors were working on a treatment plan. She didn't like this one. She was happy that the medicine seemed to take away his anxiety, but so far, she hadn't witnessed any glimpse of his lost memory returning. There were times that she almost wished they were back home, dealing with double locks, his structured meal times and goofy looking outfits, because now he only wore what they decided. He didn't seem to care what he watched; he mostly just sat in the TV room and stared blankly at the TV. He no longer cared what time he ate, because he no longer knew what time it was. It was as though he didn't have any fight left in him. They had a pattern at home. Joey always ate breakfast with her at seven- thirty. Then at lunch, when Claire's favorite soap came on at noon, and supper was straight up five-thirty, just in time for the evening news. Then it occurred to her, after all these years, that she and her mom had probably been the ones that fixed those concrete eating times in his head. It had been their scheduled life he had gotten caught up in, and he had probably been just reminding them of something he thought they forgot. Whatever this new revelation was, she knew like always, he was still a good listener. All the times she didn't have it in her to face the likes of Regina and Mona another day, she knew she could unload on Joey. Gilly knew her mom would just give her another speech about turning the other cheek, or she just needed to feel sorry for people like that. When the only person she wanted to feel sorry for was herself; he was the perfect audience. That was the only thing they had left. Just like he used to do when they sat together for hours at the dining room table and drew their pictures together. So, for the next hour, Gilly poured her soul out about everything, from taking the dead letter from the post office, to her last meeting with Leon.

"So, Joey, what do you think I should do? Do you really think I should just forget about the whole thing and pretend it never happened? Or do you think I need to confront Uncle Mack?"

Joey turned his head from the window and said, "Yes, go Gilly."

That's all he said. With that, she gave him a kiss on the cheek and a hug around the neck. She knew she got the answer she was looking for.

She would need to wait for the right time. She would have to rehearse carefully, in her head, what she would say. Gilly knew she needed to work on her interrogation skills. She would just have to keep a look out from their kitchen window, until she spotted her Uncle Mack stroll across the beach behind their apartment, collecting the trash he sold as souvenirs like he had done so many times before.

CHAPTER 17

CAMP O'DONELL
October 1943

IT WAS ON THE morning of their first day as prisoners of war, they were told through an interpreter why their captors had been so incredibly cruel and calculating in their treatment towards them, during their nearly eighty-mile death march through the Bataan Peninsula.

"You are all cowards and will be treated as such. For only a coward would willingly surrender to his enemy. We are men of honor and would rather fall on our swords and die than to surrender." That was their motto; that was their creed. It wasn't in them to try to survive captivity so they could see their families and know freedom again. The Japanese believed that their reward would be much greater in death, and their honor would be received on the other side. He went on to say "Anyone caught trying to escape will be shot on the spot, and if you should choose to come over to our side, you will be greatly rewarded," announced this unassuming, small-framed, young Japanese guard. It appeared he had no contempt in his voice, only echoing words that he had somehow been forced to repeat.

"Well, my friends, I have more reason now than ever to show them just who the cowards are. I don't know about you two, but I got plans one day and it ain't falling on any sword. But, if I find one traitor amongst us... well let's just say he's mine," Oscar announced without hesitation.

"Same for me on the traitor part, like we don't have enough problems already. You don't have anything more waiting on you, if and when we get out of here, than Joey and I have," Marty declared.

"That's where you're wrong. I'm going to use my veteran's loan like they promised me, and buy me some land and grow sugar cane. Then, I'm getting married and having me some kids. That's all I want. A place of my own and a family. I don't think that's too much to ask the big guy up there. After all, I feel like I got cheated the first go 'round, not having any real parents. What bout you, Joey? You've been awful quiet," Oscar said.

"I don't know, I guess I forgot all about that kind

of stuff. It's kinda hard to think about what's going to happen tomorrow, much less months or years from now. But you know, back when we left Fort McKinley, I had it in my head to try to figure out someway to help Eddie. I really wanted to try to be his big brother one day. Poor little fellow, just can't figure how that can happen now. There's just no telling what's happened to that place since we left. Just don't want to think about it right now. So, I guess after a hot shower and some sleep, I just don't ever want to go hungry again," Joey remarked.

"Don't worry about Eddie, Joey. I'm sure he'll be be fine. And as far as food, you come stay with me and my mom. Heck, you can even bring Eddie. She'll fatten the both of you up in no time. So, if we are just sitting around here wishing and wanting, I think when I get back home, I'm gonna start my own business, too. You know the kind of place that people have to wait in line to get in. People from all over the country will know about O'Reilly's Irish Pub. I can just see it now. I'll one day have all the whiskey, cigars and women a man could ever want," Marty beamed as he blew smoke from a pretend cigar in his right hand.

"Joey, what's that look on your face about? You don't like my idea for life after here?" asked Marty.

"No, it all sounds good. Every bit of it. It's just, that guard that just threatened to shoot us if we tried to escape, looks so familiar. If I'm not mistaken, I think that's the same one that threw food at us from the back of that Jeep. That's really strange.

Why would he feed us one minute and threaten to shoot us on the spot, the next?" asked Joey.

"Man, this is way more than strange. This is like some crazy rabbit hole we all just fell in, and someone just keeps trying to bury us alive," Marty sneered.

"Urusai! Move now!" growled one of the other guards, while pointing his bayonet in their faces. This appeared to be the only English any of the rest of them knew.

Now they were being led to their thatch-roofed prison barracks, which had been erected three feet off the ground. The floors and walls were constructed of bamboo, with no windows and only one three-by-five foot cutout for a front entrance. Their beds were the slatted bamboos floors, and the only coverings they had were the mosquito and fly-infested, pungent air. They were among thirty men who would be sharing their new ten-by-forty-foot dungeon.

They were all strangers, and Joey wanted to keep it that way. He didn't want to get too close to anyone else. He just couldn't afford to. To do so would just be one more person to lose that he cared about. Marty, Oscar and Joey had come in together and somehow, someway they were going to leave together. That is, with the prayers of Chaplain Shimley, their wits, and just plain luck.

When they were evacuated out of Manila, they had a brigade of a little over thirty-five hundred men. Their new home at Camp O'Donnell only had eighty barracks, with one set up for the prison hospital. It was almost as if the Japanese had already calculated how many men they had to eliminate along the way. By counting the barracks as they filled up, it was obvious to him that they had lost almost twelve hundred men, since they pulled out of Fort McKinley.

However, the continued brutality of the guards was ever-present, even when they weren't huddled together as migrants, on this unforeseen ship to nowhere. It didn't take long for the worst of them all to be given nicknames. The three that tormented them the most, got names first. There was Machine Gun Kelly, who took great pleasure in shooting anyone that even looked like they were going to step right instead of left. Then there was Scarface, who had a big chunk of flesh that had been carved out of the right side of his face. He liked to use his bayonet on the end of his rifle, to inflict the same disfigurement he had suffered, on anyone taller than his five-foot stature, which covered everyone in the prison camp. The most wicked of them all, was 'The Maggot.' It was though he thrived on the most sadistic torture. Even the other guards seemed to have contempt for him at times. These three would come to be called "Satan's Army." There would be no other source for the kind of evil and hatred they had in their hearts and minds, for those held in their grips, than the devil himself.

There were only three water spickets for the prisoners to draw water from. That is where

Scarface and Machine Gun Kelly spent most of their time. These were located right in the center of the encampment. The prisoners had to stand in line for hours, and if any one of them either got out of line or complained, they were either shot on the spot or lost a piece of flesh.

Oscar, Marty and Joey kept their heads down and their mouths shut, as they took turns every day hauling back small baskets of water, that they made out of woven banana leaves. There were days when water would be withheld for one reason or another. Food was scarce and they were lucky if each man got a one cup of rice at the end of the day. Once again, there were days where they were given just enough to barely keep them alive.

The entire prison had a dark cloud that hovered over it most days. These weren't the dark puffy ones formed just before a thunderstorm. These consisted solely of the swarms of flies that hovered over the bodies of those yet to be buried.

Most days, Chaplain Shimley could be found in the camp hospital, trying to keep the soldiers that were at death's door alive, just long enough to save their souls. He had not yet been able to hold any kind of daily spiritual service for the men, and he feared that without some shared message from God's Word, many would be lost forever. Most were suffering from malaria, dysentery, and diphtheria. As much as he didn't want any part of it, Chaplain Shimley made Joey his assistant with the painful and heart-ripping duty of burying the dead. He needed someone who understood that they needed a sincere, bowed head, and didn't want to be rushed through their last rites. Joey didn't want to be part of this daily dreaded duty, because at the rate things were going, he was certain they would all be gone in a matter of months. However, he relented to the man who had taken so much time comforting him during their nights in Fort McKinley. He wanted to instead concentrate on staying amongst those that were still alive, and had hope for a new life one day. How was it that Marty and Oscar woke up every morning, just happy they made it through another night? His one and only thought was that they had real concrete reasons, but so far, Joey just hung in so as not to be part of the negative force that existed every day in their fenced-in hell hole. He knew that Eddie was out there waiting for him but deep down he needed something more.

Astonishingly, there were some supplies that would trickle in from time to time, from the Red Cross. Some of the time, there would be some mail and scant medical supplies that included desperately-needed antimicrobials. Then on occasion, there would be a few cans of meat or fruit. They would only be allowed the food if Satan's Army wasn't on duty. Oscar had wished there was some way to have rat poison sent in, so he could personally serve it to all three himself. Knowing this rapidly-growing mindset was all around him, Chaplain Shimley was finding it harder and harder to penetrate the hearts that were hardening throughout the prison.

He even found himself at times wishing those three were dead, but then in his next breath, asking God to forgive them, and him for thinking such a thing.

Some letters arrived days, weeks and months too late, and Chaplain Shimley had yet another unwanted duty of informing their families that their loved ones had died. He always made it a point to let the recipients know that their young sons, brothers, husbands and fathers did not die alone, and had mercifully been given a Christian burial.

However, the letters for the fortunate few that were still alive and well enough to read them, were handed out by Chaplain Shimley. This was one assignment he was always happy to be in charge of. Joey never expected to receive anything, not even from Mrs. Gertie. She wasn't listed as his next of kin and wouldn't have been notified of his capture. Joey had been, by this point, in captivity for over a year and a half, with no word from anyone in the outside world. So, when Chaplain Shimley handed him a letter, that he said had his name on it, he was quite stunned to say the least.

"Private Joseph Stevens, I have a letter here for you."

Joey nearly squealed like a school girl, "Sir, are you serious, from whom?"

Chaplain Shimley just grinned, as he knew in an instant, he had singled out the right man, "Someone who cares. You're not as alone as you think. Don't believe for a minute that just because you don't have a family back home, that you're not in someone's prayers. What do you think has been sustaining us through all this? Our wits and charm? I know it may not seem like it right now, but God is still in charge. Something tells me that this letter is meant for you. Oscar and Marty already have their places set when they get home, now I believe you need one too. Something other than food and being Eddie's big brother one day. So, just take it and if you decide to write back, I'll make sure to get it out. I promise."

The letter was addressed to "Any Soldier, United States Army, Camp O'Donnell, Philippines.

Dear Sir,

I am part of a group of women that meets at our church every Wednesday night, to pray for all of you. Please know how much we appreciate everything you are doing to help keep our country safe and free. We will never forget the sacrifices all of you are making, every day you can't come home. We are so broken hearted to hear that you have been captured and being held prisoner.

Everyone here is doing their part to help in the war effort. We've worked together to collect and donate supplies to the Red Cross. I hope and pray that most of the things we send are getting to you.

When I'm not part of doing that, I work five, sometimes six, days a week in a factory. That's all I'm allowed to say about that.

I know this sounds ridiculous to you, considering your circumstances, but I would love to be your pen pal and do what I can do to help encourage you and keep your spirits high. Sometimes just a connection to someone that you know cares is all it takes.

I live in Shreveport, Louisiana and graduated from high school last year. The picture I have enclosed is my senior class picture, and most recent. I hope by sending my picture, you will be able to connect a face to the words in this letter.

My friend and I are saving up for a camera. When I am able to take some current pictures, I will send them if, I hear back from you.

May God cover and protect all of you in the days to come.

Sincerely,
Claire Marie Stout
225 South Banks Street
Shreveport, Louisiana

He couldn't believe it. The emptiness he had been feeling for so long was suddenly gone. It was as though he had been drowning, and suddenly his body finally had one last rush of strength, as he swallowed up his first fresh breath of air into his lungs. Even with all the weight he had lost in the last few months, he now felt as though the feast of his last Thanksgiving with his mom had reentered his soul. Finally, he had in his hand, something to dream about. Someone to fight for. These weren't just words on a piece of paper, from a stranger who is thousands of miles away. This was someone who was praying for him. This was someone that wanted to know him. And she just so happened to be the most beautiful girl he had ever seen, second only to his mom. Now if he played his cards right, he might have someone, and something, in Louisiana to go home to one day. He rushed backed to his bamboo prison barrack, and carefully composed his very first letter back home.

Dear Claire,

You have no idea what a wonderful and unexpected gift your letter was for me the moment I opened it. Far better than any Red Cross package could ever be.

Your kind words and prayers are most appreciated.

We are doing well here for now. If it were another place in time, I would love nothing more than to show you the island, along with my own personal tour guide. He knows the island well, and we could easily spend days admiring the beautiful sunset together.

But for now, your beautiful face will be

all that I need until I see another day as a free man.

As far as your request to being my pen pal, please accept my reply as my heartfelt acceptance.

I will anxiously await hearing from you again.

Sincerely,
Joseph Franklin Stevens

Joey was beginning to see this pattern in his life. Although it was irregular at times, things seemed to fall into place when he least expected them to. If he had not been so good at working on automobiles, the colonel would never have asked him to work on his car. From that, he was shown favor to visit the library for several months, where he learned to perfect his reading and writing skills. Now, even though he was being held prisoner in this horrible place, he had just received this first letter from one of the two most beautiful women he had ever seen. He didn't know yet if the letter really had his name on it, as Chaplain Shimley tried to imply, but he was absolutely certain that he would claim this good fortune as his and do whatever he needed to do to go back home and marry her one day.

To try to keep his head away from so much death, Joey came up with one of the most ingenious plans he ever thought of. He knew the guards had been working on plans to rebuild a bridge nearby, so with all the courage he could muster, he approached the only guard in the camp that spoke English. He was the one that, on their first day, called them all cowards for surrendering, but Joey somehow believed that his man had something inside that would help him. The very thing Chaplain Shimley revealed to him one night, that was usually wrapped up in ugly paper. Empathy.

"Can I speak to you about something that is very important?" Joey asked.

"What can you possibly have to say that can have any value?" asked the guard.

"I've overheard some of the arguments that the other guards have been having, and from what I can tell it appears there is some problem in designing the bridge you need rebuilt and I think I can help. I'm a builder and an architect," Joey answered.

Just like he knew the plans his mom had laid out for him years ago, he accepted that his talented hands would be his calling. Throughout the months and years since they arrived at Camp O'Donnell, he had been masterfully drawing the entire layout of the camp, with every guard, prisoner and barrack in its place. He even added the water buffalos the day they strolled by, and penciled in the handmade signs that hung over each opening, as the prisoners named each one of their barracks. The one that he and his friends had been living in was named ELLIS ISLAND. It was Marty's idea. He had fixed in his mind that they were just being held temporarily, until the ferry brought them back to the shores of his long-awaited dream. It's all he had to do to pass time, that seemed the most productive when he wasn't burying the dead. If Oscar and Marty had their future occupations all laid out, then he felt like he needed to plan his as well. How else would he support Claire and his family one day?

The guard walked into his barrack and came out with a large white sheet of paper and a pencil. He handed it to Joey and said, "Here show me."

"I just need to know the width of the opening."

"One hundred fifty feet."

"I'll be back in about two hours."

Joey walked away and prayed. He prayed he could remember. During his time at Camp Beauregard, he had seen only one bridge and it was across the same river where that young recruit had drowned. It was underneath this very bridge that his body was recovered. That picture would forever be etched into his memory, every single beam, bolt and every angle, with the young man floating underneath it. It's the way he taught himself about engines. He couldn't read well enough to follow the manuals, but he eventually learned to take snapshots of the assemblies in his head. Whether he was born with it or not, Joey also had a picture-perfect memory.

"Joey man, what are you up to?" Marty asked.

"A way to get us out of here every day, that's what," Joey answered.

Oscar blurted, "What the... You want to help them rebuild a bridge? Are you kidding me? We should be hoping we got people out there blowing them all up, not rebuilding them."

"Just listen. If I can come up with a design to rebuild that bridge nearby and we get out of here every day for a few hours to work on it, then who cares? What, you'd rather sit here and rot and let the flies feed on your body, or go work for the enemy? I think I'd rather work. At least we might get a little more food at the end of the day, a change of scenery, and some fresh air. Can't hurt to try," Joey answered.

"Sure, count me in" Marty replied.

"Me too," said Oscar.

Joey presented his sketched drawing to the guard. He stood there for a few minutes looking it over and then said, "Hm, that's really good work. You're very talented. You remind me of my brother," stated the guard. Then it was as though all his defenses suddenly disappeared. "My name is Fred. Listen, just so you know, I had to say those things to all of you when you came in. I had to follow orders just like you did when you joined. But, all of it's true. If you try to escape, you'll be shot. So don't try. I don't want to think of myself as a coward just because I'd rather live than die by my sword. I'm not here by choice. Most of us were forced to be here. I have a wife and a son that I want to go home to one day. So, I have to follow orders, too."

Joey didn't know if he wanted to laugh or cry. Here was this guard, who could shoot him right there on the spot or cut his head off if that was his pleasure, and he just introduced himself as Fred. He had a wife and a son at home, on top of that. It never occurred to him that any of these men could have a life doing anything other than tormenting other human beings. The very thought that one of them had a family at home waiting for him, was beyond his comprehension, standing where they were at that moment.

"So is Fred your real name?" Joey asked trying not to laugh.

"No, it is Ikeda, but I like Fred. My brother started calling me that because I like to dance like Fred Astaire. I saw him in a movie once and always thought I'd like to be a dancer one day just like him."

"You mean you've been to the movies? Here?"

"Well, no not here, but my home is in Osaka. It's a city probably just like you came from. We did things for fun, just like all of you did before all this."

"Man, I can't believe this. I don't know what to say. I never saw the first movie until I joined the Army. Matter of fact, I hadn't had a good day for years until I joined up. I guess I didn't figure any of ya'll had real lives other than this, that's all."

"I can't answer for any of the others, but like I just told you, I did and want to go back to it one day. So, don't mention any of this and we'll be fine. Your bridge drawing is excellent, by the way. I think this will work. Report right back here in the morning and you can bring your two friends with you. Make sure you tell them to keep quiet about everything I just told you, so we can all go back home one day."

"Oh yes sir, I will, I sure will."

The next morning, Joey, Marty and Oscar were waiting for Fred. Marty nearly busted a gut laughing when Joey told him the story. All three were so thankful to leave the prison, even if it was for a full day of back-breaking work. Over forty of the other men also volunteered for this work, out of the prison. It was a welcomed relief just to walk outside of the ten-foot barbed wire fencing. At least they wouldn't have to see and smell the stench of death for another day.

CHAPTER 18

MACK 'BUCK" MONTGOMERY
April 1973

GILLY HAD KEPT A constant eye on their personal shoreline, ever since she felt like Joey gave her the go ahead to confront Uncle Mack. After all, in her mind, what else could the words "Yes, go Gilly" have meant? She would have to live with her notion that his "yes" meant that she needed to confront her Uncle Mack. Gilly always felt like he was on her side anyway, during their one-sided conversations at breakfast, when he would just eat, nod and smile.

All her neck craning and staring, in the last few days, made her have to admit to herself that they had the most incredible picture-perfect view from their kitchen window. One that she never fully appreciated in all the months they lived here. Even on cloudy days, the blending of the sky and water was something that only the most perfect painter could do.

It was her turn to make supper, so she just stood at the window while she washed and cut the vegetables for a beef stew. As she looked out once again, the only movement she spotted was a few shrimp boats out in the gulf, and a handful of tourists straggling by. Maybe Leon was right. What good would it do at this point to drag up something that happened years ago? She certainly didn't want to hurt her Aunt Maggie, who had given and done so much for them. At the same time, why on earth would she wait all those years for the right man to come along, and then settle for an ex-con? Then, just as the doubt was rising up about whether she should follow through on confronting him, there he was, a mere twenty feet away. Mack was wearing his usual neon yellow tank top, walking in her direction. The same one that stood out in the lobby of the hospital, that morning she spotted him leaving.

"Uncle Mack, hey wait up," Gilly hollered as she flew out her back door.

"Hey Gilly, what's going on with you today? Not use to seeing you out here. I didn't think you liked the beach," he answered.

The sand underneath her feet was a good thing

right now, as it seemed to calm her down from wanting to pick up one of the washed-up pieces of wood and throw it at him. As she stood staring at him for a moment, she noticed that he really wasn't a bad looking guy. He reminded her of some of the lifeguards she had seen when she and Kat would swim at the local outdoor YMCA, back home. Although, he was more of a really old one with his tanned, leathery skin and bleached blonde hair, from too many years in the sun.

"Yeah, I still don't, but I really need to talk to you about something," Gilly said as she tried to cover her eyes from the sun.

"Yeah, sure, this is a first. Go ahead, what you got?"

"What were you doing at the hospital the other day? I saw you leaving when I was going in to see Joey."

He didn't like the sound of her voice. He never wanted to get in the way of their family time. So, he always tried his best not to go when he knew Claire or Gilly would be there. He thought he knew their schedules, so that's why he would only slip up there during the week, when he knew Claire was at work and Gilly was in school.

"I was just going to see your dad, that's all," Mack stuttered.

Gilly was in position now with her feet dug in the sand and her hands on her hips, "Why would you do that?"

"Well, I try to visit him every week. He likes when I read to him," Mack answered.

Then before Gilly could stop herself, she unleashed the same fury on him that she had on Russell Sullivan the day she confronted him about the incident at Sullivan's Grocery Store. There were no practice words or questions that she had in her mind, which suited how she felt. Nothing that was reasonable at this point would work. She certainly didn't have the patience for a long, friendly conversation with this traitorous ex-con and his feeble attempt to personally connect.

"Read to him. Are you kidding me? Read what? What story did you tell him? How you served so heroically in the war? How you had been where he had? Look, you're not like him and you never will be. I'm sure he knew the kind of person you were, and that's why he never liked you. None of us did. Now I know why. He told me a long time ago that there were traitors among us, and now I know you're one of them. Even though everyone thought his brain was broken, he must have still been able to see you for what and who you really are."

Mack couldn't believe what he was hearing. He couldn't think of anything he ever did to her or her family, that would trigger this kind of outrage. All he ever wanted to do was help. How could she have possibly found out where he came from and what brought him here? He knew Gilly was always a bit uneasy around him, but he never wanted to push himself on any of them. Maggie just told him that she thought Gilly was a little uncomfortable with strangers being around her dad, and she also knew how embarrassed Gilly was about where they lived.

He tried to keep his guard up, not knowing what else to say and not wanting to prematurely expose himself. "What are you talking about?"

"Give it up Mack, I know about your prison time. I know about everything."

He had no idea he would ever be confronted about his past. Not here in Laurel Cove of all places, and certainly not by Gilly. He knew there was no way Maggie would ever tell his story. He knew she loved him too much, to disclose his hidden shame and troubles from so long ago. That look on her face said all he needed to hear. There was no letting go of where she was determined to take this. So, he finally relented to giving it all up. "How on earth did you find out?"

"Oh, so it's true then. Never you mind how I know, don't you ever go back there again, 'cause if you do, I swear I'll tell Aunt Maggie and Mom all about you."

"Gilly, hold on for a minute. Please, just listen. You got it all wrong. You need to hear me out. Then, if you want to tell the whole town, just go ahead because to tell you the truth, I'm tired. I'm tired of hiding. I'm tired of not being able to hold my head up. I'm getting too old for this. I'd trade places with your dad right now if I could. I'd rather be where he is, than where I'm at right now. I'm ashamed, but it's not what you think."

"Oh, so you're going to tell me how to think? Give me a little credit," Gilly jeered.

"Please Gilly, let me finish. I joined the Navy because I wanted to serve my country, just like your dad did. When I was going through the pilot training program, I just kept having panic attacks. It's like I couldn't breathe, and I thought I would pass out and crash at any second. Even if I could stay up, there was no way I was ever going to be able to land any of those fighter planes on a ship. No one would listen. They just kept telling me to work it off because they were so desperate for fighter pilots. I tried. God knows how hard I tried, but I knew that if I didn't kill myself, I would wind up killing a bunch of other innocent people. Maybe I wasn't thinking clear or right, but at that time I figured the only way out would be a dishonorable discharge. I just had to figure out how to get one. I certainly didn't want to hurt anyone, not on purpose anyway, so I just started stealing supplies. I stole food from the mess hall, hundreds of tools from the hangers, anything I could get my hands on, I took. I guess it went on for weeks until I finally got caught. I knew it wasn't a good plan right away, when they threw me in prison. I told them where everything was and why I did what I did. I never kept any of the stuff, I swear. It didn't matter, they were all furious and they were going to make an example out of me, to make sure no one else got any bright ideas of trying to get out. I got a dishonorable discharge all right, but it was after I served ten years for felony theft. I stayed around Pensacola for a few years, but couldn't find any work, much less anyone that would hire me. Found myself sleeping on the beach most nights, or at some homeless shelter. All that time on the beach, I kind of learned how to make stuff out of the junk I found and sold it to the tourists. So, one day when I had enough saved up, I just started hitchhiking until I got out here one day, where I thought no one would know me. You have to admit it's a pretty hard place to find. I guess one of the tourists I sold something to must have recognized me and told you, huh?"

"Sort of, in a way. It doesn't matter how I found out. All you need to know is, I know. So, then I guess you spotted Aunt Maggie for easy pickings right away," Gilly said.

"No, it didn't happen like that either, I promise," Mack answered.

"So how did you worm your way in, to get her to marry you?" asked Gilly.

"I didn't worm, Gilly. I first went to Mimi's Diner for something to eat, and it was someone there that told me about your Aunt Maggie's apartments, that she rented out. You know, the very one you and your mom are staying in. After that, we just started talking. I'd go into the post office and send letters home, and we had lunch together a few times, and I don't know, I needed to come clean to someone or move on. She was just someone that I knew I could trust, and I just sat there in Mimi's Diner one day and told her everything."

"So, you're telling me that Aunt Maggie knows all about your past?" Gilly asked.

"Yes Gilly, every last minute of it. I may have been a thief at one time, but I'm not a liar and I'm certainly not a traitor. I'm just an old fashioned, run-of-the-mill coward."

"Well, I don't remember calling you a liar," Gilly said sarcastically.

"Look, I've always admired your family and how you and your mom tried to hold things together. I wanted to help your dad, but didn't know how. It was my idea for all of you to move here."

"I don't understand. Why would you want to help us? Why do you feel the need to go see him? Are you trying to pay some kind of penance for what you did, by visiting broken-down soldiers at the VA Hospital?" Gilly asked.

"I'm not interested in just any broken-down soldier. It's a small world, Gilly. Just when I thought it was all behind me, and Maggie had accepted my past, we visited you. Maggie wanted me to meet all of you. Do you remember that day?"

"Kind of, I guess. You didn't have much to say."

"Well, there was a reason. The minute I laid eyes on your dad—I just couldn't believe it."

"Believe what?"

"We grew up together, Gilly. My mom and his mom were friends. Her name was Gertie Montgomery, and she played the organ at our church on Sunday. Back then, your dad and everyone else called me Buck.

By this time Gilly's knees buckled underneath her, as she collapsed in the sand. The very thing that had always irritated her felt like nothing to her now, as it encroached upon her body. It wasn't fate that put her hands on that dead letter, that day. It had to be God. There was no other explanation. All those nights she silently prayed for God to help her family, and all this time he had been using an ex-con to help take care of them. Not only that, this ex-con used to be her dad's friend. She finally had a piece of his past, and he was standing right in front of her.

Mack sat beside Gilly, put his arm around her and said, "You know, Gilly, when I met your dad again that day, I thought somehow God was punishing me. I kept telling myself it wasn't right, that I still had a good mind, while your dad was all messed up. Then I just figured He somehow brought me back into the picture to help you guys out. There was no other explanation for it. If I had gone on and served in the military like the other guys, then I probably would have never seen him again, and our paths would have never crossed. So, I've just tried to give back every chance I get. You know I don't do bad selling my souvenirs every day. I told your Aunt Maggie she could quit working anytime she wants to. We have plenty of money in the bank. You know, one time I found a big, old diamond ring and sold it for over two thousand dollars. You wouldn't believe some of the stuff I've found, and how much money I've made just doing that. You need to understand, when I do find stuff, I always keep it for months before I sell it. Just in case someone comes back looking for it," Mack added.

"Okay, that's real interesting. But, I really want to know more about my dad, when he was growing up and everything. How is it that Aunt Maggie never told Mom about you and Joey? You know, that y'all used to be friends."

"Oh yeah, of course. So, the day I re-met him, I realized right away that he didn't recognize me. I've never forgotten him, though, not for one minute. He had a really bad time growing up. His mom's name was Natalie and she was so beautiful. She was such a nice lady. You would have really loved her. My mom used to give your dad all my clothes that I had outgrown, and she even sent some of hers down to Natalie. Shoot, she even bought your dad most of his Christmas presents every year."

"Why would she do that?"

"Because my mom was a good woman, like Natalie, and his old man was awful. I really think he was the meanest man in the whole town. I was scared to death of him myself. He wouldn't give her money for anything but groceries. Then one day, Natalie got sick and not long after that she died. It got even worse for Joey after that."

"What happened?"

"Hank, that was his father's name, made Joey quit school. He couldn't have been no more than eleven, and he had to work at their car repair shop all day, and even into the night sometimes. If that wasn't bad enough, his old man got remarried and kicked him out of the house. Poor little guy had to live in the shop for years, until he joined the Army. All he had was a cot in the corner. That was his world. Working on cars, pumping gas and sleeping on a cot in the corner of the shop at night. It was really pitiful. I felt so sorry for him. So anyway, my mom would send me down there some nights with food and stuff, when I could sneak in. Like I said, he was mean as a junkyard dog, and I sure didn't want Hank to see me. I still, to this day, don't understand how he survived like that all those years, and turned out like he did. I really admired him so much. As far as your Aunt Maggie letting on to your mom that your dad and I were friends, I don't know Gilly. I guess all that just got caught up in the same big secret, that she felt needed to stay where it was. I'm really so very sorry all this didn't come out sooner."

Gilly sat there trying to absorb all this horrible family history about her dad. He had a beautiful and kind mother. She died when he was young. His dad was a horrible bully. He had to quit school when he was eleven and sleep on a cot in the shop. Her Uncle Mack and his mom secretly sent him food. There was only one thing, so far, that had her confused as she uttered, "So is your name Mack or Buck?"

"It's Mack, Buck was just a nickname my dad gave me when I was little. You're way too young to know this, but Buck Rogers was a cartoon character that travelled into space. I had all his comic books. I always thought I was going to be Buck Rogers one day and fly. Kind of funny now when you think about it."

Gilly just sat there thinking about all the years that had passed, with so much contempt in her heart for this man. This man, who when he was a young boy, helped provide food and clothes to her dad. All those old feelings she once had disappeared right then and there on the beach, and now she was suddenly on the other side of things. How could she ever make things right? How would she ever repay this man for all the kindness he had shown her dad and them, even when she behaved so badly towards him?

"I'm really sorry, Uncle Mack. I had no idea. If I had known, I swear I would have been nicer to you. Really, I would have. I don't usually act that way. It's just that I was made fun of so much when I was growing up, and I just never have been good at letting new people in," Gilly said as she cracked her knuckles.

"Sounds like we really are alike, in a weird kind of way. I'm not good at that kind of stuff either. Anyway Gilly, none of this is your fault. You were just a kid when I came into the picture. It's mine. I should have come clean a long time ago. Maggie tried to talk to me about it, but I guess I was just too ashamed of the difference in choices he and I made, and how our lives turned out. It just didn't seem fair, and I just thought you would hate me if you found out. I honestly didn't want to give your mom another thing to grieve about, over how your dad was really treated growing up."

"I may not have been too particularly fond of you before, but there's no way I could ever hate you. Especially now. I just wish I knew what happened to my dad when he was in the war, that's all. Mom said he would never talk about it. He just wanted to leave it be. It may not change anything, but at least I'd know."

"Well, maybe now that we've got all that old stuff out of the way, we can put our heads together and find out."

"Really, how?"

"If you can find his discharge papers, I can start trying to track down some of the guys he served with over there. I, at least, know how to do that. They might have some answers."

"Are you kidding me? You would do that? You know Mom always said there were no coincidences in life and I'm really starting to believe her. She's got a whole box of papers inside. I remember seeing them when we moved here. Can we not tell her anything yet? At least, not until we have something to tell her. I wouldn't want to get her hopes up."

"Of course. Not a word."

"By the way, I know someone else who can help us. He's got a lot of connections. Matter of fact, he's the reason why we're sitting here right now. That's a whole different, long story that I really can't get into right now. I'll have to check with him first. He's a lot like you. He likes to keep a low profile, too."

They had been sitting outside for over an hour, which meant she only had a couple hours left before her mom got home. She knew exactly where the box marked "important papers" was, because she was the one that had shoved them up on her mom's closet shelf.

After flipping through several folders, she came across a handful of letters addressed to her dad when he was in the Army, with the biggest rubber-banded bundle being from Claire Marie Stout to PVT 1st Class Joseph Franklin Stevens, and then there were those addressed to Claire Marie Stout from PVT 1st Class Joseph Franklin Stevens. Her mom and dad wrote to each other when he was in the Army? Why didn't she tell her? Gilly sat with her legs crossed on the floor and read one letter after another. All these letters of friendship and then long-distance love, that had been the lifeline between two lonely souls, had died much like the dead letters in the post office did. The only difference was those sitting in the dead letter box still had hope, and all the dreams these two once had, had died years ago.

She carefully banded and put her parents' letters back, fiddled through several envelopes and folders, finding everything from their marriage license, birth certificates of her and her baby brother, his death certificate, and finally her dad's formal honorable discharge from the Army.

It seemed like every time Gilly exposed one secret, she had to tuck away another. Leon didn't want anyone to know that he really was finding criminals from their pictures in the post office. He made her swear not to share his hand in exposing her Uncle Mack. Her Uncle Mack and her dad were friends when he was young. Her grandfather had been an awful father and husband. Her Aunt Maggie knew all about her Uncle Mack, and now she didn't know that Gilly knew. Right in front of her, she had just read this whole beautiful story of how her parents planned their future together from worlds apart. He fell in love with a woman he never met, but at least he had a picture. She fell in love with his words on a piece of paper. From reading her dad's letters, like her mom said, her dad really was quite a romantic.

What an amazing journey this has been so far. One that she never dreamed would come about, when she flicked her dad's flashlight on under cover of darkness, unsealing that very special, hand-picked dead letter. One that she knew had finally found its rightful recipient. She is so very thankful that her Aunt Maggie had never chosen to help that one find its way. She was even more grateful that she held the beliefs she did. That it was illegal to open anyone's mail. It would have broken her heart to know that's how someone on the outside world felt about her husband. She was also thankful it barely missed its target delivery, because then who knows what the damage would have done, not only to her Uncle Mack, but to the very woman that gave so much to the people of Laurel Cove, that she now called her family.

CHAPTER 19

IT WAS A BRIDGE TOO FAR
March 1944

THE PLAN WENT EVEN better than Joey had anticipated. Oscar and Marty worked on the construction of the bridge with all the other prisoners and civilians, while Joey was made the supervisor of the job. He walked about checking every wooden board, to make sure they weren't rotten or warped, and he was in on every cut, making sure it was done by his precise architectural drawing. Then at the end of the day, just as Joey had hoped, they were given an extra serving of rice and one cup of boiled carrots. They were also given three cups of water that had to be measured and rationed out throughout the day. The only thing he could think of any better than this, would be his next letter from his sweetheart, Claire. She was always a constant thought on his mind, hoping and praying that she would love him one day as much as he loved her now. Even in the midst of all this, he would think from time to time, how did he get so lucky?

Every day he waited with all the others for something from home; some kind of care package, medical supplies or even books to read, to help them escape their day-to-day lives as prisoners of war. The Red Cross supplies that came through were never enough to sustain their needs, for time wasn't on their side. Men were dying every day from illnesses that would have been an easy fix if they were back home. If one of the members of Satan's Army was around, most, if not all of it, would have disappeared in minutes. Anything left seemed to only prolong the inevitable, for those that were slowly giving up the will to live.

Joey finally accepted it all as part of their reality, much like he did when he worked for his dad. That is until Marty got sick. For the first time since they had been captured, one of the three "band of brothers" was on death's door. He had developed malaria and had been running a high fever for days, and they had run out of medicine three days ago. He had to find a way to secure more, or he knew, like so many others, his friend would die.

There were groups of Filipino guerillas that

had fought with them, during the time they spent fighting on the Bataan Peninsula. Many of them made their escape through the jungles, right before their official surrender, and he knew most of them were still out there somewhere, fighting for their country and the men taken captive. So, every day he and Oscar tried to get a message to one of the Filipino civilians, who were working on the bridge with them, that they desperately needed their help.

"Please, if you can, we need more medicine or my friend will die. I don't have any way to pay you, but please help us," Joey begged as though he was arguing over a board that was cut wrong in order not to be caught.

"I will try, but don't ask again. Don't want to get caught. I have family," the old man answered as he walked away.

Then as the sun was setting on another day of knowing his friend was back at the camp hospital, slowly dying, all Joey knew to do was pray. Suddenly, as he lifted his head, he saw to his right, out in the deep thick brush, two sets of eyes. Since he was the supervisor on the job, Joey had more freedom than the others, to walk some distance away from the worksite.

Joey walked up to the brush, turned around as though he was viewing their ongoing construction, and just as he did a small package was thrown by his right foot. As he heard feet scuffle away, he reached down, picked up the package, and shoved it into his pants pocket. There was no doubt his prayer had been answered, and inside would be the medicine they needed. He knew that those two brave sets of eyes had not only been sent there by word of mouth, but the merciful hand of God, as well. He also knew that those two risk takers had to be none other than participants of the brave Filipino guerilla underground, doing everything they could to save the men who would one day give them their country back.

Once Joey returned to the prison camp, late that night, he was able to secretly pass it off to Chaplain Shimley, who in turn administered it to those who needed it the most. This medicine saved not only Marty, but dozens of men, including Oscar, who weeks later developed dysentery. However, after several of these drop-offs, the chaplain had a short, cautionary message for Joey.

"Look son, please be careful. I have no doubt what you're doing is real life or death for some of these guys, and they wouldn't have made it if you weren't out there taking a chance like this, but you need to watch your back. Please, whatever you do, don't let your guard down. More eyes are on you than you think. I'll be praying for all of you, that this can continue without any trouble."

Joey assured Chaplain Shimley that he had things covered. "No worry, there's no way I can get caught. The guards quit watching me weeks ago. Heck, I've even seen some of them taking a few winks in the middle of the day."

This drop-off continued off and on for the next

six months, working like clockwork, until one day this miracle delivery, along with their luck, finally ran out. Of all the guards to catch him, it would be none other than 'The Maggot.' Today was no different than all the other drop shipments, as he made his usual rounds. Their special, small package was thrown to his feet, and just as he thought it was all clear, he reached down and suddenly out of nowhere he felt an all too familiar bone crackling whack, on the back of his head. He hit the ground, but was able to roll over to see The Maggot standing over him, with his big toothless grin, as Machine Gun Kelly and Scarface pushed their way through the brush, in pursuit of the mysterious two sets of eyes. As one was shot while trying to run away, the other set of eyes was surrounded and captured.

This would be the beginning of Joey's lifelong, hellacious nightmares. To his horror, the other would belong to none other than the little boy he thought he left behind. The one he had cared so much for in the days before he left. The one that promised he would stay put until Joey came back. The one he promised himself he was going to save one day from his life on the streets. Now he was being dragged out of the bushes like an animal, on its way to be slaughtered.

Eddie didn't stay put with Father Ray like Joey told him to. He had, instead, left the safe haven of San Augustin Catholic Church, and joined the ranks of so many other young Filipino boys who became part of a group that operated the bamboo telegraph.

These young boys were small-framed and quick on their feet, as they skirted seamlessly throughout the thick jungles. They were used to spread word all over the islands of where the prisoners were held, what supplies they needed, and figuring out the safest way to smuggle them in. Eddie went a step further. He heard through the bamboo telegraph that Joey's unit had been sent to Camp O'Donnell. He just needed to see him again. He just wanted to help his friend anyway he could. Joey had been the only person that had ever treated him with so much dignity and kindness. It was as though Joey didn't see his disfigured face. He only saw him for the lonely, little boy he was, and it was Joey that made him feel like he finally belonged to the human race. Something he had never felt before.

Joey was horrified as he cried out, "Oh my God, Eddie why, why are you here? Why didn't you listen to me?"

He only stared at Joey fighting back tears, as though he didn't know him. He wanted to so badly embrace his big brother, but fought back any urge to do so. He had been trained well to never let on that he knew any of the prisoners, if he was ever captured. To do so, would ensure certain torture and death for anyone involved. Joey didn't know this rule. He didn't know that by acknowledging any connection to this young boy, it would lead to what lay ahead.

The Maggot poked his long, sharp, metal bayonet in Joey's back, as he pushed and shoved both of them back to the prison camp. He then threw them in separate four-by-six holes in the ground, covered with a lid of woven banana leaves, while they baked in the sweltering heat. For the next three days, The Maggot planned his revenge. He would have to come up with the most devious torture yet, to make sure they would never be undermined like this again. It was a seriously bruised ego for him, when one of Joey's fellow prisoners pointed him in his direction. He had allowed this smuggling to take place right under his nose. Not only that, he would never allow these two souls to reunite. The very idea that any of the civilians were willing to risk their life to help the prisoners, was a serious undermining of the future stronghold they would have one day, once the island was under their control. The fact that these two knew one another would definitely make what they had planned even more fun to watch.

The Maggot had finally worked it all out in his sick, demented mind. He pulled them out and tied Joey to one of the spickets in the center of the yard, making sure he would have the best view. He then unveiled, to the entire yard of prisoners, the most haunting torture the men had ever seen. He and the two other members of Satan's Army laughed hysterically, as Eddie's body was mangled right before their eyes, as Joey cried and screamed. There was no doubt he was now in hell, watching the devil himself as he devoured his latest innocent victim. It became too much for Joey's mind and body to sustain as he screamed and begged for them stop.

All that Oscar and Marty could do was watch, while Chaplain Shimley stayed on his knees begging them to stop. They knew better than to interfere, not for their safety, but for Joey's. Fred had to watch too, as he fought back tears. He couldn't let anyone see him care, while this poor young boy, that was only a few years older than his son, was being brutally tortured and killed. This had nothing to do with the war they were fighting. In his mind, this was nothing more than murder for someone's sadistic pleasure. Later that night, Fred threw up and swore to himself that all three members of Satan's Army would pay for this one day.

Joey spent days in the hospital, but there would be no medicine for the horror that kept replaying in his mind. Eddie was dead and it was all his fault. He would never be able to save him from his life as an orphan. He didn't get to tell him how much he cared for him, and how truly special he was. He didn't get to tell him how sorry he was. He didn't even get to tell him goodbye. He thought he had been so careful. He couldn't imagine that they could've known what he was doing. The only answer he could think of, was someone working on that bridge had betrayed him. Someone on their side had sold them out, and crossed over to their enemy for nothing more than an extra cup of rice and carrots.

Chaplain Shimley could only sit by Joey's bed, pray for him, and read aloud from both his Bible and the letters that Claire continued to religiously write. The chaplain wrote and assured her that

Joey wasn't feeling well, but he would no doubt be back in the swing of things real soon. All that Oscar and Marty could do was visit their friend, while they helplessly waited for him to come back to them.

Then one day, out of sheer frustration, Marty sat by Joey's bed and said, "Joey, man look you've got to try to snap out of it. Oscar and I know how much you cared for the kid, but he had to know what he was getting himself into. We get it that he saved a bunch of lives here, including our own, but so did you. How would you have known it was him passing that stuff off anyway? It's not like you ever saw their faces. Even you admitted that."

Joey rolled over to face Marty and finally said, "I know what you're saying is true, but why him? That kid never did anything to anybody. He was probably dumped at that church the day he was born, through no fault of his own. It just seemed like life only got harder for him the more he tried. Here he was, trying to help us, and he was... I can't even say it out loud," as Joey's voice drifted off.

"Yeah, I know. All the guys have been sick about it. Just try for a minute to look at it this way. You believe in all this God stuff, and don't get me wrong, I'm almost there, but didn't you say your mom was up in heaven watching over you?" Marty asked.

"Of course she is, and nothing is ever going to change that. I feel like she is sometimes still with me," Joey answered with a deep sigh, as tears rolled down his face towards the bamboo slatted floor.

"Then why can't you believe that's where Eddie

is right now? Look at his home, this island is pretty much destroyed by now. He had no family. Who knows whether or not all the people he did know are still alive? We need to face it, if our troops don't rally soon and get us out of here, we're going to die too. Things just can't go on like this for much longer. He just made it out sooner than the rest of us. I bet he's probably beside your mom right now, in the most perfect place. So, what about it, Joey? Remember, we all came in together and we're all supposed to go home together, one way or another," Marty said as he patted Joey's shoulder.

"I guess you're right. I didn't think about it like that. All I could think about is how much he suffered and why?" Joey said as he teared up again.

"You gotta let go of the why. That's probably one of those things that we'll never know. At least not here. Try to think about going home to Claire and the life you want with her, like you use to do. I'm going to leave you now, so try to get some rest. Oscar and I want to see you up and about tomorrow. We need you out there with us. We miss you."

"Thanks, Marty."

"No problem, brother."

Oscar was just within listening distance for Marty's entire speech. "You've been paying a lot more attention to some of Chaplain Shimley's sermons than I have given you credit for Marty, but I have to admit, that boy's death will haunt me for the rest of my life, too."

"Yeah, but at least for right now, you and I plan on having a life to haunt."

Marty's last words rang true. Joey did have plans with this beautiful woman, and he was beginning to believe that she deserved so much better than him. How would he ever be able to leave all this behind, even if they did get out? The thought of letting her go was an even bigger pain in the very heart that he thought couldn't break anymore. So, with that mindset, Joey willed himself up and out of the prison hospital the next morning. They continued to move about the camp, doing everything they could do, to keep their noses clean. Joey's days of smuggling were over. No one else's blood was ever going to be on his hands.

Fred was also grief stricken and felt like he had been a part in the murder, as he stood there and did nothing to try to stop it. He knew that such a thing would never happen there again. He had already taken steps to make sure. The only way he knew to make amends, as one human to another, was to give in a little. Oscar was finally allowed to start a garden. He had begged his captors for years to grow their own vegetables. Shortly after Eddie's murder, a small set-aside allotment of dirt quickly filled with potatoes, carrots and radishes that Oscar carefully planted and cultivated. Marty pitched in when the vegetables ripened, by trying his hand at making his first Irish stew, minus the meat. For the first time in almost three years, Oscar and Marty were able to play a part in alleviating some of the hunger pains of the remaining eight hundred prisoners, who now had three less guards to torment them. They were all certain that somehow Fred had a hand in removing Satan's Army from Camp O'Donnell. About two weeks after the murder of Eddie, all three quietly disappeared one night, and for the first time since they had all arrived at Camp O'Donnell, things didn't seem so hopeless.

However, one month later, four hundred of the prisoners were moved once again, this time to a place called Cabanatuan.

CHAPTER 20

POMP AND REAL CIRCUMSTANCES
May 1973

IT WAS A VERY public event that I had just as soon skip, since Mom insisted that they were all going as a family. I just wanted her to be able to enjoy herself and relish, if only for a few minutes, my high school graduation. All the old memories, of the last time we were all in public together, were something that I couldn't shake loose. The last few times I visited, Joey seemed to be getting more agitated and withdrawn, for the most part sitting and staring out his window. I had pretty much stopped going, giving Mom every excuse I could think of, not to see how much he was deteriorating. Uncle Mack went nearly every morning, just to sit and read to him. He said he loved The Incredible Journey so much, that he read it to him three times already. Like everyone else, he told me that I just needed to give the doctors more time. But, how much time do they need? He's been there for nearly ten months, and the most I've ever gotten out of him lately is a weak, half-hearted "Hi" and a "Bye." So, I suppose that was why I had little interest in participating in our high school graduation.

Even though there would only be twenty-two of us getting our high school diplomas, almost the whole town would probably cram themselves into the community center just to have something to do on a Friday night. Just like any event that the school held, it would be a public event of epic proportions. It didn't matter that by now most of the town knew about Joey, and why my mom and I lived alone. Even though Aunt Maggie and Uncle Mack would be there, this would be just one more thing that my mom would have to navigate, while trying to babysit a grown man that had no control over his actions. I had, in fact, managed to come out on top of the class as Valedictorian. After all the fret and worry over money for my college tuition, it all suddenly just appeared. I had a free ride to any four-year institution in the State of Mississippi. Yet, this would just be one more thing that Joey wouldn't have a clue about. Mom has counseled me more and more lately, that I shouldn't let such an opportunity go to waste. I suppose I should probably at least look into the journalism programs offered. That would be one place that I could hone my skills as a writer and perhaps work for a newspaper one day. With my graduation only two days away, in what should be a celebratory atmosphere in our apartment, things once again turned into one of those tug of wars that we haven't had since we moved to Laurel Cove.

"Mom, why? What makes you think he will even know where he is? I don't want people staring and making fun of him. Mom, please don't do this to me, to us, I'm begging you, please," Gilly begged as her eyes filled with tears.

"Gilly, honey, you haven't been to visit in weeks. You would be surprised at how much better he's doing. The doctors have tried several medications, and I think they've finally hit on something that's waking him up a bit. I haven't discussed much about his progress because I didn't want to get your hopes up, but they think there's a clear connection between him accidentally killing that dog, that may have triggered something that happened to him when he was a prisoner of war. They're not sure if it's dementia, or some kind of psychosis, but I've been taking him outside a lot lately when I go visit. I don't know, maybe its wishful thinking, but when he looks at the sky and the beach, I feel like he's in there somewhere like I haven't seen in a very long time. You know what he said the last time I was there?" said Claire.

"What, I'm hungry?" answered Gilly.

"No, where's Gilly?"

"Okay, maybe he was just wondering where that girl is that brings him all his cookies, candy and comic books. Mom, like you've always said, I'm sure he's in there somewhere, but it's all locked up and lost. Joey's lost, Mom, and he's never coming back. I promise that I'll start going back to see him. You know I love him, but I wish you would move on. When's the last time you thought about you? All you do is go to work, go see Joey, come home, and then you start over again on Monday morning. You're still a young, beautiful woman, Mom. You can start over. I mean, what's the point? I've heard the doctors talking. I've listened in the hallway when I've been there. They're just experimenting with all those people. I even heard one doctor say, once the brain starts dying, it can never come back. So why do you want to go through all this trouble, for everyone to either make fun of him or feel sorry for us, when he has no idea what he's even there for?" asked Gilly.

"Because Gilly, it's on his list of things to do. It was folded and tucked away in his tool box. I only found it a few weeks ago, when I was looking for a screwdriver to replace that broken cabinet hinge in the kitchen. I just fell completely apart when I read it. I've been waiting for the right time to share it with you, and this seems like just as good a time as any. Gilly, honey, he knew. While you and I were going about our business, doing whatever we did back then, he was planning for the day when he knew he couldn't be there for us. Somehow, he just knew something was happening to him, and this was a list of things he still wanted to one day share with you. I still can't believe how well thought out it is. Here read it for yourself..." Claire said as she slumped on the couch, trying desperately to hold herself together.

My Dearest Claire,

I don't know what's happening to me. My mind at times feels like a runaway train. Sometimes I find myself across town and I don't know how I got there. I'm scared that it's my past that's haunting me. A place I never want you to see and know about. The world is full of good and evil. I pray that only good will visit you and my darling Gilly. But when my mind eventually fails me, as I painfully know it will one day soon, please tell my precious little girl when these things come her way don't think me absent.

1. It's ok to pack away your dolls. Just put them in a safe place.

2. Be yourself no matter how small or insignificant the world tries to make you feel.

3. Always remember that great faith must endure great trials.

4. Seek the truth and take comfort in knowing it.

5. Stood the proudest when you graduated from high school.

6. Gave you the room you needed to find your way.

7. Walked you down the aisle on your special day.

8. Bounced your children on my knee.

9. Hung a tire in your favorite tree.

10. Felt your presence in the room.

Gilly just stood there, like the road map for life had been hidden from her all these years. A complete visual of her dad standing at his work bench in the garage, while writing his very own emotional and mental obituary for their future without him, was almost unbearable. It was a wave of guilt that she now felt was well deserved. Every time she had words with her mom about her dad's unwanted weight in their lives, she knew in her heart of hearts it had never been intentional. She just needed someone to blame for all their unexpected landslides.

"Mom, I'm so sorry, for everything. I've been such a rotten, selfish kid all these years. All those times that I thought I was surrounded by spoiled brats at school, I was actually one of them," Gilly sobbed.

"Oh, no you weren't. You were the bravest, smartest and most dedicated daughter your dad and I could have ever hoped for. So don't you dare feel bad, that you did exactly what you needed to do," answered Claire.

"Yeah, but I didn't need to be a jerk about it all."

Claire stood up and wrapped her arms around her daughter, "Gilly, you were never a jerk. You needed to grow up. It takes time to come into yourself. You've done that and so much more. You know what it's like to have a certain way of life and then have it taken away. No one could have rolled with the punches better than you."

"You really think so?" Gilly asked.

"I absolutely know so," answered Claire.

"Mom, will you do me a favor?"

"Sure, anything."

"Will you read Joey's letter to me? I need to hear the words out loud."

They sat down together on the couch, with Gilly's head in her mom's lap. Claire stroked Gilly's hair and read the words out loud, as though she was reading her favorite bedtime story to her little girl, before she tucked her in the bed for the night. Her dad's handwritten letter somehow made his absence in her life even more profound, and what a great man he truly was. How he thought that much ahead of what was really going to be important in her life one day, absolutely stunned her. Things that she never centered herself on, until now. For the most part, she never wanted to look that far ahead in the future. She was now absolutely sure that the grip he had on life had finally given way, just as one does on the side of a cliff when their last bit of strength empties out. Even then, the only person he thought of on his way down was her. Gilly had ebbs and flows in her life for years, as to whether Joey fought hard enough to beat his invisible demon. From now on she would never, ever doubt how hard he tried to keep being her dad.

"Sorry Hope, can't hang out today, I need to go see Joey. We'll talk later. I promise," said Gilly as she walked down the hallway. She really did need to make more time for Hope. She just wished she had the nerve to tell her not to be so wanting. If she only knew that it was actually her neediness that pushed people away. Maybe she should tell her. Maybe not. She had to admit to herself that even she had a hard time when Kat brushed her off for Martin. Maybe she should just try to be nicer. Gilly's new mindset was moving in the right direction. Hope just needed someone to invest in her, since apparently her parents were getting a divorce, too. She had some money saved up. After she visited Joey, she would make sure to stop somewhere and pick her up a nice graduation gift.

Gilly took the bus and got off at the Veteran's Hospital. She knew her way around, and had at times directed visitors up this floor or down that hall. Joey would be in the TV room with the rest of his friends, probably watching one of his new daytime favorites, 'Price is Right'. The only thing any of the guys knew to yell at the same time was 'Come on Down'. Joey would be there, sitting among all the other patients, but to Gilly's surprise he had found a new hero.

"Miss Lydia, what's going on with Joey? Where did he get that outfit from?"

"Hey, Gilly, glad to see you. Haven't seen you in a while. Joey's really been on the upswing here lately. It's been really fun to watch. He's gotten so full of life here lately. Much better than when he first got here, I'm happy to say. He has only one doctor now, who's really done wonders with how he's managing his medication. I think there were just too many hands in the pot before. Oh, the outfit he has on. I hope you're not mad. They've all been watching Superman in the morning, and he wanted his own red cape. I just picked up a big red beach towel that he ties around his neck and he's happy as a lark. You know, he's been asking about you."

"I know, I'm sorry. I've just been busy with school and work. Mom just told me he was getting better and from the look of things, he does look like he's having a good day. I guess that's all that really matters," Gilly said, not wanting to admit that her dad still looked and acted like he was still in kindergarten.

"Well, he took a deep slide a few weeks after he got here. Now he's feeding and dressing himself again. He loves hanging out with all the other patients. I know seeing your dad run around in a red cape doesn't look like much of an improvement, but he's happy again Gilly, he really is. So, don't give up on him. There are so many patients here that no one bothers to come visit anymore. It's really heartbreaking. His mind may not be where you want it to be, but he's still your dad."

"I know he is, I just wished one day that he did but if not, that's okay too, Miss Lydia. By the way, I've been meaning to ask, you spend so much time here, don't you have your own family sitting at home, wanting to spend time with you?"

"Well, I was married but we never had children. My husband, William, was killed during the war," answered Lydia.

"Oh, Miss Lydia, I didn't know. I'm sorry. Was he a prisoner too, like Joey?" Gilly asked.

"No, he was shot down somewhere over Germany. They never found his body."

All Gilly knew to do was to embrace her dad's favorite nurse, and think once again about her mom's strong spirit and words of wisdom she repeated on a daily basis. If we just take a moment to look to our right or left throughout the day, we will find ourselves much higher on the fairness scale than we would have ourselves believe. There are plenty of 'someones' more wanting than you just around the corner. Gilly was so thankful that she was finally learning how to turn that corner now. All those things that she never thought she would ever use, would be the most valuable lessons in life. She never thought this would ever be the case. She was just so glad that her dad was still alive, and it didn't matter anymore that he was flying around the room in his big red towel.

Gilly had a bag of chocolate chip cookies and some Miss Debbie cupcakes that he busted into, as soon as she handed them to him. She just sat there for a minute watching him cram one cupcake after another into his mouth. He had chocolate icing smeared over all his face and hands, just like he did at Sullivan's Grocery Store, the day they got kicked out. It was her seventeenth birthday, and another had already passed quietly and uneventfully just like she wanted. She wanted no plans, no fanfare, so if it fell apart for some reason, she wouldn't be disappointed.

"Bye, Joey. I've got to leave now. Claire and I are going to get you something new to wear. It was on your list, remember? Standing tall at my graduation. I'm going to make sure you're there for all the rest of them, I promise. We'll pick you up in a couple days, okay?"

"Okay, bye, Gilly, see you later."

Gilly would have no anxiety about Joey embarrassing her. He was dressed in a nice black suit, white shirt with a tie, and black slacks that weren't too short. His nicely polished dress shoes were tied. Like her mom said over the years, "Gilly, you don't know what he understands, the doctors don't even know for sure. So just be happy that you have both of your parents here today. Okay?"

She was happy. Happier than she thought she would ever be again, because her mom and dad were sitting together celebrating in their own special way, while Kat's and Hope's parents were now miles apart. Not only in her mind was he standing the tallest, she could once again clearly see him swinging her in that tire swing, with her pigtails and two big front teeth.

As she stood before her graduation Class of 1973, as well as the entire town of Laurel Cove, she received yet another standing ovation. The words were all well worth repeating, as she read from the same paper that she had written for her 11th grade social studies class over a year ago. LEARN NOW—USE LATER. For it may have been a different time and place, but Gilly knew without a doubt that her collection of all her mom's words of wisdom still rang true, and would stay with her forever, just like her dad's letter.

When she finished her speech, she made sure to find Hope and give her the very special gift that had her name written all over it. It was a silver necklace and charm with the words FAITH, HOPE, LOVE inscribed. She couldn't think of anyone more deserving.

As they drove back to the hospital that night, all she could think about was what an incredible week it had been. She didn't know where she would be right now, had it not been for her family. One of the things that stood out to her the most now on her dad's list. Seek the truth and take comfort in it. She had learned many truths so far, but she had one left that was more important now, than it had ever been before.

CHAPTER 21

THE LAST DAYS
November 1944

JOEY DIDN'T UNDERSTAND WHY he was chosen for another place, and different people that he wanted no part of. Why was he picked out of the hundreds of men to be moved to another camp? He thought that he and Fred had forged some kind of silent code between them, and he and his friends would be protected until the end. Fred had even shared more with him of his life before this war, late one night when everyone else was sleeping.

"My wife is a lovely woman. I miss her very much.

I can't imagine how grown up my son must be now. I hope this all ends soon, for all of us," Fred said.

"What's she like, you wife?" asked Joey.

"Her name is Mio, which means a beautiful cherry blossom," Fred smiled as he continued, "Look see for yourself," as he pulled her picture out of his uniform front pocket.

"Oh, she is very beautiful. Look this is my girl, Claire. She doesn't know it yet, but I'm going to marry her one day," Joey said as he also shared his picture. "You know, Fred, I just don't understand what this world is all about sometimes. I thought that maybe when I travelled the world, I would meet different people, but you know everybody is really the same. It's the hearts and minds of the ones that are running things that seem to keep getting us in these horrible messes."

"How so?" asked Fred.

"Well, we basically all want the same things. A safe place to live, family and good health. That's what I've been searching for all these years, and sounds to me that's all you want too, for this war to be over and to go back home in one piece."

"You're a very wise man, Joey. We must stop talking now. I don't want anyone to think I'm consorting with the enemy," Fred winked as he walked away.

He was really angry, for the first time since Eddie died. Hadn't he suffered enough, and now God was going to separate him from Oscar, Marty and Chaplain Shimley. How would he ever be able to cope without them? He no longer felt he was the sissy that his father once accused him of being. He had fought hard, made sacrifices, and sustained through more than enough death and destruction. He knew that he had never taken one step alone. No one ever does. Just like Mrs. Gertie and Buck had been there for him, all those cold and lonely nights. Joey had finally realized that family isn't necessarily some kind of blood connection. It was all about those special people that you want and need with you, on the journey of life. It was that simple.

"Look Joey, you gonna be okay, don't worry. They're probably breaking the camp up because it's all fixing to hit the fan. I feel it in my bones. I'm sure in a few days we'll all be somewhere else, too. Maybe on a ship, on our way back home, who knows," Oscar said.

"Yeah, don't forget to write," Marty snickered.

Joey just looked away and said, "Not funny."

"Look brother, I'm not trying to be. I've never been a good one for saying goodbyes. Didn't even say that to my own mom. Couldn't get it up and out of my throat that day I left, and I won't say it now either," Marty said as he shook Joey's hand and continued on, "I'm still on board with our motto, that we came here together, and we're going to leave this place together."

Leaving his friends wasn't the only thing he was grieving about. How would Claire know that he moved? What if the guards in this place would not allow him to write to her, and let her know where he was? What if the new guards were all like Satan's Army? The thought of losing her now was something that he couldn't bear the thought of.

The four hundred men who would be leaving the next day, had already been segregated just outside the camp. There was already mumbling, as to whether or not they would have yet another death march ahead of them, to their new prison. Joey left all his drawings with Oscar and Marty, in hopes they would somehow survive their remaining time there. All he had in his possession was a small bag with Claire's letters, and two banana-leaf-wrapped handfuls of rice, that Fred passed off to him. They were all situated underneath a large grove of Rainbow Eucalyptus trees, waiting for the next shoe to drop.

Joey stood up, looking back at the camp one last time, as Chaplain Shimley walked slowly in his direction. "What, did you think I was going to let you off that easy? Can't do it without you, Joey. Oscar and Marty know what they need to do here. I'm pretty certain I can count on them to take care of things. Besides, I've shared God's word all I can here, over the last three years. It's time I move on, where maybe I can help shed some light on some new sinners."

"But how'd you talk them into letting you move?" asked Joey.

"I didn't have to. I just prayed about it and God

did all the moving I needed. Fred told me to pack up and go, so here I am."

Joey felt an exhaustive relief until they were ordered to start walking. The pace would be slow throughout the day. Same conditions, different day. No food, no water, no rest. Joey held on to his banana-wrapped rice packs for himself and Chaplain Shimley, in case there were more days like this ahead. The next morning, several trucks arrived and to their relief, they were all ordered to pile in. All four hundred of them packed like sardines.

The trucks delivered them to a train station, where they were once again loaded into train cars, but this time, they would be open-air box cars. Once again, they would be packed in so tightly together that the movement of each other's chest could be felt, as each one would exhaustively try to take his next breath. These box cars were used to transport horses and cattle, and the entire floors were covered in animal waste. The blend of toxic gases from the waste-filled floors made any attempt to breathe in the fresh air above their heads somewhat fruitless. Men still died on this ride, but this time their bodies were tossed over the six-foot walls. Joey refused to participate in such despicable acts, and Chaplain Shimley condemned it right from the start. It appeared there was no turning back now. It had become more apparent than ever that some of the men had turned into the animals they had been treated as, for the last three years.

The size and overall set-up was much the same as the prison at Camp O'Donnell. The only difference here was the absence of Oscar, Marty and Fred. Once they entered, the number of prisoners was much the same, as were the sick and dying in the prison hospital.

It had once again become Joey's daily ritual, to work with Chaplain Shimley, closing the eyes of the young men who just couldn't hold on anymore. No one else would do it. No one else could stomach it. Joey knew that even Shimley's mental health was wavering, and he needed someone by his side, while he gave the men their last rites and buried them.

There was some roadwork going on outside the prison that again, Joey wanted no part of. He only wanted to be the chaplain's right-hand man, and to write Claire. The Red Cross still operated in Cabanatuan much like it did previously, and all he could do at that point was hold on, wait and pray that she wouldn't forget him.

Then one day all work outside the camp shut down. Word started to slowly filter through the Filipinon civilians, who were still coming in delivering supplies, that the American forces were gaining ground. Fred made sure to keep Chaplain Shimley informed, through smuggled hand-written notes. He wanted to go home, too. And each time, he pleaded with the chaplain for the Americans to have mercy on him, to let him live to see his family again. In his mind, that would be his honor. To be a husband and father again one day. They were no longer in the same camp. Chaplain Shimley could no longer speak on his behalf. Only their friends that remained behind, could do his bidding.

From what Joey could still put together in his head, they had been here for about three months. It had been steadily raining for over a week, and Joey didn't have the one thing that had been keeping his mind clear, and that was his daily walk around the camp. Ever since he had given up any physical work outside the camp, he picked up a daily routine of brisk walking around the camp. Something, anything to try to keep his mind off of where he was, and what he helped Chaplain Shimley with on a daily basis. This is when he would pray, "Please God, help us get out of here soon. Please take care of the ones you've given me to love."

So finally, when he saw the sun break through, he walked outside and started at the gate, making his first brisk walk and then on the second round, he thought he saw something in the thick brush and trees about a hundred feet from the camp. Again, he made another pass, but this time he slowed down to a slow gait. This time, he was sure. Joey quickly returned to the prison hospital, to inform the chaplain of what he was sure would soon be their freedom.

"Chaplain Shimley," Joey shook all over as he tried to quietly whisper, "Someone's out there. I think this is it."

"I'm not surprised. Look Joey, I would have told you, but I didn't want to get anyone's hopes up. Fred has been sending me messages that he thought it wouldn't be long. Well old pal, I think it's going to be a good day. Stay put. I don't want to lose you now. Let them do what they're going to do."

There were only two dozen or so guards in the entire prison. What few guards that were on duty, were standing around one of the spickets talking, and totally unaware that the forest surrounding them was filling up with American soldiers, Filipino Scouts and guerillas.

On January 30, 1945, in a nighttime raid, under cover of darkness, they made their move. Within a matter of minutes, the gates of their last hell called Cabanatuan were busted through with heavy tanks and trucks. After three years and six months, they had finally been freed. Joey hoped, as things quickly unfolded, that Fred would have the wherewithal to surrender, if this same action was taking place at Camp O'Donnell. Although they had been on opposite sides of this war, he knew Fred was the one and only captor who didn't want to be there either.

As they were being loaded into the trucks, most of the men looked like even death didn't want them. The ones that survived barely had the strength to lift their arms, to celebrate their freedom. Then there were the few that died in these last moments, because their hearts simply couldn't take the excitement that stirred all around them. At least for them, they knew, if only for a few brief moments, that they had, in fact, been freed. It had been the same pandemonium they all had experienced with the original attack at Fort McKinley, but this time it was one of victory.

Ironically, much like they were told on their first day of capture, not a single guard fell on his sword. Instead, every guard at Cabanatuan chose to put down their arms and fall on their knees.

Chaplain Shimley would be the last man to leave the prison alive, as he gave his last prayer for the dying and his first prayer for freedom, in over three years.

Joey wouldn't leave the same prison together with his friends, but after many frantic days, they did finally load up together again on the same ship home. Chaplain Shimley led the most victorious sermon he ever held in his life, as he preached about the Promised Land they would soon set foot on, in just a few weeks. As the men slept, ate and celebrated their country's victory, they had no idea how short- lived this victory would be for so many of them. Even though their bodies had been freed, their minds would never be able to let go of the nightmare they had just lived through.

He had only one place he wanted to go when he got home. It was that little church in Shreveport, where the same group of women still met every Wednesday night.

Their lives would all start over in different parts of the country, with each one carving out their own separate dreams. For years, many of those who survived didn't want to talk about it. It wouldn't be until twenty years later, that Oscar, Marty and Chaplain Shimley would finally break away from the prosperous lives they had carved out to have their first reunion. By this time, Joey was nowhere to be found. Unfortunately, by this time he had already been captured again.

CHAPTER 22

MASTER DETECTIVES CLUB
June 1973

UNCLE MACK WAS SO relieved that the black cloud had been lifted, when Gilly confronted him. He no longer felt like he had to hide in his souvenir shack every day. He no longer felt like he had to roam aimlessly on the beaches, looking for that magic message in the bottle that would make his past disappear. Not only had he humiliated himself by sabotaging his own personal dream, but the enormous amount of shame he brought to his own family did so much more damage. The kind that he thought he would never outlive. His father had essentially disowned him years ago, overshadowing any attempt for him to see or talk to his mother. He had no idea if either one of them was still alive, or if they still lived in the same house. Maggie held no judgment when he bore his soul to her about his intentional theft, to elude his duty in the Navy. Whether it was knowing first-hand, the personal toll the war had on her sister's life, or her willingness to let his past be, Maggie didn't care. Mack was one of the most creative, intelligent and sensitive men she had ever met. She had been lied to and cheated on by every man she had ever met, and just the idea that one would come clean, right up front, was all she needed to trust him. When he asked her to marry him, she didn't hesitate. Now, the daughter of the man that his own parents had at one time hailed a hero, had not only forgiven him, but had invited him into her life. It was something new in his life that he never would have expected. Gilly had not only opened her heart up to him, but invited him into their club. He finally felt like he was a real part of Laurel Cove, and they were now meeting twice a week, comparing notes over coke and coffee at Mimi's diner. Gilly had grown to love this place as it filled up every day, with many of the same people she had waited on at the post office. Mimi's was an institution like no other, with over a dozen tables covered in green and white checkered tablecloths, and a steady stream of hot coffee. It had a wooden counter that had taken decades of use, with sections of the edges worn down from elbow wear. She always had slices of peach, coconut, lemon and apple pie displayed on the counter in a swivel glass case. The place was always spit spot clean. Mimi would have it no other way, as she, still at eighty years old, ran the place like an army boot camp. Unlike the Double Pattie, nothing ever came out of her kitchen that was anything less than perfectly fried, grilled or baked.

"Good afternoon, Gilly, you want a piece of pie? And where's Leon?"

"Oh, he should be here any minute. He's never late, you're just early."

"Sorry, just couldn't wait to get here today. Hey, did I ever tell you how much I appreciate you letting me be involved with all this?"

"Yeah, Uncle Mack, only about a thousand times. Here's Leon now. Let's see what he found out."

"Well, have you gotten any good news yet?" Gilly asked.

"Looks like we may have hit the jackpot, I think we've found them," as Leon smiled.

Leon's work here now, no longer consisted of a small notebook pad that he pulled out of his pocket. He now carried a briefcase filled with old newspaper articles, written years ago, as told by some of the surviving prisoners of war. He had managed to collect those from some of the members of his amateur detective club, and for the time being, thought it best not to share with Gilly. Some of their experiences were hard even for him to absorb, after all these years. Even though he had played a very important role in the war, it still was something that he wished he could forget.

In all of her dad's writing to her mom, not one time did he ever mention a single person or event that took place over there. It was always about how beautiful the island was; how well they were being treated; and the plans they gradually made for their life together when he got home. She could only assume that even in their early pen pal days, he had it in his mind to never talk about what happened, when he was a prisoner of war. So, with nothing more than his discharge papers, Leon and Mack had to really dig in their heels.

They were both hot on the trail of half a dozen hard leads, to locate anyone who had possibly served in Joey's unit. One man definitely remembered Joey, but they were separated during the death march through Bataan. He suggested they contact his commanding officer, Lt. Col. Gerald Pitkins, to see if he had any information. Leon's phone conversation with the colonel was somewhat successful, in that he once again was one that remembered Joey well, but could only remember one of his buddies by the name of Marty. This lead gave them a search of twelve men named Marty from the list of infantry men, four of them had died during combat and the other two had recent death certificates on file. The other six were scattered all over the country. They had been sending out letters for weeks, hoping that one of them would respond with word that they had, in fact, been imprisoned with Joey. That they had been there. Had seen what he saw, had lived what he lived, and could perhaps, with some miracle, help him wake up from this nightmare that had once again imprisoned him. Or at the very least, tell his story of what had really happened to him all those years ago. Finally, in early June, help came.

It was called O'Reilly's Irish Pub, and Marty O'Reilly was the proud owner of this establishment. There were caricatures drawn on the walls of every famous person that had ever thrown down a pint of Irish brew, in his establishment. He had even framed the drawings that Joey left, the day when he was transferred to Cabanatuan. Marty hung them proudly, right behind the bar. He didn't hesitate to tell their story when anyone asked. Marty still loved whiskey, cigars and women and had a memory that was rock solid. When he got a hand-written letter, that his old friend, Joseph Franklin Stevens was in trouble, he picked up the phone and called Leon the same day.

Marty's telephone call gave them the whereabouts of Oscar Wilson, and the band of brothers' planned reunion was underway. Oscar Wilson returned to his hometown and had followed through with the plans he made that day, while still a prisoner. Everything he did, starting from his first day of freedom, would be methodical and much bigger and better than he ever dreamed. He used his veteran's loan to purchase twenty acres, and then expanded every few years until he had finally acquired over six hundred acres of the finest sugarcane grown in the Deep South. He married the youngest daughter of the Mayor of Rapides City, and had one son and two daughters. He had thought often, how much the stalks of the rows of sugarcane reminded him of the rows of bamboo-constructed prison housing they had once lived in. It was no surprise to him, that his old friend had lost his way. He knew Joey had not only suffered the most, but had given the most. If it weren't for him, he wouldn't be where he was. He would've died in that miserable God-forsaken place called Camp O'Donnell.

While Leon and Uncle Mack were doing their research and letter-writing campaign, Gilly was doing some of her own. Among the treasure trove of love letters between her parents, and her dad's discharge papers, she found one letter from Mrs. Gertie Montgomery. The letter was yellow, old and dusty, much like those in the dead letter box, but this one had a return address.

CHAPTER 23

IT REALLY WASN'T ABOUT THE DOG
July 1973

"MOM, I HAVE SOMETHING I need to talk to you about. I've been kind of busy doing something behind your back, and I was afraid you'd try to talk me out of it. You know how we've both wanted to know more about Joey's past."

"Yes, I'm listening."

"Okay, so it's taken a lot of time and effort, but I think you're really going to be happy after you hear what I've got to say."

"Well, I have noticed that you've been preoccupied lately, but I just thought you were working extra-long hours helping out at the post office. Aunt Maggie told me she's seen you, Mack, and one of her customers hanging out a lot lately. That one sounded kind of weird to me. So, what's going on, Gilly?"

Gilly outlined the whole story, every chapter and verse from the unsealing and reading of the dead letter, her dad's discharge papers, Leon Miller's and Uncle Mack's involvement, along with the dogged research and letter-writing campaign by them.

"Mom, we found them. We've found Joey's friends from the war. They were in prison with him. Don't you remember how he would talk about Shimley, Oscar and Marty? Well, it all came back to me. He must have said those guys' names dozens of times. I just thought he was making them all up, and never really paid him much mind. We found them and they're coming here to visit him. Almost all of them, anyway. We haven't been able to get in touch with Shimley yet. He was their Army Chaplain, but we haven't given up. Are you excited?"

Claire just stood staring at her daughter for a few minutes, in complete silence. She had worked for years on trying to make her husband's fate in life more comfortable, more bearable, accepting him as he was, for what he had become, all the while hoping for a breakthrough. It never, ever occurred to her to try to track his old buddies down. Even if she knew who they were, she would not have had the resources that Gilly's detective club did. She had just gone along for years with Joey's constant reassurance, telling her it's all in the past Claire, let it go Claire, I'm okay Claire, that made her bury any thought of resurrecting his past as a possible cure or fix for his broken mind.

"So let me get this straight. Mack was known as Buck to your dad, when they were young? Why didn't Maggie tell me?"

"Well, if she did, then she would have had to tell you all about Uncle Mack's past and stuff, and I really think she wanted you to like him. She told me that she had a lot of bad experiences with men before, and really only wanted what you and Dad had."

"I just don't know what to say right now. I'll have to have a really long sister-to-sister talk with her one day about all this, and let her know how much they both mean to us. Right now, I'm just amazed that you pulled all this off without me having a clue. All this time I've been digging in, trying to build myself some kind of career at the bank, and looks like you already have one. You're a real detective Gilly. And it's all been for the sake of what happened to your dad. Honey, I'm just so very proud of you."

"Well, I have to admit it didn't start out that way. In the beginning, I guess I was being a little nosey. Please don't say anything to Aunt Maggie about me opening that dead letter. I don't want her to think she can't trust me, and I swear I won't ever do that again. I'll find a way to tell her one day, I promise. I've even been paying the extra money for all of Anastasia's letters. Actually, I have been staying later to clean up around the post office. Aunt Maggie's desk is a mess."

"Who in the world is Anastasia?"

"Long story, Mom. I'll fill you in on that one later. What if seeing them shakes something loose in Joey's head?"

"Gilly, what you've managed to accomplish here is truly amazing. But, please don't get your hopes up. Having a few names stuck in his head is one thing, but connecting those names to people he hasn't seen in decades, is another. It would be an answer to our prayers, to at least know what happened to him. There's no doubt that Mark Cooper knew, but he would never tell me. To actually meet the guys he was over there with will be like finally meeting the rest of his long-lost family."

"You have to admit it looks like we might have a happy ending," Gilly said as she smiled and clapped.

"All I am saying is, don't get your hopes up, Gilly. He might not recognize any of those guys."

"I know, but at least we can hope for the best. That's more than we've had in a long time, don't you think?"

"You're right, and you know I've been trying to figure out something for the three of us to do together again, for a while now. Not any kind of public outing, but something a little more casual. I mean he did really well at your graduation. There's no reason why he wouldn't enjoy another get together. I can't think of anything better than this, to look forward to."

"Oh Mom, this is going to be so amazing. If Joey can only remember one thing about us one day, I would be happy."

"Yeah, me too, honey. One thing would be more than we've had in a long, long time," Claire said as she shook her head up and down.

"So, the plan is for all of us to meet up in about two weeks. Well, the when is in two weeks and the where I'm not sure yet. I was hoping you could come up with something. Our place isn't big enough and I don't want to ask Aunt Maggie. She's done so much for us already."

"Let me think for a minute. What about, I know you're not crazy about it, but your dad always loved the beach. We had some really good times coming here when you were little. We can get some chairs, ice chests, make it like a big family reunion picnic on the beach, right here behind our apartment. I can get the ball rolling for a temporary home visit for him, for a few hours. I'm sure his doctor will approve it since he did so well last time. What do you think about that?"

"Mom, don't give it a second thought about me and my quirks about sand, I would walk on broken glass right now if that would help Joey."

"Good then, we're going to have the best family reunion anyone has ever seen! And Gilly, if you're right about this, if this helps him in anyway..."

"It's okay, Mom, you carried us for a very long time, and I fought you hard along the way, too hard sometimes. You were only trying to keep things together for all of us. Anyway, I had a lot of help. If it weren't for Leon and Uncle Mack, I don't think we would be standing here planning any kind of reunion. You know, I really like Uncle Mack. He's not a bad guy after all."

"Well, I'm happy to hear you say that and you know, I think I probably need to work on getting to know him better too," said Claire.

All three members of the Master Detective Club were waiting in the lobby of the Biloxi Marriott, when Marty and Oscar walked in. Gilly knew who they were, just from the lines on their faces. The same deep kind of lines that Gilly suddenly remembered running her little fingers over on his forehead, when Joey was still her dad. She would never, ever tell either of them, her Uncle Mack's deep secret. In her mind, he was now her most unlikely hero. He had helped her find Marty and Oscar, and there was no doubt that they would help her dad find his way home again.

"Hello, you must be Gilly Stevens, you look a lot like your dad. It's so nice to meet you, I'm Marty and if you didn't already guess, this is Oscar. So sorry to hear your dad has had some problems, but we're here to help anyway we can, young lady. We owe your dad everything. Probably wouldn't be alive right now if it weren't for him. So, when do we get to see him?"

"That's right, he saved a lot of lives over there. Just doesn't sound right that he's had it the worse since we got back. I tried to find him a few times, but didn't have any luck. I guess, like so many others, he kind of fell through the cracks," Oscar chimed in as he reached out his hand.

"He saved your lives, how?" Gilly asked intently.

"Yes ma'am, he sure did. Let's walk over here, out of the middle of the lobby. I think we need to sit down for this. To start with, when we were first captured, we had to walk for days during the most God-awful heat, with very little food or water. Your dad never once let on that he was tired, thirsty or even hungry. Both Marty and I gave out quite a few times, and collapsed right where we were. That was something the Japanese soldiers didn't allow. If you collapsed, you were beaten and thrown on the side of the road to die. Each and every time a guard raised his hand to beat one of us, your dad took the beatings for us. The guards, for whatever reason, found this to be an honorable act on his behalf. After a while, their heavy hands gave way to brief moments of mercy. We begged him not to intercede, but he wouldn't have it any other way. He just said that he was used to it, and this was one time in his life that getting a beating had a good reason behind it."

Gilly's interest in hearing what she longed to know for so many years, was suddenly overtaken by a brief moment of her own memory flashback. As she absorbed her dad's selfless heroic acts, she also couldn't help being mesmerized by the story teller. There was something familiar about Oscar. A story she had heard dozens of times. She pulled herself together and said, "I'm so sorry that all of you had to go through what you did. Joey, I mean, my dad never told us anything about what happened over there. Now I understand why."

"Yes ma'am. So, when are you going to introduce us to your friends?" Marty asked.

"Oh yes sir, I'm sorry, these are my two friends that I guess I could say if it weren't for them, we wouldn't be here either. This is Leon Miller, who's a retired military intelligence agent, and Mack Montgomery, who's an amazing and talented artist in Laurel Cove, who also happens to be my uncle. My mom is still at work, but she'll be joining us later for dinner if that's alright. She should have all the details worked out of the where and when for the big get together. So can I ask you another question?"

"What? A former military intelligence agent! Where were you stationed?" asked Marty.

"Spent my time in Europe during the war. I'd really like to talk to you guys more later on. You know, compare notes and all that kind of stuff" replied Leon

Gilly interrupted, "So back to my question, please."

"Well, I don't know, it depends on what you want to know," answered Oscar.

"I can't imagine how horrible it must have been for all of you. As bad as the beatings must have been for him, is there anything else that could have happened to have triggered my dad's total mental collapse, so many years later?"

"Look, Gilly, that would take too many hours off your life, that you could never get back. How about you first tell us what happened to your dad. Was there any particular thing that made him break down?" Oscar asked.

"Well, Mom said he had his moments over the years. She said he would just have the worst nightmares. When my baby brother died, he took it really bad, and it was a while before he was able to work through some serious depression. I think my mom said he shared some stuff with our old next-door neighbor. He would never tell us anything either. Mom always thought that maybe he took it the worst, since he was the one that found little Joey in his crib that day, not breathing. I guess you can say that the final straw was one day on his way home from work, he ran over a dog. He was behind a pick-up truck that had some old hunting dogs in the back, and one jumped out in front of him and he just couldn't stop in time, and he accidentally ran over and killed it. The guy who owned the dog kept telling him it wasn't his fault, but he just kept sitting in the middle of the road, crying and rocking this dead dog. When the old man pulled it away from him and threw it in the back of the truck, he said that's when Joey just really lost it and he had to call the police. He's never been the same since. Mom and I never could understand it. The old man just said he had plenty of dogs back home and he didn't get it either."

All the color left the deep-lined, sun-parched faces of Marty and Oscar, as tears flowed down their faces. It was as though Gilly had just replayed their three-and-a-half years as prisoners of war, in less than five minutes.

"Marty, I think I need you to take over now," Oscar said as he bent over and lowered his head.

"Gilly, I'm going to tell you something that happened over there. I know you're really young and don't understand the brutally of war. It's a horrible thing, and even though one side always declares victory, there really aren't ever any winners. There are so many innocent lives that are lost, no matter what the reason is and we can never, ever forget that. Your dad got to be good friends with a young Filipino boy, right away after we landed in Manila. He spent just about every minute of his free time with this little guy. He really kind of took him in as his little brother. At least that's how he acted anyway. The kid wasn't more than ten or eleven when we left the city. As we were in the middle of pulling out of the city, your dad made him promise to stay put in the church, with the priests that raised him. I really believe that in his mind, he had great plans of maybe taking care of him one day. So once the ground war really took off, there were large contingents of Filipino civilians, many of them a lot younger than you that fought right alongside of us. Then after we had to surrender to the Japanese, we later found out about more groups that operated what they called the bamboo telegraph. As it turned out, a lot of these were really young boys, just like Eddie, delivering messages to our intelligence, where the prison camps were, as well as the numbers of Japanese soldiers and where they were camped. Not only that, they were able to smuggle in food and medicine that saved hundreds of lives. One day, your dad got involved with what he thought were regular underground guerillas, smuggling medicine that we desperately needed. So, about every couple of weeks, your dad would walk to the edge of the woods where we were working on a bridge, and one of them would throw the medicine we needed at his feet. This went on for months, until one day they got caught. One of those fellows was shot right there on the spot, but the other one was none other than Eddie. The guards figured out right then and there, after the way your dad reacted, that they knew one another. If it had been any of the other guards besides Satan's Army, it would not have been so bad. These animals had twisted minds, and torture and punishment were something they lived for. They even had a name for it, they called it 'dead runner'. They only ever did this one time, and it was to this young boy. They treated us bad, but never like this. To make matters worse, your dad was absolutely convinced that one of our own sold him out that day. He said there was no way they could have seen what he was doing, unless someone told. It was real desperate times, and some of the guys had unfortunately shut down into survival mode by this point," Marty then leaned back and took a deep sigh.

The looks on Gilly's, Leon's and Uncle Mack's faces now seemed almost catatonic. This wasn't some horror movie they were watching. This had really happened to real human beings. Not to mention, it happened to the very ones standing right in front of them, and one that was living down the street at the VA Hospital for almost a year now.

"I hate to ask, but what was dead runner?" Leon asked.

Oscar took one deep breath, when his friend, Marty, shook his head indicating that he just couldn't go on. "They took a rope and tied it around his neck, then pulled him behind one of the Jeeps, while the other raced behind. So needless to say, it wasn't long before Eddie collapsed. If memory serves me right, it was Machine Gun Kelly that was driving the first Jeep, and Scarface that did the running over, while The Maggot held your dad's face forward to make sure he had to watch the whole thing. There's no doubt in any of our minds that it was The Maggot that orchestrated the whole thing. We knew not to move, because if we did, we would all be shot. Then when they were done, they made your dad pick him up and put him in the back of the Jeep. Then, I'm guessing they just dumped the poor little fellow's body somewhere outside of the camp. Your dad spent several days in the prison hospital after that. We thought we were going to lose him then. Between good old Chaplain Shimley and a few shakes from Marty and me, he got back on his feet. Things did change a bit for the better after this. Again, it was your dad that had somehow managed to befriend one of the guards, not long after we were captured. A day or so after Eddie was murdered, all three members of Satan's Army were gone. We were all pretty sure that this guard that your dad got close to named Fred had something to do with it. Needless to say, your dad never really stopped blaming himself for not being more careful. I really think the shock of one of our own being an informant was almost as bad. It wasn't his fault, none of it was. So, him running over the dog and then having to watch it tossed in the back of the truck was absolutely, no doubt, the nail in the coffin for him."

Uncle Mack wiped the tears from his face as he said, "Good God, I heard horror stories but never, ever nothing like this. I'm just so honored to have a chance to meet you guys. I just don't think I even have the right to be in your presence right now, after all you went through."

"Can't say that I would do it all over again, but it was my honor to serve our country," Marty said, then he looked over at Oscar and continued, "Look, there's just so much more that went on over there that would really serve no purpose in sharing with you. We only told you about Eddie, so you would understand why he fell apart when he did. Honestly, if it hadn't been for those letters he was getting from his girl in Louisiana, I don't think he would have survived another day over there. I really believe that's what finally got him up and about again. We were separated later on, when your dad and Chaplain Shimley got moved to another camp. Fortunately, we all got rescued about three months later."

"So, what you're telling me is that all those years, his nightmares were about witnessing this little boy being dragged and then runover by a Jeep, while he had to watch? Oh my God, I can't imagine," Gilly said, as she cried until she almost couldn't catch her breath. Uncle Mack hugged her, as more tears poured down his face, while Leon just shook his head. Gilly pulled herself together as she wiped her face with her shirt sleeve, "No wonder he never wanted to talk about it. Just the imagined scene of this inhumane and horrible act is almost more that I can handle. I can't imagine what it had to have been like in person. And that girl from Louisiana that was writing to him is my mom, Claire Stevens, as a slight smile returned to Gilly's face.

So, it was never about a dog, but about an innocent young boy named Eddie. One that was not only her dad's friend, but his want-to-be adopted little brother that he somehow felt responsible for. One that helped them to survive, when they had no hope. Gilly just sat there and thought about all the complaining she did when she was Eddie's age. All the things that she thought she had been cheated out of. How unfair she thought life had been to her.

How her dad had ruined her birthday, that day in Sullivan's Grocery, standing there like a big goofball, with Miss Debbie chocolate icing smeared all over him and the freezer door. How she had wanted to be anywhere but there in that moment. Now she had just been told a story, a true story of this brave, freedom-fighting young boy who lived and hid in the jungles, and whose only goal at the end of the day was to help her dad and the other soldiers. For that, he was dragged to his death behind a Jeep, and run over like an old dog. He would never have another dream. He would never have another chance. This would certainly be one more life lesson she knew she needed to inventory and never forget. Just because you didn't understand someone's pain, doesn't mean it isn't real.

It suddenly became clear to her that her dad had not suffered all these years for what happened to him. He had been suffering for what happened to Eddie, and so many others like him. It wasn't his mind that had broken into a million pieces that day, when he accidentally ran over the dog. It was his heart.

CHAPTER 24

TIME CAPSULES, CASTLES AND DREAM PARTNERS
August 1973

BEFORE THE WEEK WAS out, Leon had finally gotten in touch with Chaplain Shimley. He said not to start without him; he would drive all night if he had to. When he returned to the states, he pastored several churches, finally settling down at a small church outside of Houston, Texas. He married a woman that had many of the same qualities as the women Joey told him about, when they were tentmates at Fort McKinley; Natalie, the wonderful mother who raised him, and Mrs. Gertie, the woman who stepped in after she died. He would never forget those talks. How much Joey missed his mom, and how much Mrs. Gertie still meant to him. Much like Mrs. Gertie, Shimley's sweet Olivia felt it was their responsibility to meet the needs of their community, even if it meant reaching into their own pockets. At the beginning and end of each day, Mr. and Mrs. Shimley thought they were the richest people in the whole world. Their home had always been filled with the sounds of unending joy and laughter, from the four children they adopted that the world had so cruelly rejected. It had been Joey's last selfless acts, before they evacuated Manila, that the chaplain also never forgot.

Chaplain Shimley never stopped praying for his friends, and had always held out hope that they would one day ALL be reunited. It is true that Joey and Eddie were responsible for saving countless lives with their smuggling operation. But it was Chaplain Shimley that helped in saving hundreds, if not thousands, of souls. Each and every name would forever be etched into his heart. He wondered many times about how he managed to continue on with the memory of so much heartache and loss. There were so many young men that never had a chance for a decent burial during their death march, much less shown any mercy when they could no longer go on. Even the ones that were buried in the prison camps did not have their loved ones there to say their final goodbyes. He had struggled, just like so many of his fellow soldiers, all during their imprisonment and years since, trying to find it in his heart to forgive his captors for the atrocities that took place over there. Each and every time he thought he was slipping into his own darkness, some unexpected miracle would occur, such as the telephone call from Leon Miller.

After they were freed, the prisoners, scattered about in different prisons, were quickly hauled away from their torture chambers and the island they were built on. He never had the opportunity to tell them just how much they meant to him. All the times they thought he had been the one that held them together, it had been their courage and individual sacrifices all along that kept him going. They had no idea how many times he had secretly broken down and cried, when no one was looking. It also amazed him at how creative those three young men were, in the worst of times. How Oscar talked the guards into letting him plant a garden, and Marty could make potatoes, radishes, beans and rice taste like you were eating in a gourmet restaurant. The new bridge that Joey sketched for the guards, which made them show him the favor to be trusted to work outside the camp as a supervisor on the job. With that he was able to acquire the medicine that healed so many. How they held him up on his darkest days, when he didn't think he could make it another day, when they would tell him how much his sermons and prayers meant to them. He had reunions before, but none like this one would surely be.

More excitement was building in the Stevens'

family, as Claire and Gilly planned on a day of new clothes shopping, when Claire announced, "I've been waiting on the right time to talk to you about something I think you might be interested in. I just opened a new account for a customer, that plans on opening a new business right here in town. He said it might take him awhile to get things off the ground, but he's looking to hire at least two people. It's the kind of business I think you might agree Laurel Cove needs."

"Mom, I appreciate it. I admit when we first got here, I thought this place was pretty awful and I didn't want to leave Kat. But, it turns out that was probably the best thing that could've happened to me. I had to take some chances with people that I probably never would have, and I've made some really good friends. These friends, I'm pretty sure, are the kind I will keep the rest of my life. You know, my thinking that Laurel Cove didn't have a lot of what we were leaving behind, well, I've come to realize that sometimes less is more. Matter of fact, Mimi's Diner beats the Double Pattie any day of the week. And Hope has turned out to be a pretty good friend. So, for now I really like working for Aunt Maggie. I've really gotten attached to some of the customers that come in," answered Gilly.

"That's wonderful, Gilly. It sounds like you've grown up quite a bit while I wasn't looking. I'm so happy that you're comfortable calling Laurel Cove your home. But, do me just one more favor and go talk to him. Here's his card." Claire reached in her purse and handed Gilly a small, white business card that read, EDWARD HAYEN, EDITOR IN CHIEF, LAUREL COVE NEWSPAPER.

"Mom, are you serious? Is this for real? When you said new business, I thought maybe you were talking about another diner or hardware store. A newspaper, that would be amazing! You think he would hire me? I mean, I can't believe this. I might have a chance to be a reporter. Wait until Leon hears about this," squealed Gilly.

"I think you have more than a chance. I told him some of the work you did to track down your dad's friends, and he was really impressed. There's no reason why you can't go to college and major in journalism. I bet he'd even let you work part time."

Gilly just stood there not knowing what to make of how the most important things in life had come to her here. This place, this town that she thought was full of stupid people with nothing to do. How angry she was for how Joey controlled their every move. Now she knew the heartbreaking reason why. All those reasons made up her journey, one that she would have never walked, had it not been for Eddie. A young boy that lived and died decades before, and only knew rejection before he met her dad. It was definitely one of the saddest events that was not only part of the world's history, but hers now, and one that she hoped would never be repeated. Just like Marty said, no matter who wins during a war, there were never really any winners.

She already had her first story. She wouldn't

need to do any further investigating for this one. She would never, ever tell anyone else about the dead letter she opened and read by flashlight, under the covers of her bed that night. And she would never let her mom know she read the letters that probably saved her dad. No, her first story would be about Laurel Cove. Pop 851 and what an amazing little town it turned out to be.

Claire and Gilly giggled like two teenagers as they walked through JC Penny, shopping for Joey's new beach outfit. Gilly would hold up one Hawaiian style, tropical shirt after another while Claire would give thumbs up or down. They both agreed on a short sleeve, light blue button-up shirt, that had small, yellow, tropical flowers printed on it, white shorts and brown flip flops for his first meeting with his long-lost friends in almost thirty years.

Gilly would not have any anxious thoughts on how Joey would behave this time. They had the beach behind their apartment all to themselves. Only the people that knew Joey and where he came from would be there. Besides, from here on, she promised herself that she wouldn't care anymore what people thought or said. Not only was he 'The Incredible Hulk' and 'Superman' all wrapped up in one, he was now her very special hero.

Joey dressed himself, with every button on the shirt perfectly aligned, in every button hole. As they walked out of his room, Claire made sure to tell Gilly that he even knew how to put his pants on before his shoes. He picked up his left foot and said, “Look Gilly, I got flippy flops just like you.”

Nurse Lydia walked up, wanting to check up on her favorite patient and said, “You’re going for a ride, Joey. Today’s going to be a fun day at the beach with some of your friends. Remember, we’ve been talking about this for a few days. Are you okay with it?”

“Yes, let’s go, Gilly, I’m Superman ready.”

Once out in the parking lot, Gilly opened the back door of their new four-door buttercup yellow Pontiac Catalina, and Joey hopped in. Gilly crawled in up front and turned on the radio, while Claire put the car in reverse, as they glided back out of the hospital parking lot. The radio once again played a song, that this time, well suited the occasion. If only her dad knew the words, if he could only follow the tune, instead Gilly softly sang, “If you could read my mind love, what a tale my thoughts could tell, just like an old-time movie, bout a ghost from a wishin’ well…” Gilly knew that if Claire Marie Stout and Pvt 1st Class Joseph Franklin Stevens had to do it all over again, they probably wouldn’t change a thing. For there were plenty of ‘someones’ out there that didn’t have what they had, after all they had been through. As she looked over, she knew those were happy tears that flowed down her mom’s smiling face, while Joey’s body swung to the rhythm.

Once Aunt Maggie found out about the big beach party, she involved herself whether they wanted her to or not. It was a beautiful, clear sky-blue August

Sunday and she had arranged everything in perfect order. She had the ice chests full of drinks, chairs set up, blankets spread out, and umbrellas up. Uncle Mack had the BBQ pit spitting fire, while waiting to slap his first round of hamburgers on.

Everyone was there. Aunt Maggie, Uncle Mack, Leon, Oscar, Marty and Chaplain Shimley all stood and grinned when they walked up. Gilly was nervously cracking her knuckles, while looking over her shoulder for two more special guests. She hoped and prayed that her gut feeling was right. The detective work she did this time was solely on her own.

"Joey, you have some old friends here. Do you recognize anyone?" Gilly nervously asked.

"No, I'm hungry," answered Joey, as he shook his head back and forth.

"Okay, we're going to eat in a minute, I promise. Let me introduce you to someone then, his name is Oscar."

"Nice to see you again, Joey. It's been a long time."

"Yeah, can I have your hamburger if you don't eat it?"

"Sure, man you can have anything you want."

"Gilly, I have something for Joey, but I don't want to overstep how much he might can handle right now," Marty said.

"No, don't worry about that, he loves presents. Especially the unwrapping part. Mom said that was always his favorite. I just hope I haven't overstepped myself either."

"Huh," Marty sounded confused.

"Nothing," said Gilly. "Joey, this is another old friend. His name is Marty and look, he's got a present for you."

"Oh boy, I love presents. Is it my birthday?"

"No, but I think it's a special day, kind of like your birthday. Here, open it."

Joey sat down in the sand and carefully tore the paper away, pulled the folds of the box open, and for one moment it was as though the gravitational pull of the Gulf of Mexico did forget to work. Only this time, rather than the waves swallowing them up as she once feared, it sounded as if the waves had been held back, for even the seagulls held their breath. There was dead silence, for what seemed like an eternity.

Then Joey cried out, "Mama, I made it, I did good, just like you said."

Claire and Gilly had no idea what Joey had seen to stir this kind of unexpected and overwhelming emotional reaction. As they peered over his shoulder, they could see that inside the box was Joey's Cuban Cigar box, a small Bible, a bag from Edgardo's Souvenir's Shop, a camera and a stack of photographs. Marty had flown back to the Philippines a few years after the war, and dug up their metal foot locker.

This special time capsule of memories had been unsealed, and it was all the good ones. Not only was Joey holding his old black Bible and his mom's handmade hearts in his hands, but Marty had all of Joey's rolls of film developed. There were pictures of the island before it was bombed, along with pictures of him and Eddie in front of the store where they met, sitting in the cart with a hat-covered pony, and Eddie opening the first wrapped present he ever got, of a new pair of shoes. Joey's voice filled with joy and laughter, as he flipped through them, pointing to his long, lost little brother. The one he had been grieving for all these years. Eddie was back in his hands now, right where he could forever keep him safe.

Out of the corner of Gilly's eye, she could see Mr. Bolton walking up with the last two guests for their reunion. Gilly turned to her dad's handsome, dark haired, brown-eyed, long-lost friend who grew up to look just like Rudolph Valentino, with a perfect strawberry birthmark on his right wrist.

She quietly whispered, "Oscar, I believe with all my heart that the woman dressed in that purple and white polka dot dress is your mother," as she directed him to Anastasia. Then she looked at the other woman and said, "Uncle Mack, I think you already know yours."

Gilly walked away, feeling a great sense of accomplishment; however, this wasn't the happy ending she had hoped for. They had dropped off Joey, almost one year to the day, at the Biloxi Veteran's Hospital, where the doctors were supposed to help Joey remember who she was again. This wasn't the ending she had dreamed so long for. She sat down by Joey and her mom, picked up a handful of sand, allowing it to slowly filter through her fingers. Meeting his long-lost friends appeared to stir nothing other than old memories, that she had no part of. Gilly's next thought was at least she had a part in reuniting two other broken families. Maybe that's what this was all about. Maybe this was God using her pain, for the good of others. Gilly decided that being with her parents, together again on this beautiful day, was enough as she watched Joey pack a bucket of sand and flip it over. Then he slowly removed the bright green plastic bucket, ever so gently revealing his long-awaited new masterpiece.

"See Gilly, I told you the castles were getting close."

Tears flowed down her face as a flood of memories from their days of building sand castles on the beach, emptied out. Suddenly these tiny grains of sand became the very thing that, in the most unexpected way, mended two broken hearts.

Then Gilly, with her big grown-up smile, reached for the bucket and said, "You sure did, Dad."

THE END

About the Author

Ann C. Purvis choses to publish under her birth name, Elizabeth Collums; this is her true roots and where she has drawn from many of the experiences she writes about. Ann retired from the USPS and lives in Denham Springs, Louisiana. She enjoys decorating and DIY projects. She has two daughters, a step daughter, son-in-law, two amazing granddaughters, and her dog Daisy.

Dead Letters of Laurel Cove

by ELIZABETH COLLUMS

Reading Group Questions and Discussion

1. One of the first things we learn about Gilly is that she hates talking in front of people. We also learn that it's not because she is shy, but because she feels judged for things in her life that she has no control over. Do you ever feel like you are being judged over something beyond your control? Does it make you feel defenseless?

2. In her report on how one can have a positive effect on society, Gilly states at the end: "Come to an understanding within yourself of your passions, energy, strengths, your weaknesses and most of all, of your dreams. And don't let anyone tell you that you can't. Find a dream partner. Write it down. Go back and read it, change it if you must, but make it your revision, not someone else's." What are your dreams? Just like Gilly suggests, write them down, find a dream partner or someone who shares your vision, and go back to read the list often, change as you grow, and revise as you want. Let no one revise your dreams but you!

3. After the report, we learn that all of those suggestions were actually some of her mom's daily doses of advice. What are some of your mom's pieces of advice that you have used in your own life? Share how they changed your mindset, or direction.

4. Gilly feels that she will always be on the "wrong side of the tracks." Why do you think she is caught in such a negative mindset? Do you have anything in your own life that you feel you are stuck in a negative mindset also? How do you think you could change to start looking at life more positively?

5. Gilly is embarrassed about Joey. She blames him for the fact that both her and her mom don't have many friends. Do you have a family member that you feel ashamed of sometimes? Do you find yourself blaming them for things that are less than perfect in your life?

6. Gilly thinks often how much she wished she could go back to "before" and have things be like they used to be. Is there a tragic event in your life that you feel that way about? How did it change your life? How often do you find yourself wishing you could go back to "before" it happened?

7. In chapter 4, Claire mentions the saying, "Some things are best left unsaid if it changes nothing." Can you think of a time in your life when you learned something you wish you hadn't? Or something that would've been better left unsaid? If so, why?

8. Just like with Joey, Claire, and Gilly, out of nowhere our lives can be altered dramatically. Do you have an event that changed your life and the course you thought it would take? If so, what event and how did it change you?

9. When Gilly lashed out at Mrs. Weaver, did you think it was justified? Do you ever find yourself lashing out in anger to someone, only to feel remorse for it later? When that happens, do you tell yourself you are never going to do it again? Has anyone ever done it to you? How did it make you feel?

10. Gilly admits that she reads a lot and that helps her with her feelings. What do you do that helps you with your feelings? How did you find that outlet?

11. When Gilly set out to find what happened to the mind of Joey, did you feel it would lead to hurt or understanding? Have you ever wanted to understand why someone in your life acts the way they do? If so, what did you find?

12. In the beginning of chapter 8, when they were driving to Laurel Cove, did you feel the same defeat and heartache that suddenly overcame Gilly? Have you ever thought your life would be better without someone in it, only to find that when they were gone you missed them tremendously?

13. On page 123, Gilly feels jealous over Joey's happiness in his new home. How can you relate to what Gilly is feeling?

14. After hearing about Leon Miller, Gilly got excited about being in Laurel Cove and felt that maybe there was a good reason for her to be there after all. When in your life have you met someone, or heard of them, and knew you were meant to be right where you were? How did that situation end for you?

15. On pages 132-133, after reading the letter from Kat, how did you feel? Did you feel Gilly was too harsh in her feelings about Kat's letter, or justified? Why? Also, the letter sparked insecurity in her about all the relationships she had. Do you find that when you feel insecure about one relationship it can make you feel that way about others in your life?

16. After spending time with Hope, Gilly started to admire the way Hope looked at life. Do you feel more like Gilly or Hope? Why?

17. When Gilly opened the dead letter and read it, what were you first thoughts? Did you agree with Gilly or disagree about who the letter was talking about? Do you think asking Leon to help her was the right choice?

18. Gilly's desire to be a detective fueled her need to find out the truth about her Uncle Mack. Have you ever felt the need to find out other people's secrets? What did you intend to do once you found the truth? What did you end up doing, and how did that work out?

19. When Leon revealed Mack's secret to Gilly, what where your first thoughts? How did those thoughts change when you learned he did ten years in prison for it? Did you agree with Gilly that she should tell her Aunt Maggie?

20. After confronting Mack, Gilly felt remorse for the way she had judged. What did you think about how Mack explained himself? What about his childhood? Have you ever pre-judged someone only to find out later that you were wrong? Have you ever been judged unfairly? How did those things make you feel? How did it change you?

21. When Gilly's mom, Claire, gave her the list of "things to do" from Joey, how did it affect you? When Gilly apologized to her mom, how did that affect you? Have you ever made a bucket list? If so, have you completed any of the things on your list?

22. On graduation day, when Gilly was no longer worried about her dad embarrassing her, how free do you think she felt? What other revelations do you think led to her overall newfound happiness? How do you think letting go of what others think of you or those you love could free up your life?

23. "Seek the truth and take comfort in it." What does this statement mean to you?

24. How did you feel when Marty and Oscar told Gilly about Eddie and how he died?

25. “No matter who wins during a war, there were never really any winners.” Do you agree with this statement?

26. When Claire and Gilly picked up Joey for the big beach party did Gilly’s sentiments mirror yours or oppose them? What event in your own life came to mind?

27. The ending of this book reflects all of our lives. What things in your life did you wish at some point would go back to the way they used to be, only to find that they are actually exactly as they should be?

Want more reading and book group suggestions?
Visit: www.ropeswingpublishing.com

ACKNOWLEDGEMENTS

I really do believe that we should all try to lead a purposeful life. And the core of that is tapping into the God given skills and gifts stored deep inside our hearts and minds. What we dream about, what we want to become. We all have them. Some more than others. I had, in fact, written down my dream to become a writer decades earlier in a profile for my ten-year class reunion.

Dreams come with risks, and risks come with failure. After I wrote my first book, I sent dozens of queries to book publishers all over the country. It took several weeks before I finally heard from one, only to tell me that they weren't interested. That's when I knew I was a writer. I had been turned down! I was now among the millions of other rejected want-to-be writers, but I was now officially in the club.

Fast forward a few months when later, by chance I was introduced to who would become MY dream partner, friend and publisher, Michelle Jester. My heartfelt thanks and appreciation to Michelle for not only making it possible for my first book, *PASSENGERS*, to see the light of day, but she also knew this one would come to past before I did.

# acknowledgements

There were two specific biographies that gave me great insight into the real-life struggles that occurred during this wartime period. *Bataan Death March, A Soldier's Story*, By James Bollich and *Days of Anguish, Days of Hope* by Billy Keith. I then sat for hours watching *YouTube* videos of the few remaining survivors of the Bataan Death March. Many of them had different memories of the number of days and miles they walked, but in the end, their stories were the same. It was all about their faith, hope, and survival. I hope this story honors them in some small way.

Thanks to the incredible cleanup crew that were there again in my corner. Deborah Dawn Hall, Alexis Jester, and Sherry Cook Reamer for their careful dots, commas, and lane changes. And of course, last but certainly not least, Larry Jester for his military and history knowledge.

And as promised to my friends still plugging away at the Walker Post Office, there is a little something in here for all of you. I learned so much from the hundreds of customers that I waited on every day for over twenty years. And for the most part, the most valuable lessons that I got to take with me were two of the most important we can ever learn, empathy and gratitude.

Also from Elizabeth Collums

A mysterious letter arrives from America to the village of Highland Way, where Annie, the oldest daughter in the Ewing Family, was left to care for her mother and younger sister after her father left to find work in Dublin. Soon, Annie, Lily, and Katy find themselves on a harrowing journey.

The hand-written note not only will expose deep secrets, it will also challenge the strength and fortitude of the Ewing women, leading each member into their own soul searching voyage.

Follow this extraordinary passage that begins in Ireland and leads each woman to uncover their own courage and truths in this new world.

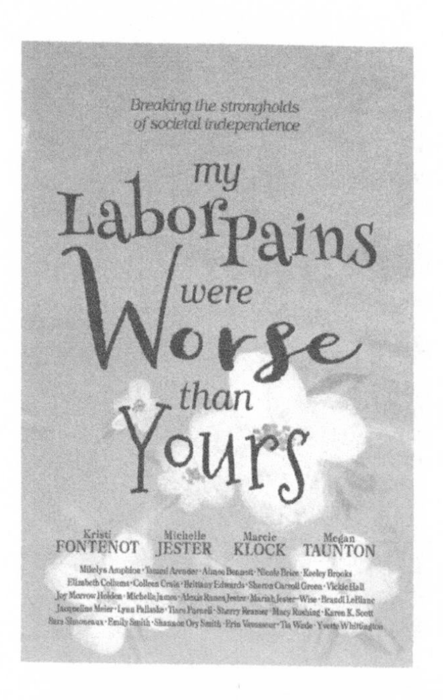

Ever wonder why being the independent woman we are told we should be often times simply leads to us battling our problems alone, or worse, competing with other women? Why, at every single baby shower, do most women share their harsher tale of labor and delivery in unnecessary one-upmanship? Why most women are left with feelings of unworthiness?

We often find ourselves facing struggles alone and isolated in a society where women are made to feel they must be independent to be productive. God did not intend for us to walk through our battles without support.

Join women from different backgrounds as they come together to share their own experiences of pain, perseverance, and encouragement first-hand and in heartwarming detail. We hope that through their stories, you find you are not alone. Because we all have struggled and we all have survived; we need to learn to struggle and survive together.

Made in the USA
Coppell, TX
15 December 2021